BREACH
OF TRUST

Books by Rachel Dylan

Deadly Proof
Lone Witness
Breach of Trust

ATLANTA JUSTICE

BOOK THREE

BREACH OF TRUST

RACHEL DYLAN

BETHANYHOUSE
a division of Baker Publishing Group
Minneapolis, Minnesota

Published by Bethany House Publishers
11400 Hampshire Avenue South
Bloomington, Minnesota 55438
www.bethanyhouse.com

Bethany House Publishers is a division of
Baker Publishing Group, Grand Rapids, Michigan

Printed in the United States of America

Library of Congress Cataloging-in-Publication Data

Names: Dylan, Rachel, author.
Title: Breach of trust / Rachel Dylan.
Description: Minneapolis, Minnesota : Bethany House Publishers, a division of
    Baker Publishing Group, [2019] | Series: Atlanta justice ; book three
Identifiers: LCCN 2018033932| ISBN 9780764219825 (trade paper) | ISBN
    9780764233166 (cloth) | ISBN 9781493417247 (e-book)
Subjects: | GSAFD: Suspense fiction.
Classification: LCC PS3604.Y53 B74 2019 | DDC 813/.6—dc23
LC record available at https://lccn.loc.gov/2018033932

Cover design by LOOK Design Studio

Author is represented by the Nancy Yost Literary Agency.

19 20 21 22 23 24 25   7 6 5 4 3 2 1

CHAPTER
ONE

Mia Shaw gripped a bundle of brightly colored helium balloons with the word *congratulations* splashed all over them. The elevator chimed, and the doors opened onto the tenth floor. She stepped out, almost running into a tall guy who was trying to get on. "Sorry," she muttered as she glanced up. She quickly brushed by the man with her armful of balloons, anxious to get to her friend's apartment.

Mia walked down the long hallway and banged on Chase Jackson's door. She didn't know why he wasn't answering his phone or responding to her texts. They'd agreed to go out to dinner that evening to celebrate his first successful year as a partner. They both worked at the prestigious Atlanta firm Finley & Hughes. Mia, like Chase, worked on high-stakes litigation defending huge corporations.

Unlike her two best friends, Mia worked on the "dark side," as they called it. But her life wasn't like theirs. She had a six-figure debt weighing her down from law school at Emory, and working at Finley & Hughes was the best way to pay that off. She also wasn't on a moral crusade to save the world like her friends. She was just trying to get by.

Mia had been slammed at work today, but she wasn't going

to let this anniversary go unnoticed. Many people crashed and burned after being elected partner. They couldn't take the heat or the pressure, but not Chase. He had taken on the extra responsibility and thrived in his first year in partnership. Chase was not only a great friend, he was savvy and willing to help Mia negotiate firm politics. Since he was three years ahead of her, she relied on his insight and advice.

"Chase!" She banged on the door again. "I know you're in there. You're probably working, but I told you that I'm taking you out to celebrate." She tapped her black heel on the floor as she waited. "We have a reservation in Buckhead, and we're going to be late."

It was only the second week in January, so their billable hours had started over for the year, and Chase would be eager to get a jump on making his objectives, just like the rest of the lawyers at the firm. He was even more of a workaholic than she was, and that was saying a lot, but she didn't want him to ignore this big career milestone. Once he got out of the apartment, he'd be glad she made him go.

Deciding to take matters into her own hands, she tried the door, expecting it to be locked, but it wasn't. *Strange.* But she wasn't deterred. She was bound and determined to drag Chase out to celebrate.

Mia walked through the door and yelled his name again. But she only got a few steps inside before she stopped short. The hair on the back of her neck stood up as she took in the scene of disarray. Her grip on the balloons loosened, and they floated up to the ceiling.

She took a few steps farther into the living room, which looked like an F5 tornado had gone through it. Two lamps were smashed on the floor, the bookshelf was turned over, and the navy cushions were pulled off the couch and strewn on the floor.

What in the world had happened?

"Chase?"

She worked her way through the apartment room by room. When she entered his bedroom, she heard herself let out a piercing scream.

Blood. There was so much blood.

Her friend's body lay on the bedroom floor. His blue eyes were open, but there was no light behind them.

She knew he was dead, but she had to check for a pulse. Her hands shook as she made contact. The life was gone from his body.

Slowly she backed out of the bedroom, shaking, unable to bear the grisly scene any longer. Tears started to well up in her eyes, and anger quickly followed. She pulled her phone out of her purse and dialed 911, trying to keep her breath steady.

"This is 911. What is the nature of your emergency?"

"My friend was murdered."

─◁◇▷─

Mia sat at the Midtown police precinct, still reeling from the horrid events of the evening. What was supposed to have been a night of celebration had turned into her worst nightmare. She'd given her statement to the detectives, but it felt like she kept repeating herself over and over. Now another detective had come into the room to talk to her.

"Let's talk about the maintenance man," Detective Rossi said. "You told Detective Smith a few things, but I want to start at the beginning for myself."

Mia wasn't sure why the detectives had traded off, but she was willing to stay all night if it meant catching Chase's killer. "I don't know his full name. I just know that Chase called him David. Chase had multiple run-ins with the guy. The most recent one was an actual fight."

Detective Rossi opened his notebook. "Tell me about that."

"There's a history there. It started shortly after David began working at the apartment complex. Chase got frustrated because the guy was always running behind or was a no-show on multiple occasions when he was supposed to fix things. Chase felt disrespected because he'd taken time off work to meet David and had been stood up. But things changed when Chase came into work last week with a black eye. He told me the two of them had seen each other out the night before. From what I understand, David had been drinking heavily at the bar. The two of them got into it, and David provoked Chase, so he took a swing at him. Unfortunately for Chase, David swung back and connected hard. The fight was the last straw. Chase was planning to go to the building manager and even higher up the chain to the corporate office."

Detective Rossi's dark eyes locked onto hers. "Do you know if Chase made that threat known to David?"

Mia nodded. "He told David to his face that he was going up the chain. It was also a pretty hot topic in the office because everyone wanted to know why Chase had a black eye. It's not every day that happens. He was asking if anyone at the firm had contacts with the company that owned the building."

Detective Rossi jotted down a few notes. "So Chase could go to corporate and get the guy canned?"

"He didn't say that exactly, but I think at the very least he wanted David to know that he had the power to do that." She took in a breath.

"Did Chase ever mention being afraid of him?"

She couldn't help but smile. "Chase wasn't afraid of anyone or anything. But he also wasn't stupid. He probably knew better than to get into an all-out brawl with the guy, so David must have really ticked Chase off for him to take a swing. But I could never get the exact details of why Chase punched first." It hit her in that moment that maybe Chase *should* have been afraid. "Are you going to track down this guy?"

"We're actually bringing him in now. His name is David McDonald."

Hearing his full name sent a chill down her spine. "He could be the killer."

"We'll get to the bottom of this. For now, you should go home and try to get some rest."

She knew sleep wouldn't come easily tonight. Her first priority was to start looking into David McDonald.

—◈—

The next day, Mia sat in front of her laptop at home, trying to find out everything she could about David McDonald, but his social media presence was nonexistent. The more she looked and came up empty, the more suspicious she became. Who was this guy?

Given the circumstances, she wasn't going into the office today. She needed some time to get her head around what had happened, and everyone at the firm was more than understanding about it. From the calls she'd gotten, the entire office was reeling from the news.

When her doorbell rang, she jumped up to get it, knowing who was on the other side. She opened the door and grabbed her best friend, Sophie Knight, in a bear hug.

"Why didn't you call me last night?" Sophie asked.

"It was so late when I got home from the police station, and I knew you'd get out of bed and come over."

Sophie's blue eyes softened. "Of course I would have. Please let me know what I can do."

Mia had cried last night in the privacy of her home with no one around, but right now she didn't need tears—she needed action. "Just you being here is important to me."

They walked into the living room and sat beside each other on the couch.

"What are the police saying?" Sophie asked.

"They brought in the maintenance manager—a guy named David McDonald." Just uttering his name made her sick.

"Do you know him?"

Mia shook her head. "No. But Chase told me all about him. He seemed a bit unstable, with a bad temper, and had a rocky relationship with Chase. Including an actual fight last week. What if this guy lost it and killed Chase? Chase was threatening to go to corporate about him. Maybe he feared for his job."

"Murder isn't exactly the best way to keep your job, though," Sophie pointed out.

"You're right, but this guy seems like a wild card. He doesn't even exist on social media."

"At all?" Sophie asked. "That is really strange. How old is he?"

"He's thirty-nine. That much I was able to glean from scouring the internet. I've only made my way through basic social media, though. I still have a lot more digging to do."

"You didn't sleep, did you?" Sophie asked knowingly.

The dark circles under Mia's eyes were probably betraying her. "What can you expect?"

Sophie grabbed her hand. "You don't have to be so strong right now. You witnessed an atrocity. It's okay to need time to grieve and vent and get your feelings out."

Sophie was the emotional one of their friend group. Mia had gone to law school with Sophie at Emory. She still remembered meeting the tall, thin blonde and initially making prejudgments about why Barbie was at law school. Mia had felt so average by comparison—average height, average build, average brown hair and eyes. But Sophie had taught her an important lesson about not judging a book by its cover. Sophie was the furthest thing from an airhead that Mia could have imagined. And once they'd shared their first coffee and Con Law outlines, it had been an instant friendship. They'd met the third member of their tight-knit group, Kate Sullivan James, through the Atlanta Women Attorneys group.

Mia looked at her friend. "You're much more in touch with

your feelings than I'll ever be. Honestly, I think I'm still in shock. I don't think it's fully hit me that Chase is really dead and I'll never see him again." As those last words came out in a shaky voice, the tears threatened to come back.

But then her cell phone started buzzing. Mia looked at the screen. "It's the police."

"Get it," Sophie urged.

"Hello," Mia answered.

"Is this Ms. Shaw?" a male voice asked.

"Yes."

"It's Detective Rossi."

"What is it?" She held her breath.

"I wanted to let you know that we've arrested David McDonald. He is in our custody."

She blew out a breath. "Thank you." She considered for a moment and then said, "I tried to do some digging into who he is, and frankly, he's a blank slate. I hope you'll have more luck than me."

"He's a former ATF agent. That probably explains the lack of public information on him."

She hadn't seen that coming. "ATF?"

"Yeah, do you know about the ATF?"

"Yes, I've heard of them. They mainly deal with guns and arson, right?"

"That's part of it, yes, although they do other things."

Her mind couldn't process this new information. How did this fit into the overall picture? "I'm a little shocked that he's a former Fed. Why was he working as a maintenance manager?"

"We're looking into all of that," Detective Rossi said. "But those jobs can be really tough, especially if there's undercover work. Please don't feel like you need to carry on your own investigation here. We'll keep you fully apprised. He's in lockup right now and can't hurt anyone else."

"Thank you, Detective."

"Let us know if you need anything."

She hung up and looked at her friend.

"What is it?" Sophie asked.

"Chase's killer was a former ATF agent. That's why I couldn't find anything out about him. They've arrested him, though."

"The police have to have something on him. Maybe they found some evidence to tie him to the murder." Sophie paused. "I don't know that it would be healthy for you to get too deep in the weeds on this. The police are doing their jobs. You've told them what you know."

"I hear you." Mia knew Sophie was right, but rational reactions weren't her strong suit right now. She looked at her friend, who was a prosecutor in the district attorney's office. "I'll need your help navigating the criminal justice system. I want to understand each step of the process."

Sophie nodded. "Whatever you need."

"You should get back to work." Mia hated that she was taking time away from Sophie like this.

"Don't give it a second thought. Kate has a hearing this morning, or she would be here too."

Mia was fortunate to have such loving friends, but she also knew that getting through this was going to be a highly personal process. At least now she knew what she needed to do. She walked Sophie out and then picked up her phone to make a call.

"Hey, Mia," Walt Fitzpatrick answered. "I hope you've reconsidered my dinner offer."

She smiled. Her law school friend was an assistant US attorney at the Department of Justice working in the Northern District of Georgia. Lately he'd been trying to get her to go out with him. "Hi, Walt. That's actually not why I'm calling. I need your help."

"For you, just say the word."

"I need you to see what you can find out about a former ATF agent. His name is David McDonald. And I think he's a murderer."

CHAPTER
TWO

Noah Ramirez sat at his small but highly functional desk at K&R Security. He'd founded the security firm with his best friend and former Atlanta police officer, Cooper Knight. Now K&R had a private investigations wing headed up by his other good friend, Landon James. It was great to have his friends as his business partners. He knew they would always have each other's backs. And in his book, that meant a lot more than money.

Noah reviewed his email and worked on his status report of open cases. Business was good, and he enjoyed being his own boss. He had also loved his time as an ATF agent, but the private sector suited him even better. He'd learned during his time at the University of Georgia that he had a real knack for technology, and now he got to put those skills to use every single day.

His phone rang, and he picked it up. "This is Ramirez."

"You have a collect call from the Fulton County Detention Center. Will you accept?" a computerized voice asked him.

Noah had no idea who would be calling him from jail, but his curiosity got the best of him. "Yes."

A moment later he was connected. "Noah, are you there?"

"Who is this?"

"It's David McDonald."

Noah's old ATF buddy, but this clearly wasn't a social call. "David, are you okay? Why are you calling from jail?"

"I need your help, man." David's voice was deep but unsteady.

Noah tapped his fingers nervously on his desk. "What happened?"

"They're holding me for the murder of an attorney named Chase Jackson."

His immediate thought was to ask whether his friend had done it, but he quickly put that out of his mind. David wasn't a killer. Yeah, he had his past issues with the ATF, but this was something else entirely. Noah knew the real story about the ATF, and that made him even more sure that David was innocent. But he also shouldn't ask David because this phone call was recorded, and Noah wasn't his counsel. "You need me to find you a lawyer?"

"They've assigned me a public defender. I'm going to meet with him before the preliminary hearing."

"When is that?"

"Tomorrow," David said breathlessly. "Will you come?"

"Of course. But why me?"

"You're one of the only people left on this earth I actually trust. I didn't do this. I promise you that. Someone is setting me up, and I think it has to do with what happened before."

Noah didn't know whether David was calling him as a friend or wanted to hire him to help with his case. But it didn't matter. There was no way Noah was going to let down the man who had once saved his life. "Sure. I'll be there."

"Thanks, buddy. I knew I could count on you."

—◁◇▷—

Mia walked into the Fulton County courthouse, and a sick feeling that started deep in the pit of her stomach spread throughout her body. It had only been a few days since she'd found Chase brutally murdered in his apartment—his body butchered by the knife of a lunatic. A lunatic she was going to make sure paid and paid in full. Hopefully with his own life, if she had anything to say about it.

While she realized that her newfound faith should tell her to forgive the perpetrator, she couldn't bring herself to do it. The murderer deserved to pay.

She closed her eyes for a moment before she actually walked into the courtroom, wondering if God would give her strength. Today was the preliminary hearing for David McDonald, and there was no way she was going to miss it. While she knew that preliminary hearings were usually run-of-the-mill, she wanted—no, she *needed*—to see the face of the man who had done this.

The nightmares came every night, and they were always the same. She knocked on Chase's door, he called out for her to come in, but once inside, she found his bloodied body.

In her dreams, there was always a faceless man standing over Chase's body. She needed to be able to put a face on the culprit. At least that way she'd have someone concrete to direct her anger toward instead of the faceless creature of her nightmares.

"Mia, did you hear me?"

Mia turned and saw Sophie standing beside her. "Sorry. I was in another world."

Without hesitation, Sophie embraced her tightly.

Mia stepped back and squeezed her friend's hand. "Thanks again for coming down."

"You don't have to thank me." Sophie's blue eyes misted up. "You know I'll always be by your side."

"Let's go in." Mia walked into the courtroom with Sophie. "Do you know the prosecutor?"

"Who is it?"

"Anna Esposito."

Sophie nodded. "Yes. She's very aggressive and won't pull any punches. I don't know her personally, because my work doesn't really overlap with hers and she came into the office after I started in the white-collar unit. I think she was a prosecutor in Macon before moving up to Atlanta. Word on the street is that she has her sights set on bigger and better things."

Mia considered that a positive. "That's good. I don't want anyone going soft on this guy, and maybe if she's that ambitious, she'll want to nail him to the wall. I met with her once already so she could hear my story."

It was going to take every piece of strength Mia had not to strangle McDonald with her own hands. Sophie had been her rock, letting Mia cry on her shoulder and praying with her. Bringing her home-cooked food and making her eat it. Basically, being the best friend a girl could ever ask for.

Sophie was the main reason Mia had found faith in the first place. But since she'd only been a believer for about nine months, she didn't have the solid foundation that Sophie did. What she did have was a ton of questions. How could God have allowed something like this to happen to Chase? She didn't have an answer to that, but it was another reason she was up at night. At least now, though, for the first time in her life, she didn't feel completely alone. There was something she couldn't put her finger on about believing and actually feeling that God was there.

Mia and Sophie took their seats in the courtroom gallery and waited. A few minutes later they were joined by Harper Page, the managing partner at Mia's firm. Harper was tall and lanky but wore his black designer suit well, and he had a full head of salt-and-pepper hair.

"Are you sure you're able to handle this?" His bright green eyes questioned Mia.

"I have to be." She would find the strength from somewhere. Maybe God would help her. One thing she knew for sure: nothing could ever be as bad as finding her friend's body. She could handle a hearing. It was her mission to make sure this case didn't go off the rails. She knew she wasn't a prosecutor, but she could still exert pressure on Anna and others in the DA's office if she had to.

"You've already been through so much," Harper said quietly. He had also been a rock throughout this process. His support meant the world to her. The fifty-three-year-old partner was a shark in the courtroom, but she was quickly coming to see a softer side of him that she'd never known existed. The death of one of your own would do that to you, she guessed. Harper took it personally, and of course she did as well. In fact, the entire Atlanta legal community had given an overwhelming show of support.

It wasn't long before Mia got her first glimpse of the monster when McDonald was led into the courtroom. She sized him up immediately. Probably about five ten, with a light buzz cut and facial hair. He looked like he could have been the guy next door, but she knew better. He briefly looked into the audience, but he didn't make direct eye contact with her. She wished he had. Her fingernails dug into her hands, and she tapped her foot nervously under her seat as she waited for things to start. Time was passing so slowly.

The judge entered the courtroom, took her seat, and the preliminary hearing began.

Mia listened as Anna Esposito rose from her chair and questioned the lead detective running the case, trying to present enough evidence to show probable cause. As Mia understood it, the bar was very low at this stage in the game, and there was no concern on her part about the case moving forward. This was all just part of the criminal process.

But as Mia heard the words come out of the lead detective's mouth, a wave of nausea washed over her. She prided herself on being a strong and independent person, rarely showing her emotions or letting down her guard. But no obstacle in her life could have prepared her for what was about to happen.

As Anna continued to question the detective, a large photo popped up on the screen. It was a picture of Chase at the crime scene.

Mia heard herself suck in a breath. Sophie grabbed her arm and gave her a reassuring squeeze.

"You don't have to look," Sophie whispered.

But Mia couldn't turn away. Wouldn't turn away. She'd seen the actual body, so she could push through and handle this picture. She had to stay strong.

She glanced over at Harper and saw that his spray-tanned face had turned pale. How could you not be impacted by such a horrific image?

Anna pushed a dark curly lock of hair behind her ear and turned toward the witness stand. "Detective Rossi, the suspect, David McDonald, is a maintenance worker at the victim's apartment complex, isn't that right?"

The detective nodded. "Yes. Mr. McDonald is actually the maintenance manager."

"And did you find evidence of Mr. McDonald's presence at the crime scene?"

"Yes. We found fingerprints that match Mr. McDonald's in the apartment. We also found a pair of Mr. McDonald's work gloves, and most telling, we found hair follicles matching the suspect on the victim's body."

Anna focused her attention on the judge. "Your Honor, I submit that the state has more than met the probable cause burden."

"Anything from the defense?" the judge asked.

"Not at this time, Your Honor," the public defender said.

Mia leaned over to Sophie. "Is that weird?"

Sophie shook her head. "He's an experienced public defender. He knows the drill. The case is going to move forward."

"Why wouldn't he question the witness, though?" To Mia,

that seemed very odd. It was like letting one side completely have its say while not even trying to fight back.

"Because he's overworked and underpaid," Sophie said flatly. "And there's not much to gain by doing that at this juncture."

There was a lot about the criminal justice system that was foreign to Mia. She knew her way around a courtroom, but all in the context of civil cases.

The next few minutes passed by in a blur as the hearing finished and the judge ruled that the case would be turned over to a superior court judge to proceed.

Mia sat still as she heard voices and movement around her. Harper exited quickly, saying he was headed back to the office, but she couldn't make herself leave.

"Noah, what're you doing here?" Sophie asked.

Mia looked up and saw Noah Ramirez standing in front of them. The last time Mia had seen him was at Sophie's wedding. They had both been in the wedding party. Sophie and Cooper had a short engagement and got married in August. She'd never seen Sophie happier.

Someone called out to Sophie. "I'll be right back," Sophie told Mia as she walked away to speak to someone in the crowd.

That left Mia alone with Noah. With smoldering dark eyes, thick black hair, and broad shoulders, he was exactly her type. But she feared he was too straightlaced for her. He might look dangerous, but she knew better. He was a Boy Scout. She might have turned her life around, but she still wanted someone with a bit of edge and spontaneity.

"So what *are* you doing here?" Mia repeated Sophie's question since he hadn't yet answered.

"David's an old ATF friend of mine," Noah said.

"Are you serious?" She couldn't believe this turn of events. He nodded. "Yeah, we worked together there."

"So you're, what, defending him?"

"Well, I'm no lawyer, but I've got his back, yes."

19

"He killed my friend. You saw those pictures." She heard her voice rising with each word. Raw emotion she wasn't used to feeling bubbled up. "I'm the one who found his body."

Noah took a step closer to her. "I'm so sorry about your friend, but I know David didn't do it."

"You heard the evidence. How can you deny it?" She knew Noah was a smart guy. He had to be in his line of work. He must have been blinded by his friendship.

"Yeah, I listened to what the detective said. David worked in the building. He did maintenance in Chase's apartment. It's no surprise there was physical evidence that he'd been there."

"And the hair found on the body?"

"That could've been planted. If you know what you're doing, you could make that happen."

"That's a stretch." Noah was loyal to his friend, but she was confident that once all the facts came out, he'd see that David was guilty.

"How are you holding up?" Noah asked.

Mia looked into his big dark eyes, struggling to find the words. "It's tough."

"If there's anything I can do, just let me know."

She squared her shoulders. "Help me put your friend behind bars."

Noah shook his head. "That's the one thing I can't do. I'm sorry."

"Then there's nothing you can do to help."

"It's my job to protect my friend and prove his innocence."

"And it's my job to make sure Chase receives justice." She turned away from Noah, fighting the memories of those awful pictures that had flashed up on the screen.

⊰◇⊱

The next day Noah sat in the main conference room of K&R Security for a team meeting, waiting for his partners to arrive.

He was totally preoccupied with yesterday and what had happened at the preliminary hearing.

He hated seeing Mia suffer, but in this instance, she had the wrong guy. He couldn't blame her for being angry and hurt. He couldn't even begin to imagine what it had been like to find Chase Jackson's body. Finding any dead body was hard enough, but when it was someone you knew and cared about, it only amplified an already awful situation. Not to mention the fact that this was a particularly brutal murder.

Noah had barely slept last night and had replayed everything he knew over and over in his mind. What concerned him the most was that this wasn't a gunshot wound to the head. This was a butcher job, and to him that indicated that it was highly personal. If David had wanted to kill someone, and that was a big *if*, there would have been many ways for him to do it that were much cleaner.

Noah's two business partners and friends, Cooper and Landon, entered the room. The three of them had met as freshmen in college at UGA and had been friends ever since. Noah and Landon had experienced a rough patch over Noah's ex-girlfriend, but Noah had long since put that behind him.

"What's up?" he asked, knowing immediately that something was wrong by the looks on their faces.

Landon shifted. "Coop and I got ambushed by our wives about you working on this McDonald case."

"What do you mean?"

"They don't want you doing it," Cooper said flatly.

Unbelievable. "They don't get a say in my cases now, do they? I didn't realize that came along with the marriage deal." He might sound defensive, but this was ridiculous.

"Absolutely not," Landon said. "We just wanted to give you a heads-up. And we want you to do what you need to do to help your friend."

"But reading between the lines here, guys, are you saying I'm on my own?"

"No." They answered in unison.

"We wouldn't do that to you," Cooper said. "We just want you to be aware of the situation and know that it might get a bit delicate. But we're in for whatever you need. We'll handle the flak at home. They would never allow us to have any control over their legal cases, so it works both ways. At the end of the day, they're just trying to protect Mia."

"Understood. And I don't want to put you guys in an awkward position with the ladies. I could see the hurt in Mia's eyes yesterday, but I also can't turn my back on an innocent man. A man who saved my life."

Cooper nodded. "We hear you. If he's innocent, then that's all the more reason for you to be involved."

Landon cleared his throat. "But . . ."

"Spit it out," Noah said.

"As your friends, we also want you to be prepared for the possibility he did this."

"What happened to innocent until proven guilty?" Noah asked. "Wouldn't you want me to defend you guys if something like this ever happened to you?"

"We just don't want you to get hurt," Landon said.

Noah held his tongue at that comment coming from Landon. *God, give me patience.*

"I see from that scowl that we've pushed you too much," Cooper said. "But you're too nice to tell us what you really feel."

Noah ran a hand through his hair. "I'm just trying to do the right thing here, guys."

"That's our Noah," Landon replied.

Noah wasn't exactly sure whether Landon was being sarcastic or sincere. They were closer now than they had been in years, but the past was always going to be there.

"I think we're done here." Noah rose from his chair and left the room to get some air. There was no way he was going to let an innocent man take the fall.

CHAPTER
THREE

Harper had asked Mia to meet with him in his office first thing. She twirled her long dark hair up into a bun and made her way down the main hallway with its fancy chandeliers to the elevator bank. Harper's corner office was two floors up from hers. She didn't know whether he just wanted to check on her after the preliminary hearing or if this was strictly business.

Managing partners at large law firms could have quite the reputation for being ruthless businesspeople, and Harper was no exception. But he had shown only kindness to her during this horrendous ordeal. That let her know what type of person he was, and she was thankful to work for a man like him.

She needed all the help she could get at this point. Chase's death had rocked her to the core, but it had also pushed her closer to God in her new relationship with Him. She kept praying, but the pain was still there. Though she also felt that if she didn't have her beliefs to stand on right now, she'd be even more desperate and hurting.

Until last year, she hadn't even thought God existed. Her mother had taught her to be tough and independent—because her mom had been just the opposite and had insisted that Mia turn out differently. Her mother had never been antifaith, but she'd never been profaith either. All of that led Mia to be fairly agnostic—about everything. She prided herself on being rational and logical, and she had a hard time figuring out how belief in God could fit into that.

But that was before Sophie was almost killed in a car bomb in a church parking lot. The only reason Sophie was alive was that she'd left her phone inside and had gone back to get it. Coming to grips with how Sophie could have been killed—but wasn't— pushed Mia to take a hard look at God for the first time in her life. It hadn't been easy, and she was still taking it one day at a time, but she had a peace in her heart now that she'd never felt before.

God, please take this hurt away.

Harper's door was open, but she still knocked to get his attention.

He looked up and smiled when he saw her, then took off his reading glasses. "Come on in."

She took a seat in one of his large ivory chairs. Everything about his office was immaculately decorated, from the furniture to the wall hangings and modern art. That was what more than five million a year in base salary would get you. Not to mention the bonuses. But Harper hadn't gotten to be managing partner without having the goods to back it up. He was one of the firm's top rainmakers, meaning he brought in business. *Big business.* And that meant big bucks.

"Mia, how are you doing? That was tough to see and hear at the hearing."

"Yeah, tell me about it," she muttered.

"Are you sure you don't need to take some time off? I promise it will in no way impact your partnership progression. I know there's always hesitancy to step off this hamster wheel for fear of getting left behind, but these are highly unusual circumstances. You have the backing and support of the entire partnership. I give you my word on that."

Hearing that did make her feel a lot better, but she had a different plan in mind. "I appreciate the offer, but I really need to keep working. Honestly, sir, it's the only thing that's keeping me sane right now. Work brings a sense of normalcy back to my life. If I didn't have this, I think I might totally lose my mind."

He smiled. "We're more alike than you probably realize."

"I can definitely keep up with my work. I don't want you to worry about that." The last thing she needed was for him to take her cases away. She'd beg if she had to, because she couldn't be idle right now. Having cases meant a way to channel her energy.

"I have confidence in you, Mia. That's why I'm about to make a big request. A huge request, really. And before I do, you should know that it's okay to say no."

She had no idea what Harper was going to say. "All right."

He took a deep breath and looked right at her. "I'd like you, if you're up to it, to take over the Lee Corporation International case. Chase was running it, and we need someone to step in."

Her heart thumped loudly. "You want to give me the LCI case?"

"If you want it."

"Of course I want it. That case was Chase's top priority. I want to do right by him."

He leaned forward. "Good. I'll get you plugged in to the files and make sure you have the list of other associates working on the case."

"Will a partner be involved?"

"Only if you need me. I'll be available, but you'll run this thing day-to-day. This will effectively be *your* case now. Not mine."

"Thank you." What an opportunity for her. She hated that it had come about this way, but Chase would have approved of her taking on the LCI case. She couldn't fill his shoes, but she'd try her best.

25

"Get to work, then. I'll set up the necessary client introductions, but I'm sure they'll love you. I'll go ahead and send some emails to get it started."

"Thanks." She stood up and felt filled with purpose.

"You can also review Chase's hard-copy files and whatever he had on the system to start getting up to speed."

She nodded.

"Sorry. I hope it doesn't bother you to hear his name."

"No. I want to honor his memory. And we can't do that if we're afraid to talk about him." She paused. "I'd also like to be the one to pack up his office. I know we haven't touched it yet, given how fresh this is to everyone, but I'd like to do that, if you'll allow it."

"Whenever you're ready. No rush. I've given strict instructions for it not to be disturbed yet."

"Thanks again, Harper. For absolutely everything. I don't know how I could've gotten through this without you."

"Chase was part of the firm family, as are you. That's what matters. We're all like family around here."

And wasn't that the truth.

―◁◇▷―

Mia dashed up the stairs outside the prosecutor's office. She was running late for her meeting with Senior Assistant District Attorney Anna Esposito. The prosecutor had been skeptical of Mia from the start, and Mia wasn't sure why. It wasn't like she had done anything to get on Anna's bad side—or at least she didn't think she had.

But when her phone rang, she stayed outside and took the call because it was Walt. Anna would just have to wait a little longer.

"Hey, Walt."

"Mia. Sorry, I know I haven't had much for you so far, but I've been having to work my sources and connections."

"Let me guess. It's hard to find out anything about McDonald."

"Hard, yes, but not impossible. I just had to get to the right people who had the intel that we needed. So, here's the thing. Your guy has a very storied history at the ATF. Turns out he left under suspicious circumstances. I don't have all the details, and I'm having to read between the lines and put together info from a few different sources, but I can give you the bottom line."

"Please do." Her heartbeat sped up in anticipation.

"He was working deep undercover, and an op went sideways. He was the fall guy. The antigovernment militia group he infiltrated is highly dangerous. It was his job to bring the group down, but the leader is still at large. There was a showdown of some sort, and a couple of ATF agents were injured in the cross fire. The militia group also suffered a couple of casualties. Needless to say, it was not a good scene. He got forced out of the ATF."

"So a man like that is more than capable of this type of violence." She'd told the entire story of Chase's murder to Walt in great detail so he had the full context for his search.

"Oh yeah. These deep cover guys are capable of anything. Most of the time they're working for the good guys, but sometimes they can crack. The pressure they face in the field is tremendous. Maybe he couldn't adjust to his new normal life and things took a turn for the worse."

"He could've just snapped," she said.

"Definitely a possibility."

"Walt, I can't thank you enough. Please let me know if you hear anything else."

"Will do. And I know you're in a rough spot right now, so I won't push my dinner offer again, but maybe once you're feeling better, we can talk about it."

"Thank you, Walt. You're the best." She was noncommittal on dinner, but he had done a lot for her, and she appreciated it.

She ended the call, walked into the DA's office, and talked to the receptionist. After a few minutes, she was escorted back to Anna's office.

Anna stood to greet her. "Mia, so good to see you again. Please, come in and have a seat."

Mia took a tentative step forward.

"Mia, I won't bite. Please." Anna motioned for her to sit down.

"I'm sorry. I'm still not myself." Mia unbuttoned her coat and placed it on the back of the chair. She was still thinking about her conversation with Walt.

Anna's dark eyes softened. "You've been through a tremendously traumatic event. You shouldn't have to apologize for how you're feeling."

"What would you like to talk about?" Mia asked.

"I know we've gone over your witness statement, but I wanted to get a better feel for you and Chase. I know it's difficult to talk about, but in my position as a prosecutor, knowledge is absolutely power. I don't want any surprises in the courtroom. This case is too important. So if my questions seem intrusive, I apologize in advance, but that's how I need to operate."

Mia cocked her head to the side. "All right." She didn't know what she was about to jump into, but if it would help the case, she would answer questions for hours.

Anna gazed directly at her. "Were you and Chase romantically involved?"

Mia felt her eyes widen. "No. It wasn't like that with Chase." She didn't know why people couldn't accept the fact that sometimes men and women were just friends.

Anna set her pen down on the legal pad in front of her. "Mia, this is the time to be completely honest with me. Colleagues at firms have relationships all the time. If yours crossed the line into something physical, then you need to let me know right now." All the kindness had left her voice.

Mia took a breath, trying to keep her cool. Freaking out wouldn't do anything to further the cause. "I would tell you if there was something more there. Chase and I were very close.

But it was always like a brother and sister. Nothing more. He helped me navigate my way at the firm. He was like family."

Anna still didn't seem fully convinced. "How did you meet?"

"We worked on a large case together. At that point, I was just a junior associate, and he was a midlevel. I think he saw that I was a hard worker and eager to learn. We became friends, and we grew closer as we spent more time together."

Anna jotted down some notes. "Let's shift gears for a moment. You told me when we first met about something Chase told you involving an altercation with the suspect."

Mia nodded. "This was a week before he was killed. Chase came to work with a black eye because he'd gotten into a fight with McDonald. The law firm was abuzz over it."

"So they exchanged punches?" Anna asked.

"Oh yeah. Chase told me he connected with McDonald's jaw, but Chase wasn't exactly a trained fighter. I think he got the worse end of things. I wished he could've just let it go and walked away. Maybe he would still be alive now."

"There's no point in coming up with those types of hypotheticals."

"What can I do to help?" Mia blurted. There had to be something she could do. She felt so helpless.

"Just answer when I call and make yourself available for witness prep when I set up those meetings. Since you found Chase, I will most definitely call you as a witness. You also bring the human element to the picture, and that will be absolutely critical for the jury to hear and see."

"I can help in other ways too."

"I understand that you're a lawyer and want to get in on the action, but criminal law is my area of expertise, not yours. Let me do my thing. You're a witness here, nothing more. Not my second chair. Understood?"

Ouch. Anna wasn't pulling any punches, but Mia didn't respond. She refused to commit to staying out of this. Too much was at stake. If Mia thought she could help, she was going to do it regardless of what Anna told her.

"I have a question," Mia said.

"What?"

"What do you know about McDonald's history at the ATF?"

"The detectives are doing the full rundown on that."

"They haven't told you anything yet?"

Anna arched an eyebrow. "What are you getting at?"

Mia didn't want Anna to know that she'd been snooping so directly. She just wanted to put ideas out there, and hopefully Anna would find the truth herself. "I have questions, like why he left the ATF. Did anything happen to him there that could've caused him to snap? Those kinds of things."

Anna nodded. "Your instincts are right on. Believe me, we'll fully examine all of that."

"Good. Because I think that could be important to explaining the full story here."

Anna rested her elbows on the desk as she leaned forward. "If the defense attorney has any skills whatsoever, he'll try to point the finger elsewhere. Is there anyone you know of, either in the firm or outside, who would have any grudge against Chase?"

"No. Everyone loved him. I mean, he had his quirks just like the rest of us, but he really was a blast to be around. Even when things got stressful on a case, you could always count on Chase to be positive. He was a life-of-the-party type of guy." It felt weird to talk about him in the past tense.

"Any issues with clients, past or present?"

"Nothing that I've ever heard of. You can ask Harper too."

Anna nodded. "I'll do that."

"From what I know, his clients loved him too. It's one of the things that helped him get promoted to partner last year. The clients raved about him. He was highly responsive, he had a strategic mind, was always aware of all the intricacies without losing the big picture. . . ."

Anna patted her arm. "It's okay."

"It's just so hard and strange talking about him and realizing that he isn't here. That he won't ever be here again." Mia paused, but this time instead of sadness washing over her, the anger returned. "Please tell me that you're not going to offer McDonald a plea deal."

"No way. Not on this one. If they bring something to me, I'll have to consider it, but I doubt that will happen. This is first-degree murder. It's not a crime of passion. He had the time to lie in wait and plan the murder. David McDonald went into Chase's apartment that night with the intent to kill him. He had plenty of time to cool off, but instead he went back to finish the fight. The jury will not be sympathetic to that."

Mia felt a fire growing in her belly. "I want justice. I want the death penalty."

"The particularly heinous nature of the crime does call for it, in my opinion, but let me focus on getting the conviction first, okay? I never like to get ahead of myself. It needs to be one step at a time. We need that guilty verdict."

"I hear you. But know I'll do everything in my power to make sure he pays."

Anna's eyes narrowed. "Mia, please do not take matters into your own hands. You're hurting, but you have to let the justice system take care of this. There is a process, and we follow it. That's what separates people like us from people like McDonald. We can't lose that. Please remember that."

"I know. I just want you to understand that I am here for whatever you need. Nothing is too small. Just ask."

"Thank you. I think that's all for now. But I'll be in touch."

Mia rose from her seat and exited the office. She knew Anna was supposed to be a competent prosecutor, but there was so much on the line. An acquittal would mean that Chase's murderer would go free.

That would happen over Mia's dead body.

Noah sat in his black Grand Cherokee, trying to plan next steps. He'd just met with David at the jail. Talked to him through the glass. It tore him up to see his friend like that—accused, beaten down, defeated.

His mind went back to his time at the ATF when he and David were on an undercover assignment together, working jointly with the DEA to try to take down a key cartel player. Noah's cover had been blown, and he was two seconds from having a bullet put through his brain by a member of the cartel. David had literally taken a bullet for him.

He knew he couldn't face this challenge alone. *Lord, I know that David could not have done this. Please help me and show me the way I can prove his innocence.*

The first step in trying to accomplish that goal was to make a phone call. He dialed former prosecutor turned defense attorney Patrick Hunt and then started up his Jeep. He pulled out of the jail parking lot while waiting for Patrick to answer.

"This is Patrick," he said.

"Patrick, hi, it's Noah Ramirez."

"Hey there, how are you doing?"

"Okay." They had worked together on a case involving Sophie Dawson, now Sophie Knight after her marriage to Cooper.

"What's going on? Hope you aren't in any trouble."

"I'm not the one in trouble, but I need your help." At least he hoped Patrick could help him.

"Shoot."

"Have you heard about the McDonald case?"

"Yeah. The murder of the Finley & Hughes attorney."

"Exactly."

"It's been the talk of the lawyer circuit since it happened."

"McDonald and I are former ATF colleagues, and I'm certain he didn't do this, Patrick. I think he's being set up. I know you switched jobs and now work on the defense side with Ashley Murphy."

"I did and I do."

"I need a top-notch defense attorney willing to take on David's case pro bono. And given your background and the type of guy you are, I thought you'd be perfect." Noah held his breath, waiting for an answer. Patrick was his best option.

"I can tell by the sound of your voice that this means a lot to you."

Uh-oh. Noah was about to get the brush-off. "David took a bullet for me. He's the only reason I'm alive right now."

"I'm completely sympathetic. And one of the reasons I moved over to the defense side was to do exactly this type of work, but I can't take on any new cases right now. I head to Europe next week to teach a legal clinic for a semester."

Noah blew out a breath. What was he going to do now? "I get it." He couldn't give up, though. "Do you know anyone who might fit the bill?"

Patrick laughed. "Definitely not my partner. Ashley doesn't do pro bono. Or at least she hasn't up to this point." He paused for a moment. "But I actually do know someone you could try."

"Who?" Noah's pulse sped up.

"A guy named Tyler Spencer. He goes by Ty."

"What's his story?"

"He's a well-known defense attorney who has a heart. He really has a passion for social justice. This type of case would probably be right up his alley. If you want, I can give him a call myself and see if I can drum up any interest."

"Thank you, man. As you can imagine, time is of the essence here. The public defender isn't cutting it."

"I'll call Ty now and let you know."

"Thanks. I owe you."

"Just doing the right thing, that's all. I'll let you know what I find out."

Noah thanked him again and hung up. Maybe, just maybe, this Ty Spencer was the answer to his prayers.

Mia sat in one of the Finley & Hughes conference rooms on the thirtieth floor of the building, overlooking the beautiful Midtown skyline. She was waiting to meet the clients from Lee Corporation International. Four of the executives were coming to the meeting today. The CEO, Lew Winston, the chief technology officer, Howard Brooks, and the VP of business development, Edward Clark. In addition to those men, the general counsel, LCI's chief lawyer, Owen Manley, would also be attending.

Butterflies swirled in her stomach as she prepared for the meeting. She only had one chance to make this first impression, and even though Harper had faith in her, if the clients started complaining, he would have to intervene. At the end of the day, their happiness trumped everything.

She'd done her due diligence reading their online business profiles and reviewing the paper files in Chase's office that were marked as background research on the executives. Nothing too crazy stood out to her. They all had stellar academic and professional credentials, but that was to be expected for such a huge company. They would only hire the cream of the crop.

She'd started reviewing Chase's hard-copy files and getting up to speed on the work that had been saved into the electronic system, but there was a ton of material to wade through. She wanted to make sure she actually absorbed what she was reading and wasn't just skimming. The files had also been a bit of a mess, which made things even more difficult.

It wasn't long before Harper entered the room, flanked by the three executives. Harper made introductions, and she shook hands with each man, making sure she gave a firm shake. She'd learned early in her career the importance of a firm handshake coming from a female attorney.

"You gentlemen are in great hands with Mia. She'll pick up right where Chase left off," Harper said. "There shouldn't be any delays."

Lew took a step toward her. "Mia, I want to express to you our greatest sympathy from everyone at LCI. I understand you and Chase were very close." His hazel eyes focused on her.

Now wasn't the time to get emotional about losing Chase. Not in front of the client. She could actually hear Chase's voice in her head, telling her to stay strong for the executives.

She thanked Lew for his words, but it was time to focus on business. She needed to show these guys that she could handle this case.

"Please, gentlemen, have a seat, and let's get to work."

They all gave her a smile except Howard Brooks, who eyed her with a healthy dose of skepticism. She didn't know if it was because of her age, gender, or just the fact that she wasn't Chase.

They took their seats around the big table in the large conference room. According to their bios, all three men were in their fifties. Howard was the youngest at fifty-one, while Lew was the oldest at fifty-nine.

Mia opened her laptop. "I'm starting to get up to speed on

the case, but I would love to run by you my current understanding of the state of play."

"That works for me," Lew said. "Ed, Howard?"

"Fine by me." Ed's brown eyes made contact with hers.

"Me too," Howard said flatly without looking at her. He seemed very defensive. The other two men seemed much more comfortable and engaged with the idea of her taking over this case.

But she'd worry about Howard later. Right now it was show time. She wanted to prove that she could jump in and talk about the facts with a keen understanding. "LCI has been sued by Electronics Pursuit Group, or EPG. EPG claims that you breached a contract with them valued at one hundred million dollars."

Howard held up his hand. "But, of course, there's no truth to that. This is just a money grab by EPG."

She could already tell that Howard was going to be her challenging client. "I understand. I'm just trying to lay out the allegations." Howard nodded, and she continued. "EPG claims you backed out of a joint venture in which they would have supplied a device that you would've put new cutting-edge software on."

"It's not that simple, but on a basic level, yes," Lew said.

"So what's the LCI position?" She looked at each man, waiting for a response.

As a moment of silence ticked by, the conference room door opened, and a tall blond man entered the room.

"I'm so sorry I'm late. I got tied up."

"Mia," Lew said, "I'd like to introduce you to our general counsel. This is Owen Manley."

Mia rose from her chair and offered her hand to LCI's GC. She knew this relationship would be an important one right from the get-go.

Owen gave her a warm handshake. "Mia, nice to meet you. I'm so sorry for your loss."

She met his big blue eyes. He was a bit younger than the

executives but probably still a good ten years older than her. "Thank you."

He took a seat beside Lew. "Don't let me interrupt things. Please pick up where you were, and I can catch up."

Mia didn't want to jump back into things without setting the table. "We were about to talk about the LCI response to the allegations."

"Great," Owen said.

"Yes, we entered into the agreement," Lew said. "But the contract was contingent on EPG providing a very specific working prototype that they never came through with. They provided a substitute that didn't cut it. We examined the prototype and didn't feel like it held up to the specifications we wanted, and that EPG had assured us they could provide."

"That wasn't a condition of the contract as I read it, though." She was thankful Finley & Hughes was not the law firm that had drafted the contract. In her opinion it was very poorly worded, and that fact could have a big impact on this litigation.

"Those exact words might not be in the contract," Howard said, "but that was the deal. Both parties understood it. Our software is groundbreaking. We can't put it on a subpar device. What they've presented is too large and unsightly. If we had gone through with it, it would've been awful for our brand. Sometimes you have to make the hard calls for the greater good of the company, even if it does come with some short-term heartburn."

"Is there any appetite for settlement?" She had to ask that question.

"Not at the number their lawyer initially floated—basically eighty million," Owen interjected.

That was crazy. "I agree," she said. "That's too high."

Lew put down his pen. "That's exactly what Chase said."

The references to Chase made her both happy and sad, because she knew that at some point others would forget him.

But she never would. "From everything I've read, both sides have served discovery requests, and we've started collecting documents."

"Yes. Chase said this would be a highly expensive phase of litigation," Ed said.

Owen cleared his throat. "I'd like to keep costs down as much as possible."

Spoken like a true GC. As the chief attorney at LCI, it was Owen's job to keep costs under control. "We'll do the best we can, and we did give you our projected budget, which I have reviewed and agree with. Unfortunately, defending this case will be expensive. It's the nature of the beast. I'm sure you've seen how quickly it can add up from your other cases."

"We want you to aggressively litigate this case," Lew said. "If we're going to pay to defend it, we want to make EPG feel the pain too. They shouldn't be able to coast along while they're bleeding us dry."

She straightened her shoulders. "You don't have to worry about that. This case is my top priority. Finley & Hughes prides itself on our aggressive litigation tactics. This case will be no different."

"That's great," Owen said. "We need that type of top-notch representation."

As she listened to the men talk, she realized this case was more complex than she had first imagined. It also appeared that Howard was going to be the contrarian. Owen, on the other hand, seemed pleasant and would hopefully be good to deal with. Ed seemed very introspective, and Lew seemed reasonable. But she knew how quickly all of these first impressions could change. "I'm going to jump into the documents and see what our team has found. If you can think of any potentially troubling emails that you either sent or received, I definitely need to know about them."

"I don't think you'll find any smoking guns. We aren't young pups, and this isn't our first rodeo," Lew said.

"And I completely appreciate that, but I'll ask again." She wanted these men to respect her in the same way they had clearly respected Chase. "If there's anything, no matter how small, I need you to tell me. We need to find it before the other side does." She made a point of making eye contact with each man.

"Gentlemen?" Lew asked.

"I'm good," Howard said.

"Me too," Ed replied.

Owen leaned forward. "I'll reiterate what Mia said. Now's not the time to hold back."

But no one said anything else.

"Okay." Mia closed her laptop. "If I find anything, you guys will be the first to know."

"Is there anything else we can do for you?" Ed asked her.

"Just be available for issues as they arise and questions as they come up. That's what I need most." She took a breath. "I know how much this case meant to Chase, and I want to honor his memory by doing anything and everything I can to defend LCI to the fullest. I want you to know that I'm all in."

Lew gave her a kind smile. "If you're anything like me, working helps you manage the grief. I lost my best buddy five years ago after a long battle with cancer. Continuing to build this company helped me get through it one day at a time."

"I appreciate that." She immediately had a respect for Lew. She thought she was a good judge of character, and everything out of his mouth had seemed sincere. She wasn't so sure about the others just yet. She needed more time to get to know them. "And it goes without saying that if you need anything from me, I'm reachable 24-7." That was the nature of working in Big Law. There was no such thing as time off. If a client needed something, she would be there for them, no matter the time of day or what her previous plans were. Client service was everything. "And given you each had a personal relationship with Chase, I also want you to know that I'm going to do everything in my power to make sure justice is served. I'm obviously not the prosecutor, but that doesn't mean I can't be involved."

The men rose from their seats. "We understand," Lew said. "And we have the same wish for justice. We'll all be following the prosecution very closely."

"Let me see you out." As she escorted the men out to the elevator, she wondered if she was really ready to take on this challenge.

—◅◇▻—

Ty Spencer walked into the Fulton County jail. He had spent the last two hours in his office, reviewing every news article that was out there on Chase Jackson's murder. He'd also done his best to do background research on the suspect, but his public profile was uncommonly sparse. Patrick had told him that McDonald was a former ATF agent, so that might explain it. Those types didn't exactly have an active social media presence, and for good reason.

It was decision time. Would Ty be willing to take on this case—and take it on pro bono? There was only one way to know for sure, and that was to visit McDonald and look him in the eyes man-to-man. There was no substitute for a face-to-face meeting under these circumstances. If he was going to stick his neck out, and do it for free, it needed to make sense. He took his responsibilities as a lawyer very seriously.

As a criminal defense attorney, he often represented men and women who were guilty, but he prided himself on taking the tough cases to prove the innocence of those who had already been convicted in the court of public opinion. His calling was to help those wrongly accused. He could be doing a lot of other things with his law degree, much to the chagrin of his parents, who had both hoped that he would be a fancy corporate partner. But working on the defense side held a special purpose both in his heart and mind. That was why he was particularly careful about who he took on as a client.

This case was especially dicey, because the victim was an attorney. Ty wasn't one to back off of a challenge, but he wanted to make sure he was emotionally invested. That was why meeting McDonald in person was key. Then he could make an educated judgment.

He greeted the officers in the jail, whom he knew all too well. After the normal bureaucracy, he was escorted into a room provided for inmates to meet with their lawyers. Although he hadn't taken the case yet, he wasn't going to get tied up on that technicality.

McDonald was brought in by the guard and took his seat. He was probably just under six feet with an athletic build. Although he seemed hesitant as he gazed across the table, he looked like he could hold his own. "Did Noah send you?"

"You're fortunate to have such a good friend," Ty said to put him at ease. "Noah contacted another attorney he knew, and the case got referred to me. I'm Ty Spencer. I want to talk to you about your case."

McDonald nodded. "Whatever you need to know. I'm an open book."

It was best to not beat around the bush. That wasn't Ty's style. "Did you do it?"

"No." McDonald didn't flinch.

"Then why are your prints all over the apartment? And your hair on his body? And what about your gloves?"

"I'm the maintenance manager. I've been to Chase's place multiple times since I started this job. The last couple of times, I was working on the heating unit. And someone stole my gloves and planted them and the hair on the body. That's another reason I'm convinced this was a setup."

Admittedly, Ty was intrigued. "I'm listening."

"Full disclosure, I didn't like the guy. We'd gotten into it multiple times since I started working there. The worst being an actual fight that I'll fully admit I provoked."

"Tell me about the fight."

"There's a restaurant a couple doors down from the apartment building. Chase and I were both there one night, eating at the bar. I was doing more drinking than eating, though. I'm still messed up from my time at the ATF. I had a few too many drinks and was looking for trouble. I started talking to Chase about the pretty brunette he has a picture of in his apartment. I'm not proud of what I said, but needless to say, it wasn't something a man should say about a woman. I knew he cared about her, so I was just saying it to get a reaction out of him. Well, if I was looking for a fight, I got it. Chase hauled off and punched me good, but he wasn't really a fighter. I hit him back hard and leveled him with one punch to the face."

"And when exactly did this happen?"

"A week before he was killed." McDonald paused. "Yeah, I realize how bad that looks."

It was time to move on to another area of inquiry. "I tried to do some recon on your background, and you're an elusive man."

McDonald nodded. "I don't know how much you know or have heard, but I worked at the ATF for ten years on deep undercover, high-risk assignments."

"That's how you know Noah Ramirez." Ty had a feeling there was a lot more to all of this, and that only further intrigued him.

"Exactly. But on my last assignment, I made a mistake. A mistake I'll live with forever. Because of that, I left the agency disgraced and under a cloud of suspicion. I'm telling you this because you need to understand that I bring a lot of baggage with me. I'm not sure what will come out in the trial, but I want to be open with you."

"Did you talk to your public defender about this?"

"I tried, but he wasn't that interested. I got the impression that he was overworked and didn't have time to dive into the sordid details of my past."

"That's pretty typical for public defenders. Their caseload is unthinkable, and they don't have the ability to go deep in the weeds. Tell me more about the ATF incident."

McDonald looked down. "It was a disaster. I was on a deep undercover op, embedded in an antigovernment militia group. I'd been with them for over six months. They were up to their necks in illegal arms, explosives, and drugs. Everything was going great until I got really suspicious of the group's leader. Deep in my gut, I thought I was blown. I signaled for the larger team to storm the compound. Unfortunately, two ATF agents were badly injured. Multiple members of the militia group were killed, including the leader's cousin. The evidence we needed to prosecute anyone was destroyed. And to make matters worse, the leader wasn't onsite, and they were never able to charge him."

Ty had an idea where this was going. McDonald was the one who took the fall for the failed op. "What did they do to you?"

"They opened an internal investigation. Tore me to shreds. Questioned my mental state. Said I'd gotten in too deep in my legend."

"Legend?"

"The persona I took on. When you go undercover, you have to live it, believe you *are* that person. If you don't, that's the quickest way to get yourself killed. But the shrinks at ATF said I couldn't distinguish my real self from the legend, and they claimed I was unfit to return to duty in the field—I had to be tied to a desk job. Which I totally disagreed with. I made a mistake, that's for sure. I misread the situation, but it wasn't because I was confused about who I was." McDonald paused. "I think someone connected to the militia group could be trying to set me up to take the fall for this."

That twist caught Ty off guard. "That's a big allegation."

"Yeah, and one that might be too dangerous for you to tackle. That's one of the reasons I wanted Noah involved. This is more his wheelhouse. If you decide to take my case, please use him and see if you can figure out an angle there."

"What's the name of the militia leader?"

"Van Thompson. He's a very dangerous man and has a large group of loyal supporters. I don't want to put you in harm's way, so that's why I think you should work with Noah on this. If anyone can figure out what's going on, he can. I just know that I didn't do this and someone wanted me to take the fall. Why Chase was the target, I'm not sure."

The more Ty listened to McDonald talk, the more he empathized with him. But this ATF story also complicated things and would make his job as a defense lawyer even more challenging. He had to gauge how much he could trust the words coming out of McDonald's mouth. "How would you answer the argument that the ATF incident put you over the edge? You had a fight. You were emotionally unstable, and you cracked—killing Chase Jackson in cold blood."

McDonald averted his eyes for a moment before making contact again. "Look me in the eyes right now and tell me whether you actually believe that."

Ty knew this was tough, but he had to push McDonald. "It's not a question of what *I* believe. It's what a jury will think. Will they believe that you're a good guy who had a bad thing happen to him and one day you just snapped? That it was all too much for you? I can hear the prosecutor now, making that closing statement. She'll be extremely persuasive. And the fight you had with Chase makes it all the worse."

"I'm not a killer. After leaving the ATF, I got the maintenance job. It wasn't exactly glamorous, but I don't need much to get by."

"Besides Noah, is there anyone else you can trust?"

McDonald shook his head. "No. He's the only one. As you can imagine, most of my ATF colleagues decided it was better to cut ties. I don't hold that against them. It's just the way it is. But Noah didn't do that. He was willing to take the heat and stuck by me."

"Sounds like a true friend."

McDonald cleared his throat. "So if I'm reading between the lines here, you're trying to decide if you want to take my case?"

Ty shook his head. "No."

"Then why are you here?"

"I'm not still trying to decide. I've made my decision." Ty had no idea whether McDonald had actually done it. From his own mouth, he'd said that he was an expert undercover operative, which meant he was an expert at deception. But there was something deep inside of Ty telling him to do this.

McDonald raised an eyebrow. "And?"

Ty knew his answer. "Let's try to get you out of this mess." He hoped he could make good on that.

CHAPTER
FIVE

O wen Manley sat in his office at LCI. It was evenings like this, going on eight o'clock, that he questioned whether he'd made the right decision five years ago to jump off the partner track at Peters & Gomez. The renowned firm based in Atlanta had given him every opportunity in the world, but being an associate there had come at a hefty price.

He'd told himself that if he moved in-house to work in a corporation, he'd have more time for a life. He could actually date someone, settle down, and start a family. But the in-house gig wasn't all it had been described to be, and his dating life was still as nonexistent as it had been while he was at the firm. In some ways, his social life might even be worse, because at least at the firm he was around a lot of his peers. Here at LCI, he spent the majority of his time around the executive team, which was comprised of mostly older men.

He'd taken a substantial pay cut to leave the firm, but he'd been told the quality-of-life difference would be more than worth it. Unfortunately, that hadn't been true in his situation. At all. Maybe he should've taken *a* corporate counsel position instead of being *the* general counsel, but when this opportunity fell in his lap, it was far too good to turn away. Or at least that was how he'd felt at the time.

A knock at his door broke him out of his little pity party. Howard Brooks popped his head in.

"Come on in, Howard. I see you're here late too."

"You know how it is." Howard took a seat across from Owen.

"What can I do for you?" Owen served a lot of roles as the head lawyer for the company. Sometimes the executives just wanted to use him as a sounding board. And since Howard was the chief technology officer, he often dealt with a lot of legal issues.

Howard rubbed his chin. "What do you think about our new lawyer?"

The question caught Owen off guard. "Mia Shaw?"

"Yes."

"I thought she sounded like she was on top of it. I also did some asking around, and she has a solid reputation outside of the firm."

Howard crossed his lanky arms. "Don't you worry that she won't be up to the demands of this litigation? Her friend was just killed. I can't imagine that her head is in the game. Why do you think she got assigned this case? It doesn't make sense to me."

"It might be *because* she and Chase were so close. This gives her a good way to do something for him, just like she said. I imagine Harper was sensitive to that. He wouldn't have given her the case if he didn't think she was up for it. He wants to keep LCI as a client."

"But Mia also said she's going to be working on the prosecution too, didn't she?"

"She isn't the prosecutor, so I think that was probably her providing moral support." Owen didn't know what Mia had in mind, but he hoped she could keep it separate from the LCI case.

"I don't want to sound like a crotchety old snake, but our

primary concern is our company—not her feelings. We can't afford to serve as her grief counseling."

Owen tapped his finger on the side of his desk. "How about this? We give her a trial run. See how she handles things. If, after a few weeks, you still don't think she's up to it, then I'll have a direct conversation with Harper."

Howard frowned but then nodded. "I guess that sounds reasonable."

"I think we need to give the girl a chance. And think of it this way: I bet she'll work ten times harder on this case because she is so personally invested."

Howard tilted his head to the side. "I hope you're right."

"Did you share your concerns with Lew and Ed?" Owen wanted to know if everyone was concerned about this.

"Yeah, and they both said to talk to you. They didn't seem quite as bothered as I was about the whole thing. But you know Lew can have a soft spot, especially for the ladies."

Owen laughed. "Yeah, I know." Lew had quite the reputation as a ladies' man. He'd never been married but had gone through several high-profile relationships over the years.

"We're trusting you to stay on top of all of this."

"That's my job." Among a million other tasks.

Howard stood. "I'll see you tomorrow. Don't stay here all night. We don't pay you enough for that."

Owen watched as Howard left the office. Hearing Howard's concerns did give him pause. It would probably be good to have a one-on-one with Mia and set expectations. He'd give her a call tomorrow.

—◁◇▷—

Kate had invited Mia over to her house for dinner. What Kate had failed to tell Mia was that this wasn't a girls' night out. Landon and Cooper were both in attendance when she arrived. She didn't mind that her friends wanted their husbands around. She totally got it, although it made her feel like the odd one out. Besides, it was too late to cut and run. She was stuck for the evening, and she'd just have to suck it up and try to put on a smile.

She only felt happiness for her two married friends, but Mia didn't think she'd find love anytime soon. She was so different from the two of them. Watching her mother struggle with one dead-end relationship after another had taught Mia an invaluable lesson: the only person she could ever fully count on was herself. Definitely not a man. They often made promises to get what they wanted, only to walk out when times got tough. She'd seen it happen countless times, and she was the one left with her mom to pick up the pieces. Mia thought back to many a night when her mom struggled to even put food on the table. Mia had promised herself that she would never be like her mom.

Mia stood beside Kate in the kitchen while the guys grilled on the back patio with Sophie, taking advantage of the mild winter day. Atlanta was known for having big swings in temperature in the winter. Today the high had been almost sixty.

Mia listened to Kate tell a story about a crazy client as they chowed down on chips and dip. Mia loved Sophie's homemade spinach dip and took another big bite.

The doorbell rang. "Can you get that?" Kate asked. "I need to pull the casserole that Sophie made out of the oven."

"Sure." Mia wasn't sure who else would be coming over. "Are you expecting someone?" she asked over her shoulder, but Kate must not have heard her. Mia headed down the hallway to the front door.

She opened the door to find Noah Ramirez standing on the other side.

"Can I come in?" he asked as she stood there like a dummy without saying a word.

Blinking, she nodded and stepped aside.

"I take it from your response that you aren't happy to see me." As he walked past her, his shoulder brushed her own.

"I just didn't realize you were coming."

He smiled at her. "Landon called and invited me over. I was assured I wouldn't be a third wheel."

That comment made Mia give a little smile. "Yes, I know that feeling all too well. The guys are out on the back porch."

He gently placed a hand on her shoulder. "Can we talk for a minute first?"

"Sure." She looked up at him, acutely aware of his touch. His piercing dark eyes felt like they could see deep into her soul. She didn't know why, but she felt exposed.

"I said it before and I'll say it again: I'm truly sorry. I know what it's like to deal with the sudden loss of someone you love."

"You do?" she couldn't help but ask.

"My dad died of a heart attack last year. No signs or warnings whatsoever. I get that it's different from homicide. I do. But I can empathize with the pain of loss."

Her heart softened a little toward him. But that didn't change the bottom line. She planned to nail his friend to the wall for what he had done.

"I've been thinking about you since we talked in court. I'm praying for you," Noah added.

She considered her response. "Thank you. There was a time when I would've rolled my eyes at you, but the past year of my life has really changed everything. Although after Chase's death, I have to wonder if my prayers are being heard. I'm having a hard time trying to make sense of all of it. You probably don't understand."

"More than you know, actually. I went through a time when I wondered if God was hearing me."

She knew that Noah and his circle of friends were strong men of faith, so this surprised her. "I just assumed that if you had been doing the faith thing for years, you wouldn't have these doubts like I live with. I'm fairly new at it and still trying to find my footing. My life has been so different from what I imagine yours has been or that of my friends. It makes the whole faith thing super complicated."

"It can be complicated for all of us. Even if we've been doing it for decades." He gave her an encouraging smile.

She softened a little more, but she didn't want him to get the wrong idea. "I'm sorry about your father, but that doesn't change how I feel about David McDonald. He killed one of my best friends."

"What if I told you that I'm working to prove his innocence?" Noah asked softly.

"I'd say that you're a great friend but that you're wrong. You don't know all the facts, do you?" She couldn't hold her tongue. She didn't have anything against Noah, and the last thing she wanted was for him to be duped by his friend.

He raised an eyebrow. "What do you mean? I heard the facts at the preliminary hearing."

She took a deep breath. She hated to be the one to break this to him, but she would want to know if she were in his position. "Did your friend tell you that he and Chase came to blows the week before Chase was murdered?"

Noah's handsome face said it all. He'd had no idea about any of this. "And you know about this how?"

She lifted her chin. "Chase's black eye, for one, but he also told me about the fight. Why are you such a staunch defender? It has to be more than just because he's a former colleague." Any information she could gather about McDonald might be useful. She could pass it on to Anna.

"David saved my life. Took a bullet for me on an undercover operation."

"So you feel indebted to him?"

"Not in the way you think. I know him and that he'd never kill someone in cold blood. It's just not him. I want to be upfront and let you know that I'll be actively working his case. You and I have a bit of a tangled web between us, and I know that Kate and Sophie have expressed their disapproval."

"What?"

"You didn't know?"

"No. But you shouldn't pick your clients based on me or what the ladies think. I wouldn't want that. Of course, I think you're wrong here, but that's beside the point." She couldn't believe Sophie and Kate had spoken up on this. She appreciated their zeal, but she also didn't want to rock the boat in their relationships. "Don't change what you're doing on my account. I'm not going to try to dictate what you and the guys can work on. I'm just telling you what I think the reality of the situation is."

"I didn't want there to be any surprises. I'm openly telling you this now."

"I guess we'll both be working on this case, then. Just on different sides." And they would probably end up butting heads over it. "I'm obviously not the official prosecutor, but that doesn't mean I can't help. If I find evidence that supports McDonald's guilt, I can give it to the prosecution."

Noah frowned but didn't respond.

Kate walked into the room. "There you two are. Come on, we're ready to eat." She walked ahead of them toward the dining room.

Noah placed his hand on Mia's right arm. It was her instinct to shrug him off, but for some reason she didn't. "Can we call a truce for the night?" he asked.

As she looked into his dark eyes, she appreciated that he was so loyal to his friend, even if he was wrong. "Yeah, I can do that."

"Good." He smiled and gave her arm a squeeze.

She wondered if he wasn't dangerous after all.

―◁◇▷―

Noah looked to his right and made brief eye contact with Mia before she shifted into a conversation with Sophie.

There was no doubt Mia Shaw was an intriguing woman, and he had to admit he was attracted to her. But those big chocolate eyes held a lot of pain and shadows. And he knew all about shadows.

As the son of a preacher, faith was just about as natural to Noah as breathing, eating, and sleeping. But his faith journey had been anything but a straight line. In fact, he'd had a total faith blowout after his girlfriend had cheated on him with Landon. That type of deep betrayal from both of them had almost been too much for him to bear.

But he'd always had some connection to God, even when it was really strained. Mia seemed to be early in her journey. He was thankful that she had God in her life, because going through what she had alone would be very difficult. He understood why she would question God, but just the ability to have those conversations was a positive thing.

He wasn't the best at talking about his faith with others. That wasn't his strength. His dad, on the other hand, truly had that gift. Noah still missed his dad like crazy. One moment he was there, and the next, gone. In that one awful phone call, Noah's life had forever changed. But he was so grateful for the time he'd had with his dad and the example his father had set for him. And he was certain that in this circumstance, his dad would want him to stand up for his friend.

Something told Noah that he and Mia were going to be seeing more of each other. He had no intention of backing off of David's defense, and Mia seemed just as focused on his conviction.

"Earth to Noah." Cooper nudged him.

"Sorry, what did you say?" Noah turned to his friend.

"I asked if you wanted to help us on cleanup duty."

"Sure." If it put some separation between him and Mia, it

was probably a good thing. He followed his friends into the kitchen, his hands full of plates.

"So what gives?" Landon asked.

"What do you mean?"

"The tension between you and Mia was filling the air," Landon said.

"And it wasn't just about the case," Cooper added.

Landon gave his shoulder a little punch. "The glances the two of you were exchanging were pretty epic. I'd say there's something brewing there."

Noah couldn't help but laugh loudly. "You guys are out of it. I know you want to find me someone, but the looks Mia was giving me were anything but friendly."

Landon and Cooper exchanged their own look. "She's clearly upset about this case, but when she thought no one was looking, she kept eyeing you," Landon said. "And it wasn't in a negative way."

Noah thought his friends were stretching, but they were coming from a good place. "She found her friend brutally murdered, and I'm doing everything I can to try to defend the suspect. I'd say that's pretty much a nonstarter on the romance front." And why was he even talking about romance? He was the one who needed his head checked.

Cooper smiled. "Let's just see how it plays out. On a serious note, though, what's going on with the case?"

"I talked to Patrick Hunt, who put in a call to a great defense attorney who is taking David's case. I spoke to him yesterday, and he agreed to do it pro bono after meeting with David."

"That's good news, right?" Landon asked.

"Yeah, definitely. His public defender couldn't devote the time needed. And as I told you guys, I'm working this too. Also pro bono. I'll keep up with whatever else you need me to do, though." Noah was the technical whiz of K&R, so he was often called upon.

"We know that, Noah," Cooper said. "You've always been there for us. You've never once complained about anything, no matter how crazy it got. We're here for you now."

Noah was so thankful for his friends. Yes, he and Landon had been torn apart for a while on the cheating episode, but they were in a good place now, and their friendship was stronger than ever. Landon had acted badly, but he had been dealing with the serious trauma and pain of war. Noah had long since forgiven him. But the fear of betrayal was still there, and it made him cautious about giving his heart again. Because when he gave, he gave everything he had. There was no doing anything halfway with him, and that included love.

"Don't look so down, man," Landon said. "With you on the case, you're bound to find evidence that can help exonerate him."

"That's the plan."

Now to execute it.

⬦

Ty rubbed his eyes as he sat in front of his computer. He checked the time. It was after ten. It wasn't unusual for him to work late into the night. He definitely wasn't a morning person.

His decision to start his own firm was one of the best he'd ever made. He enjoyed working and dealing with a complex and challenging case. He'd started his career out of law school at a small firm specializing in criminal defense, but after a few years, he'd learned the ropes and was ready to strike out on his own. Do it his way and not have to report or account to anyone else.

Ty hadn't become a lawyer to get rich. He knew from the moment he stepped through the University of Georgia School of Law doors that he wanted to dedicate his life to being a criminal defense attorney. And if he could especially serve those who had been wrongfully accused or convicted and try to get their convictions overturned, then even better.

He kept replaying his conversation with David McDonald in his mind. The entire story from start to finish had an odd ring to it, but he couldn't put his finger on what was troubling him.

In some ways, David was the clear and obvious guilty party. He had means, opportunity, and motive. He also had at the very least a troubling past at the ATF, and at the very worst a disastrous past. No doubt Anna Esposito would air out all the dirty laundry at trial. Ty didn't know how much of David's files would be off-limits for security reasons, but even if Anna couldn't get her hands on the official files, prosecutors had ways of getting the info they wanted from the Feds. The way they saw it, they were all on the same team. Even if Ty didn't put David on the stand, Anna could call his former boss at the ATF to expose the damaging parts of the story.

There were a few nagging questions floating through Ty's brain. Could David be suffering from PTSD? That wouldn't be a defense, though. It would only help prove the prosecutor's probable theory that David had snapped. Maybe Ty could use it as a mitigating factor, but it wouldn't rise to the level of an insanity defense. He knew David wasn't criminally insane as defined by the law, and it would be difficult to find any doctor to qualify him as so.

What Ty needed to do was see if there was any merit to the theory that the militia was trying to get back at David for what he'd done. But something else was bothering Ty. Chase's apartment had been ransacked. Whoever had killed him was also looking for something. And in Ty's mind, that didn't jive with David as a suspect. Maybe the murder was connected to one of Chase's cases? Could he have brought home confidential client files that the killer was trying to find?

Although it was late, Ty still picked up the phone and dialed the number David had given him for Noah Ramirez. After only two rings, he answered.

"Noah Ramirez? This is Ty Spencer, David McDonald's lawyer. Sorry to call so late."

"You can call me anytime. What's up?"

"I'm sitting here thinking about building out the defense, and I need to do some digging that hopefully you can help me with."

"Shoot."

"I need you to run down everything you can about Van Thompson and his militia and figure out if there's any way there could be a connection here. But don't stop there. We need other alternatives too, if that one ends up being implausible for a jury. David said you were willing to work on the investigative side of his defense. Is that still right?"

"Absolutely. I'm on it. And anything else you can think of, don't hesitate to ask."

Ty hung up the phone, motivated to keep working. The more he thought it over, the more convinced he became that he had an innocent man's life in his hands.

CHAPTER
SIX

Owen waited in the ornate lobby of Finley & Hughes for his meeting with Mia. When he'd called and asked if they could meet to discuss the case, she'd immediately given him her availability.

Finley & Hughes was actually the chief competitor of his previous law firm, Peters & Gomez. Normally, an in-house counsel like himself would try to give work back to his old firm, but in this case, he couldn't. Peters & Gomez represented a competitor of LCI, so they couldn't take the work because of conflicts of interest.

Both firms employed the cream of the crop as far as attorneys in Atlanta went. Being in the Finley & Hughes offices brought back a lot of memories for Owen. All the things he had left behind—chiefly, the amenities and luxuries of a big firm. Everyone assumed that a big corporation would be the same as a firm, but that was far from the truth. The company cared much more about cost cutting and shaving off anything that wasn't an absolute necessity. He got a vending machine instead of a cappuccino bar, and a water fountain instead of chilled sparkling water.

"Owen, great to see you." Mia walked toward him. Her long

dark hair flowed well past her shoulders. She wasn't cover-model gorgeous but had more of the girl-next-door look, with big dark eyes and a warm smile. But Owen was her client, and she was completely off-limits in his eyes. Plus, he probably needed someone a little closer to his age. They weren't that far apart, though. He was only forty-three, and he figured Mia was in her low thirties, based on the law school graduation date posted in her firm bio.

Owen smiled. "Thanks for taking the time."

"Come with me to the conference room."

He followed her down a long hallway and into one of the firm's many conference rooms. This one was smaller than the one he'd been in previously, but that made sense, because it was just the two of them. It still boasted a magnificent view of the city. He didn't think there was a bad view from anywhere in the office.

"We have coffee and water," Mia said. "Please help yourself."

At the word *coffee*, his ears perked up. He grabbed one of the red Finley & Hughes logo cups and filled it to the brim. Then he took a sip after dosing it with some sugar.

Mia also poured herself a cup, and they took their seats. "What can I do for you?"

"First I want to thank you for stepping in on the case. I know you've been through a lot lately, and we appreciate it."

"Of course."

He needed to decide how up front he was going to be with her. The last thing he wanted was to bring her down or dash her confidence. "I'd also really like to be kept in the loop more than you probably would in a normal litigation."

"I know you're probably concerned that I'm still a senior associate and not yet a partner, but I assure you that I can handle this case."

"I was right where you are not that long ago. I'm less concerned about seniority than I am about you being able to take this on, given everything that's happened. And actually, I'm not that concerned. But some of the business is. Especially given the ongoing legal proceeding in Chase's case and your vested interest there."

She bit her bottom lip. "I promise you have nothing to worry about. I can handle everything I need to do both on your case and in making sure that Chase's murderer is put away."

"I think you're probably right, but I wanted to do you the professional courtesy of letting you know that you might be under the microscope, so you could handle yourself accordingly."

Mia blew out a breath. "I appreciate your honesty. It's actually refreshing."

He grinned. "We don't get a lot of it in our line of work, huh?"

"Not nearly enough." She paused. "I've got a team meeting set up for tomorrow to make sure everyone is still running full speed ahead. I haven't gotten any reports yet of any hot documents, but we're still early in the review process."

At the sound of *hot documents*, Owen cringed. He knew all too well that hot documents meant *bad* documents. And the fewer they had of those, the better. "You're giving me law firm flashbacks."

Mia laughed, and for the first time, her eyes brightened. "I take it you don't miss it, then?"

"Actually, I miss a lot about it. Being an in-house attorney is much harder than I expected." And that was just the tip of the iceberg.

"Really? Hearing everyone talk about the benefits of going in-house, I thought it was like the pot of gold at the end of the rainbow."

Now it was his turn to laugh. "I make less money, work almost as much, and still haven't found time for a life."

"You ever consider going back?"

He took a big gulp of coffee. "Every single day. But bringing in business isn't my strong suit, and we both know that's critical to surviving in Big Law as a partner. What about you? Are you going to stick it out on the partnership track?"

She nodded. "I'm not sure what my long-term plan is. Right now I need this job to pay off my debt from Emory, but whether being a partner is actually something I want, I'm not sure. So I'm operating as if I'm full steam ahead to make sure I have that option. Thankfully, the partner track is so long here that I don't have to figure that out right now."

Owen was enjoying this conversation with Mia. They could relate on many fronts, and he found that a nice change of pace. He just hoped she could perform on this litigation. "Don't assume that the grass is greener on the other side." He looked down at his watch. "I've taken enough of your time. Really all I wanted to do was to give you the heads-up."

"Thanks. I'll be in contact after my staff meeting and as we go through the documents. One more thing, though—do you have a settlement number in mind?"

"Nowhere near the number EPG is at. For strategic reasons, I'd like to put some heat on them through the discovery process and see if we can get them to offer up a much lower number."

"I think that's a good idea. But at the end of the day, are you willing to try this case?"

That was the million-dollar question. Or multimillion-dollar question. "I'd obviously prefer not to. But I can't get authorization for the type of settlement EPG is seeking. We're on different playing fields right now."

"I know you don't want to hear this, but EPG's claim isn't frivolous. They have some good points, even if your guys don't think so. I'm speaking purely from a legal perspective here."

He'd thought the exact same thing, but the executives had been bullish about defending this case. "It's good to hear you say that, because I had the same concern. But at the end of the day, we can only advise the business. We can't make all their decisions for them."

"You have much more influence than I do because you're the company's lawyer. We might get to the point where you'll need to hard-sell them on trying to reach a resolution if we can close the gap on the settlement numbers."

"I get that." Owen was impressed by Mia's strategic thinking. She wasn't like some litigators who wanted to try the case regardless of the merits. Reaching a settlement through a business resolution was always preferable in his opinion. He just didn't know if it would be feasible. "We'll speak again soon." He took the last sip of his coffee.

"I'll walk you out."

Owen felt much better after this meeting. In his opinion, Mia Shaw was up for the job.

—◁◇▷—

Mia took a deep breath of fresh, crisp air before entering Chase's apartment building. She hadn't been back since the day she had found his body. Her hands shook a little, holding the key as she waited for the elevator in the main lobby.

Mia had met Chase's mom at the funeral and then had coffee with her again yesterday. His mother reminded her so much of her own. They both battled the same demons—namely drug addiction. Mia hadn't missed the telltale signs.

She was pretty sure Chase's mom was still using and knew she had gone through ups and downs. Surely Chase's murder only made it worse for her. And that was why Mia wasn't completely surprised when his mom asked if Mia could help box up Chase's things. She'd said she didn't have the strength to do it right now.

Mia didn't know how she was going to find the strength either, but she at least had a clear mind. And Chase would have wanted her to help. They shared a special bond over their moms, and she owed him this.

I can do this.

Before she was ready, she stood outside Chase's door. His

apartment was no longer an active crime scene. The police had gotten everything they needed and given Chase's mom the all clear to return. Given what Mia knew the room had looked like, she had suggested a cleaning service to remove the blood, and his mom had agreed.

She closed her eyes for a moment, and the awful memories flooded back, threatening to overtake her as she fought the nausea bubbling up her throat.

"Mia." A hand was laid on her shoulder. "Are you okay?"

She opened her eyes, and Noah stood there, looking at her. "What're you doing here?"

He didn't immediately respond.

"Are you following me?" she asked.

"No. I was here doing some recon of the building, trying to figure out how the perpetrator could've gotten in and out. What are you doing here?"

She blew out a breath. "Chase's mom asked me to help box up his things."

"She didn't want to do it?"

Mia shrugged. "She probably wanted to, yes, but I don't think she's capable at this point. She has some struggles of her own in addition to the grief of losing her only child."

"That's asking a lot of you. Especially considering the circumstances."

What Noah probably meant was that she had found his body in the apartment. "I'm used to taking on a lot."

He put his hand on her shoulder again. "Let me help you."

She stepped away to break the contact. "I don't think that's a good idea."

"You shouldn't have to go in there alone. I'm here, and I'm more than able. Please."

She looked into his eyes and desperately wanted to say yes. "You can't view this as a chance to dig around and help your friend. Do you understand?"

"The only person I'm trying to help right now is you, Mia."

In that moment, with just the two of them staring at each other, she believed his words. And even though she knew she shouldn't be, she was drawn to him.

"All right." She stuck the key in the lock and started to turn the doorknob.

"Wait." He grabbed her arm. "Do you know what condition the place is in?"

"We had a cleaning crew come in, so I think it will look a lot different than when I saw it last."

"Please let me look first," he urged. "Just in case. I'd hate to put you through something again for no reason."

She accepted his kind offer and waited outside the door until he returned. Visions of blood and death flitted through her mind. She tried desperately to stop them. *Lord, please help me.* Would He hear her prayer today?

"It's good," Noah said.

She realized she'd been holding her breath and exhaled. Maybe her prayer was being answered.

"You don't have to do this, Mia," Noah said quietly.

"I do. I definitely do." Taking another breath, she stepped into Chase's apartment. She stood for a moment, looking around. Even though she knew it was clean, she still half expected to see blood somewhere. But thankfully there was no sign of gore. At least not yet.

The cleaners had tried to tidy the place up in addition to the deep clean she'd requested. The cushions were back in the sofa, the broken lamps had been removed. The shards of glass were long gone.

"It's almost eerie. You'd never know that this was the same place," she said.

"Why don't you take a minute, and then we can get to work. It'll be better for you to take it in first, I think."

She noticed there were plenty of flat boxes stacked in the

corner along with packing supplies. She'd ordered them, and the building manager had brought them inside. She thought he felt sorry for her, but she accepted his help. She'd been accepting more help lately than she was accustomed to. The fact that Noah was with her now was evidence of that. But wasn't it in times of crisis that you were supposed to accept help? That didn't make her weak, did it?

Mia was quickly growing tired of her own self-analysis. What she needed was to step into action and stop wallowing.

She looked around the kitchen and living room but found herself reluctant to go to the bedroom. She wasn't sure what she would find there. It would be easier to push that off until the end. Deal with the stuff right in front of her first and not go to the actual scene where she'd found the body.

Noah walked over to her. "Let me know what I can do."

Avoiding the inevitable trip to the bedroom, she looked up at him. He normally had a bit of scruffy facial hair, and today was no different. "Why don't we get some boxes and start packing up in here and in the kitchen?"

"Sounds like a plan." He went to the other side of the room and grabbed an armful of boxes.

She focused back on the task at hand and decided to tackle the kitchen first. Noah also entered the kitchen, and as she placed things in the boxes, he arranged and taped them up.

They worked in silence until the kitchen was almost done. Then Mia had to speak. "You know you don't have to be here."

"I know. But I want to be here. You shouldn't have to do this alone." He paused. "I'm surprised you didn't ask Kate or Sophie to join you."

He had a good point. "Honestly, I'm not sure why I didn't. It just felt like something that would be easier to do solo."

"Do you think that's true now?"

She looked at him. "No. I appreciate the company, I really do. I've never gone through an experience like this in my life. I hope and pray I never have to live through something like this again. I think a second time would really do me in."

He moved to her side. "You're not expected to just be okay. It doesn't work like that. You need time to grieve and to grapple with the circumstances. Those things take time—a lot of time. There are no instant fixes for this."

"Don't you understand that's one of the reasons the prosecution of this case means so much to me?"

Noah nodded. "I do, but I also know you want and need the *right* guy to be punished."

Mia didn't feel like arguing that point right now. "I know we have different opinions on that, so let's just not go there."

"Of course. Living room next? There's not a ton there."

She walked into the living room, followed by Noah. Her focus went directly to the mantel. Chase only had two framed pictures displayed there. Her eyes started to fill with tears as she zoomed in on them. She'd been to Chase's place countless times, but she'd never paid a lot of attention to the pictures.

The first and largest picture was of Chase at his law school graduation with his mother next to him. She looked remarkably lucid, and Chase had confided in her that his mom had made a special effort at sobriety for his graduation day.

But it was the other picture that really got her. A picture of her and Chase in front of the Fulton County courthouse, celebrating arguing her first case. She picked up the photo and held it tightly in her hands. Everything that she'd been holding back threatened to burst out like a tidal wave.

Noah moved closer beside her. "Remember those good times, Mia."

They were both smiling widely in the picture. "What a senseless taking of such an amazing guy." She sniffled but held back from crying.

They packed up the remainder of the living room, and then it was time to go into the bedroom.

"I'm not sure I can do this," Mia said. She stood frozen like a statue, locking eyes with Noah. A pit of despair formed in her stomach.

"I can do it, if you'd like. I really don't mind. You shouldn't push yourself to go in there if you're not ready. No one would blame you for that."

Mia considered his offer. "That's sweet of you, but I think I need to go into that bedroom and see how it is now. I think it might be important for me to do."

"Whatever you think is best. We've done a lot so far. You could always come back."

"We're trying to clear everything out by month's end so the apartment can be rented."

Mia knew deep down what she needed to do. She made her way through the living room and into Chase's bedroom.

When she stepped through the door, she could feel the world closing in on her. Dots danced in front of her eyes. The smell of death flooded back to her, filling her senses.

And then she collapsed.

─◁◇▷─

"Mia, can you hear me?" Noah knelt on the floor beside her. He'd been just close enough to break her fall. One moment she was fine, then she started wobbling, and before he knew it, she was going down.

Her long dark eyelashes fluttered, and she looked up at him. "Noah?"

"You had a little fainting spell." He hoped she would be okay. This was a lot for any person to take. The fact that she'd been as sturdy as she had was a surprise. "How are you feeling now?"

"Light-headed."

"Have you eaten anything today?"

She shook her head. "No. I didn't think I could hold anything down. I was so nervous about this."

"You need to eat and stay hydrated. I'm going to sit you up, all right?"

"Yes."

He pulled her gently into a seated position.

Suddenly she looked down at the hardwood floor and started shaking. Her skin noticeably paled. "This is where his body was. I have to get up. I have to get out of here." She started to stand, and he steadied her. She clearly wasn't at full strength—either physically or emotionally.

He guided her out of the bedroom. "Take some deep breaths. There's a coffee shop right next door. Let's get you something to eat and drink."

She didn't argue as they walked in silence out of Chase's building and into the coffee shop.

"Take a seat. I'll get you something." He grabbed a bagel, a muffin, and some flavored water before joining her at the table. "Please eat and drink."

She gave a weak nod and tore off a piece of the blueberry muffin. "I'm sorry. I feel really embarrassed. Nothing like that has ever happened to me. Ever. I didn't even realize people actually fainted."

"This is what trauma can do to a person. Believe me. I saw this happen all the time at ATF."

"Tell me more about ATF. I need to think about something else." She opened the bottled water and took a big sip.

"The ATF was my first job out of college. I had a knack for computers, and they had a void there. But I also trained and learned a ton of other things. I worked joint operations with the DEA and even did some undercover work."

Her nose scrunched. "That sounds dangerous."

"I'm not going to lie, it was risky. But it also came with a big adrenaline rush." He paused, wondering how much he should tell her. "I told you before that David saved my life."

"Yes, you did," she said warily.

"We were on one of those dangerous undercover assignments. I was much more inexperienced than him. I made a bad decision, but he stuck his neck out for me, putting himself in imminent danger to save my hide."

"You're telling me this to try to explain that he's a good person?"

He desperately wanted her to understand what type of person David was. "He's not a murderer, Mia. I know it as surely as I know that I'm not. He's a good man who was loyal to his team." Noah ran his hand through his hair. "His last op, the one that got him ousted, was a very complicated situation, but David would've never knowingly put his team or anyone at the ATF in jeopardy. When ops go bad and people get hurt, there's always a need to provide answers, and even better if there's someone the higher-ups can point a finger at and discipline. Or even allow to take the fall. In this instance, David made a judgment call based on faulty info and turned out to be wrong. Just like I had made a wrong call the previous year and nearly gotten killed."

"You're saying it could've just as easily been you," she whispered.

"Yes. That's a risk we take going into that line of work. David was never charged with any crime. He was given a formal reprimand and demoted to desk duty. He decided it was best to resign. He wanted to protect the rest of those he worked with. He took the fall so that his teammates wouldn't get any blame."

"You think it was actually someone else's fault."

"David would never admit that, but that's truly what I believe happened. Things are often not how they appear, and the truth can be hidden deep beneath the surface."

"That final operation involved a militia group that was heavy into arms trafficking and drugs," she said.

"That's right."

"I made a call to a law school friend who's an AUSA in town. It appears the exact details of the internal investigation at the ATF are closed to the public, but I was able to learn a bit about the type of work McDonald was doing. I would think he was under a lot of stress in that kind of undercover work. I'm not saying that justifies his actions, but playing a cold-blooded militia member had to have an impact on his psyche. Maybe he never adjusted back to reality."

"Or maybe he was set up by someone who didn't like that a Fed infiltrated their group and caused the deaths of two of their own."

Mia frowned. "You really think that's a possibility, don't you?"

He nodded. "It makes a lot of sense to me."

"Do you have any actual evidence to support it?"

"Not yet, but I intend to keep looking until I find it."

She leaned forward. "I want to be involved."

"Why? You don't believe that's what happened. You think he's guilty."

"I do, but I think his history at the ATF could actually help me prove that."

"You really shouldn't be making phone calls inquiring about all of this."

She lifted her chin in defiance. "I know you don't want me looking into this, but I have to."

He shook his head. "It's not like that. It's just that this militia group is bad news. These guys are deadly. People asking questions can lead to dangerous things."

Mia looked at him for a long moment. "All the more reason we should work together."

"Are you sure you want that?"

Her expression softened. "I just want whoever did this to pay, and until I see evidence to say otherwise, I believe that your friend did this. If you can show me something else, I promise I'll look at it. I owe you that for all you've done to help me."

"You don't owe me anything. You only owe yourself one thing."

"And what's that?"

"The truth."

CHAPTER
SEVEN

Noah sat in his office with Cooper. He needed a trusted outlet to bounce ideas off of.

"What's on your mind?" Cooper asked.

"I think someone related to David's last assignment is setting him up to take the fall for this murder." Ever since Noah had gotten the phone call from Ty Spencer, he'd been thinking a lot about this and trying to put the pieces together.

"Why? What makes you think that?"

"There wasn't just fallout on the ATF side from that op. The militia group that was dealing in arms trafficking lost two of its members that night—including the leader's cousin. What if this is them seeking out their revenge?"

Cooper frowned. "How would a militia group member even know how to set up David?"

Noah wasn't deterred. "They could've been tracking him. What if they had him under surveillance? They saw an opportunity with Chase and took it."

Cooper rubbed his chin. "I think you might be grasping at straws, man."

Noah blew out a breath. He realized he might be too, but he

had a gut feeling that wouldn't go away. "David thinks he was set up. I believe he didn't do it. So the next step is to think about who had the motivation to set him up. He worked on many ops over the years, but this was the freshest, the one where his cover was blown, and the one with the fallout."

Cooper tapped his pen on the desk. "So you're thinking revenge for the death of the cousin. They frame him for murder? Why not just kill David as payback?"

"Yeah." Noah knew it sounded flimsy. "What if they thought making him go to prison for a crime he didn't commit would be even worse punishment? Especially for a former Fed."

"You have a good point there. Prison is not a good place for law enforcement inmates."

"Humor me for a minute. Supposedly there was this fight out in public where Chase and David came to blows. If someone was following David, they could've witnessed the fight and seen an opportunity."

"It's plausible, yes. I'm still doubtful, but it's worth playing out. You need to be careful, though. These guys aren't people to mess with. If they find out that you're nosing around and asking questions, you could put a target on your back."

"I'll be discreet. Don't worry."

Cooper didn't look convinced.

—◁◇▷—

Mia gathered up her things and headed toward the conference room. Yesterday had been a particularly trying day. She was still mortified that she'd passed out on Noah, but he took it all in stride. She'd called Chase's mom and let her know that everything was done except the bedroom, and his mom agreed to finish up. That was good, because Mia didn't think she had the strength to go back. She prided herself on being a strong woman, but this type of pain was on a different level.

She'd taken Sophie's advice and turned to God repeatedly.

But even that only did so much. It definitely helped her not feel so alone, but the pain still ran deep.

Then again, if she wasn't in pain, that would be a bad sign. If one of your best friends was killed, it should hurt. But why he was killed was the bigger question. Was this really all about a stupid grudge? It was so hard to wrap her head around that.

Mia sighed. Feeling sorry for herself wasn't going to get the job done. Too much was on the line.

This would be her first team meeting on the LCI case, and Mia wanted to make sure everyone was on the same page. One of the good things about working at a mega firm like Finley & Hughes was the staffing. She was never a one-woman show but had almost unlimited resources at her fingertips. And given the circumstances surrounding why she was taking over the case, she had Harper's full support. His words rang in her mind. *All you have to do is ask. Whatever you need, consider it yours. We want to keep LCI happy.*

At the end of the day it was all about the client's happiness, which in turn meant they would keep giving the firm work. Mia had once been a bit naïve about how law firms worked, but she'd long since shed that innocent vision. It was always about the bottom line.

She'd had a long talk with Harper yesterday morning because she'd become concerned while reviewing everything Chase had in his office. Files that she expected to find weren't there. And the files that were there were a complete mess.

Harper had reassured her that Chase was running fast and furious before his death. He was trying to bring in new business, which was key for a partner, especially a newly minted one, while also trying to handle the LCI case. Harper felt like she was probably making a mountain out of a molehill. She didn't want to complain for no reason, but Chase's LCI case files were in complete disarray, and she had known Chase to be a very meticulous lawyer.

That not only meant that her job was going to be harder, but she wondered why Chase had kept his LCI case files like that. A more sinister thought crept into her mind: Had someone been rummaging through his office? His apartment had also been ransacked. She didn't want to entertain that train of thought, so she turned her attention to the team meeting.

Mia entered the large conference room that was already filled with the rest of the team. When she walked in, everyone stopped talking. She might not be a partner yet, but as a very senior associate, she should be able to get the attention of those more junior—or at least she hoped so.

Unfortunately, Mia didn't have a tight-knit relationship with these associates, and she definitely wasn't known as being the life of the party like Chase. It would be interesting to see if the team accepted her stepping in and taking charge. At the end of the day, they didn't have much choice, and she didn't either. Harper had spoken on the issue.

"Thanks, everyone, for getting together this afternoon." Mia took a deep breath. She couldn't just jump in and act like this was no big deal. There were things that had to be said first. "I'm not going to pretend like this is a run-of-the-mill change in team members. Everyone in this room knew Chase and cared for him. I can't fill his shoes, but I do plan to honor his memory the best way I know how—and that's by picking up where he left off and putting on the absolute best defense of our client that we can."

Her statement was met with some yeses and nods. "I know everyone is knee-deep in reviewing the slew of documents that we collected so far from our client. We will also be getting the first wave of documents from EPG. After this meeting, I'll send out assignments as to who I'm going to move over to start reviewing the EPG documents."

That got their attention.

Nancy Wayne cleared her throat. "What's the reporting structure going to be like? Who is the *partner* on this case?"

Mia tried to keep her facial expression neutral. They all assumed there had to be a partner, but in this case, there wouldn't be. Harper had been crystal clear about that. "Given the unique circumstances, there won't be a partner on this case. I'll be managing things. If you have any issues, you come to me."

By the looks on their faces, Mia had vastly underestimated the level of resentment these associates were going to have, reporting to her without there being an ultimate partner in charge.

"Are we still going to be on a mandatory ten-hour document review schedule?" Tameka May's brown eyes honed in on Mia as she asked the question.

"I know it's rough to sit at your desk and review documents on a computer for ten hours a day. But I checked with our internal practice support, and they've run the numbers. Given the amount of data we have to get through, the discovery deadlines in place, and the number of people we have working on this case, the answer is still yes. But that doesn't count weekends."

That last comment got a laugh out of the group, because they all worked weekends.

"If you spread out fifty hours over seven days, then that's a little over seven hours a day. Which should still give you time to work on other things."

That statement was met with many wide-eyed stares. She wasn't telling them anything different than what they'd heard from Chase, but she was an outsider jumping into their well-formed team. Chase had a much better sense of humor than her and a more affable personality.

Well, they were stuck with her.

"And what if we'd like to work on another case?" Nancy asked.

Mia stared into Nancy's brown eyes. Before she could respond, Nancy kept talking.

"I'm not asking for myself, but I know there are others who want off this case, especially now that Chase is gone and there's no partner face time."

77

Mia clenched her fists, surprised at how bold Nancy was. "I know I'm not a partner . . . yet. But you should want to do your best work for the client regardless." She surveyed the room of ten associates, making eye contact with each and every person. "If you want out because you don't want to report to me, then let's figure that out now."

Not a single person moved an inch.

Mia let out a breath. "Now that the drama is behind us, can we talk substance?"

Silence. Good.

"Let's talk about what you're finding in the documents."

"Nothing incriminating," Tameka said. "I think EPG is trying to take us on a wild fishing expedition by asking for so many different categories of documents. I haven't seen a single discussion between the decision makers that would be incriminating."

"Let's think about it another way, though." Mia leaned forward. "The contract is poorly worded. We're banking on an understanding that isn't clearly defined in the agreement. Putting aside whether we'd be able to introduce evidence outside the four corners of the document, we need to be searching and thinking of it that way. Did we have discussions with EPG in which we told them exactly what we needed? Did we ever say why a certain type of device was needed for our software to function properly? Did we have discussions on specifications at all? The client is saying we did, so we need to find those documents and then worry about admissibility."

"I think we should make a settlement offer," Nancy said.

"And that's based upon what?" Mia tried to keep her cool.

"The fact that LCI most likely will be found in breach. Why not manage this thing now? Reach a business solution."

If Nancy had any client contact, which she didn't, then she would have known that LCI was not interested in making a settlement offer because they already knew the number EPG was demanding. "That's not going to happen right now. We have our marching orders."

"Isn't it our job to convince our clients that they need to talk settlement?" Nancy asked.

Nancy was openly challenging Mia now for the second time. Mia wasn't sure where all this hostility was coming from. She'd only had limited contact with Nancy in the past. "It's our job to advise our clients, but ultimately they make the call. Not us. We're outside counsel. We're not the client."

Nancy rolled her eyes, and Mia had had enough.

"Unless anyone else has something to say, I think we should all get back to work." No one said anything, so Mia walked over to Nancy. "Let's talk for a minute." She waited until the room had cleared out, then took a seat beside Nancy. "You obviously have some sort of issue with me. Let's get it out in the open."

Nancy crossed her arms. "You're not Chase."

"And you think you have to remind me of that?" Mia heard her voice get louder as she spoke.

"Chase was always talking about you," Nancy said.

"We were very close," Mia said quietly. The memories rushed back as she thought about that framed picture in Chase's apartment.

"But he still loved me."

"What?" Mia had to have misheard Nancy. Loved?

Nancy lifted her chin in defiance. "Chase and I were dating."

Mia raised an eyebrow. This was news to her. But could that explain why Nancy was so unhinged about everything? "I had no idea."

"We were very private about it, since he was a partner and I'm just an associate. But we were in love."

"I can see the need to keep that private." As Mia looked at Nancy, she was having a hard time believing this. Chase had confided in her about a lot of things. Wouldn't he have told her about his relationship with Nancy if there was one? But now that Chase was gone, there was no point in debating the issue. "Maybe it might be best if you take yourself off this case and start fresh on something new."

Nancy shook her head. "No. Chase wouldn't have wanted that. Whether you realize it or not, I'm the best midlevel associate you have on the team. You need me."

Okay, if that was how she wanted to play it. Mia was about to get real. "One of the things about becoming more senior is being a leader. And your attitude today in front of everyone didn't exhibit leadership qualities."

Nancy laughed. "You're one to talk. You have one of the worst reputations at the entire firm."

"For what?"

"For being a coldhearted witch only out for yourself."

Mia gasped. That couldn't be true.

Nancy's eyes widened. "What? You didn't know?"

Mia couldn't find any words. She'd never gotten the feeling that was her reputation at Finley & Hughes. She tried her best to be a team player.

"You didn't." Nancy smirked. "Chase was the only person who spoke well of you. Now that he's gone, I'm sure it will only be a matter of time before you're off the partner track. Then you'll get the 'talk' that you need to start looking for 'other challenging opportunities,' but they won't be with Finley & Hughes."

Mia started to wonder if she was going crazy. Was there any truth to what Nancy was saying? Regardless, if Nancy was sticking on the team, then Mia would have to find out a way to manage her. The last thing she wanted to do was run to Harper. She needed to handle this herself.

"I'm sorry you have such a low opinion of me, Nancy. But we're going to be working together, so you need to put any personal issues aside."

Nancy huffed as she stood up. "I give you a month before Harper takes you off this case. If that."

Mia sat in the chair, unable to move as Nancy left. What in the world had just happened?

—◁◇▷—

The next day at his office, Ty watched from down the hallway as Anna Esposito tapped her black-heeled foot while she waited for him in the lobby. The small lobby held only a couple of chairs and the reception desk.

Ty felt that Anna had a deep-seated distrust of defense attorneys. He guessed that she'd been burned too many times at the beginning of her career, and now, a decade in, she wasn't having any of it. But Ty wasn't like all those other lawyers. He tried to live by a different code, one that allowed him to sleep at night. Fighting for justice in a way that might not make sense to some but made perfect sense to him. He'd learned early on in his career that justice was often not cut-and-dried or applied evenly. Those with power and money lived in a different world from those without. And Ty wanted every person to be equal under the law. That was what drove him.

Ty had two younger attorneys who worked under him, but he didn't have anyone else on his level. Overall, it was a pretty small operation he was running, but he knew he was effective in the courtroom. And being able to perform in front of a jury was the most critical part of his job—and his success.

He gathered himself and walked into the lobby. He ran his fingers through his hair, trying to comb it.

"Please don't tell me you went to court looking like that," Anna said.

Ty laughed and ran his hand through his hair again. "Hello to you too. And no. I've been working on a brief for a death penalty case, and when I get in the zone, I tend to end up looking like this. Sorry to make you wait, but I had to finish my thoughts. Life and death, you know." He realized his shirt was untucked, but he wasn't one to care about appearances.

She looked away. "Okay, now I feel like scum for making that comment."

"Don't give it a second thought. Come on back to my office." He ushered her through the door and down the hall to his no-nonsense office. It wasn't quite as sparse as a prosecutor's, but it wasn't exactly luxurious either. He did well for himself, but he also took on quite a bit of pro bono work. Like the death penalty case he had just mentioned. And those cases didn't keep the lights on.

"Please sit," he said.

She did as he asked and sat across from him as he settled in behind his desk.

"So what is it you wanted to talk about?" she asked.

"I want to take your temperature."

Her eyes narrowed. "On what?"

"A deal."

Anna's jaw clenched. "You called this supposedly important meeting to ask me about a plea deal? Have you completely lost your mind? I think you need some sleep."

Ty shook his head. "I promise I'm thinking clearly. And once you really sit down and go over everything, I think you'll agree that your case isn't as strong as you might have initially thought."

"Whoa. Are you saying that I haven't properly evaluated my case? How would you know what I've done?"

He raised his hands. "There's no reason to get defensive. We're both just doing our jobs here and doing them the best we can. I'm telling you that if you take a good hard look at this, then things won't add up."

Anna leaned forward. "You can't truly be looking at me with a straight face and claiming his innocence."

"Yes, I am, because I think there's a very good chance that he is innocent."

Her nose crinkled. "Then why try to get a plea for an innocent man?"

"Because I know how the system works. And honestly, I wanted to plant the idea of his innocence in your head."

She laughed. "It'll take a lot more than you looking at me with those big puppy dog eyes. My first and highest obligation is to obtain justice for the victim."

"Bingo! And what justice is there if the wrong man is convicted? That means the real murderer is out there going free and an innocent man will be wrongly incarcerated. I can't believe that you'd want that."

"Let me guess—you have another prime suspect you want to serve up?"

Ty shook his head. If only he did. "Not yet. But I'm working on it."

"I think you've wasted enough of my time." Anna rose from the chair.

"Anna, wait a minute." Ty also stood. "I know you're a great prosecutor who will leave no stone unturned. I'm telling you that I'm going to find evidence to exonerate my client. And when I do, I have faith that you'll do the right thing."

"I try my best at my job," she said. "And right now, all the evidence I see only says one thing: guilty."

CHAPTER
EIGHT

That night Mia's feet pounded the pavement as she ran the winding jogging trails at Piedmont Park. She wasn't an avid runner, but she did enjoy jogging to clear her head, especially in the cooler weather. She'd tried other forms of exercising, but nothing helped her like a good jog. Taking in a deep breath of cool air, she let it fill her lungs.

As beads of sweat started to slide down her face, she replayed the conversation she'd had yesterday with Nancy. She wasn't sure what bothered her more: the possibility that Chase had actually been dating Nancy, or that he might have hidden it from her.

She racked her brain, trying to think of any clues that Chase had been having a secret relationship, but she couldn't come up with anything. Chase wasn't chatty about his love life, but given their work lifestyles, she didn't think he had much time for anything remotely serious. Nancy had made it seem like they were on the brink of marriage, and Mia wasn't buying it.

She realized that from the outside, people might think she was jealous. But it wasn't like that. She just didn't want to believe that one of her closest friends had been dating a woman like Nancy. Every word that came from her mouth seemed poisonous. Mia was trying her best not to surround herself with people like that these days.

Mia pushed herself to up the tempo, willing her legs to move faster, trying to sweat out all the stress bombarding her. It didn't help that Nancy had also twisted the screw by commenting on what people at the firm thought about Mia.

She felt like she'd lost all perspective. She was usually so level-headed and guarded with her emotions. After Chase's murder, the world seemed like it was crashing down on her. Now she had a team of associates who clearly didn't want to work for her and didn't seem to respect her. She had no idea how much Nancy had stirred the pot before Mia even came into the meeting, but after giving it some thought, it seemed like a distinct possibility.

Mia would have to figure out a way to be a true leader and get them on her side. She'd never convince Nancy, but she could win over the others. Nancy clearly had a different agenda. Mia even considered the possibility that Nancy might be mentally unstable—and that idea scared her. Could Nancy have hurt Chase? The evidence didn't point in that direction, but Mia had a queasy feeling about things.

As far as the rest of the team, maybe she'd try to have more one-on-one meetings instead of group sessions. That way she could build a relationship with each of them. Why did it bother her so much what they thought of her? Maybe because she didn't want to let Chase down, and they clearly had respected him so much.

Mia was tired of these thoughts, and for a minute just focused on pushing her body to its limit as she wound down the trail in the park. She'd gone farther than she had originally intended, but it was all for the best.

As she rounded the next corner, a tall man jumped out in front of her, startling her. She tried to go around him, thinking it was just a mistake by someone running the opposite direction.

But before she could get out of his way, the man grabbed her shoulders and threw her to the ground. She landed with a thud on her back and yelped in surprise and pain.

He approached, looming over her, wearing a long-sleeved T-shirt and jeans, and a ball cap pulled down low over his eyes. He gripped her arms and lifted her off the ground before slamming her back down again, knocking the breath out of her.

He leaned down so that his face was only inches from hers and squeezed his hands tightly around her neck. His stale breath made her sick. "You need to stop asking questions and mind your own business. Do you understand?"

She looked into his eyes, and a flash of recognition hit. She'd seen this man before.

Fear shot through her, but with the fear was bubbling rage. She was not going to let this man hurt her more than he already had. She'd taken an entire summer of self-defense classes a few years ago with some women from AWA. And now she was going to put it all into practice.

She raked her nails as hard as she could down his cheeks, drawing blood. He howled and staggered back a step, releasing her throat, and she started screaming at the top of her lungs. He reached down again, trying to grab on to her, and she lashed out with her feet, forcing him to dodge.

She jumped to her feet, and when he started to come at her again, she gave him a swift kick in the groin before turning and running as fast as she could—still screaming for help.

It wasn't long before she met a couple of male joggers coming from the other direction. They stopped when she called to them. Her entire body was shaking.

"Are you okay?" one of the men asked.

"No. No, I'm not." She tried to catch her breath. "We need to call the police. I was just attacked."

—◁◇▷—

Noah walked into the Midtown precinct of the Atlanta police department. He'd gotten a call from Cooper that Mia was being interviewed about an incident that had taken place tonight. Details were really sketchy, but apparently Mia had called Sophie in a panic.

When Cooper had contacted him, Noah felt the need to go down to the station to check on Mia. Yeah, they weren't exactly close, especially given the circumstances right now, but Cooper and Landon were on an overnight assignment in south Georgia, and it seemed like Mia could use some help.

Noah greeted a couple of officers and explained the situation—making sure to include the fact that he was former ATF. He waited a couple of minutes, and then Mia emerged with a man who was presumably a detective, based on his suit.

When her big brown eyes met his, they widened in surprise. "Noah."

He immediately noticed the bandage on her neck. There were also some scratches on her arms.

"Ms. Shaw, do you have a way to get home, or should we take you?" the detective asked.

Without hesitation, Noah answered, "I can take her."

The officer looked to Mia for her approval. She nodded. "Thank you, Detective Sykes."

"We'll be in touch to follow up." Detective Sykes gave Noah a little nod and left the two of them alone.

Noah placed his hand gently on Mia's shoulder. "What happened?"

She bit her bottom lip. "Can you please get me out of here? Then I'll explain."

"Sure."

He walked close by her side as he led her out of the precinct and escorted her to his Jeep. She was visibly shaken, and anger bubbled up inside him as he wondered who had hurt her.

"Do you want to go home?" he asked.

Mia shook her head. "Can we go somewhere else and talk?"

"How about my place? I'm only a few minutes away in the Highlands. No one will mess with you there. I guarantee it."

"Thank you."

She sat in silence while he made the quick drive from Midtown to the popular Virginia-Highland neighborhood. He'd bought his classic bungalow when he left the ATF and started his own business. He loved the area, as he could walk to restaurants and shops, and he was only a couple of minutes from their office downtown.

"Let's get you inside."

He took her gently by the arm, and they walked up the steps onto his big front porch. He opened the door for her, and she stepped inside.

"Come into the living room and sit down."

She took a seat on his large beige couch.

"Do you want some water or Coke?" he offered. "Or I could make coffee."

"Water would be good for now."

He left her alone for a minute so he could grab a bottle of water from the kitchen. He was ready to learn what had happened to her, but he didn't want to push her. He purposely gave her a moment to collect herself. He took a deep breath, trying to steady himself as well before heading back into the living room. The last thing he wanted to do was make her uncomfortable by being too amped up.

Noah stepped into the room and handed Mia the bottle of water.

"I don't even know where to begin," she said breathlessly.

"Just take it one step at a time," he encouraged her.

"I've been feeling stressed out from everything that has happened—Chase's murder, obviously, and now taking over his case—so I decided to go for a jog in Piedmont Park. Everything was going fine, and then all of a sudden a man jumped out of the trees and threw me to the ground."

He could see the distress marring her pretty face. "Take your time, Mia."

"I fought against him as hard as I could. I scratched his face. By that time, I was in a bit of a rage. I was scared, but even more than that, I was angry that this man was trying to hurt me, and I was not going to let that happen."

"You were very brave."

"I kicked him, and then I just started running as fast as I could in the opposite direction, screaming my head off. I saw a couple of joggers, and they helped me call the police right then and there."

"Did you get a good look at the guy?" Noah asked.

She grimaced. "That's what I need to talk to you about."

"Go on."

"He spoke to me. He told me to stop asking questions. To back off. As I was fighting, I looked up at him. It was pretty dark on the jogging trail, but I looked into his eyes, and I remembered where I had seen him before." She took a deep breath. "I ran into him getting off the elevator at Chase's apartment building the night I found Chase's body."

Noah's head snapped to attention. "Are you sure? Did you tell the police?"

She nodded. "Yeah, but I think they thought I was just confused and distressed by the attack. I didn't press the cops about what he said, though."

"Why?"

"I needed time to process it. To figure out what it means."

"Because you think it could help prove David's innocence."

She shook her head. "No. I honestly hadn't gotten that far yet, but I do know that I recognized the man. I don't think the police actually believed it was the same guy or that there even was a guy at Chase's place. They believe I'm just confused and too tied up in all of this to think clearly."

"What did he look like?"

"Well over six feet. Strong but not overly bulky. He wore a hat, so I couldn't really see that many details, but he was Caucasian, probably in his thirties or forties. His eyes were definitely dark. I gave the best description I could to the police."

"You did the right thing." Noah held back all of the anger that threatened to overtake him. What a scumbag to attack an innocent woman like Mia. He wasn't naïve. He knew that evil existed. He'd seen it too many times in his career. This was just the type of thing that got his blood boiling. "You realize that this bolsters my theory about the militia connection. You told me you'd been making phone calls. Have you done any further follow-up?"

She sniffed. "Yeah. I've talked to my DOJ contact a few times, but he's a good friend. He would never do anything to put me in jeopardy."

He didn't think Mia realized just how dangerous those phone calls could be. "It's more complicated than that. These groups have sources and informants all over the place. All it takes is someone mentioning an inquiry. Your friend could have the best intentions, but if he asks someone who then asks the wrong person, it could get messy. Real messy. And it sounds like that may be exactly what has happened."

"You think I'm in danger, then?" Her voice cracked.

Noah needed to be honest with her right now to keep her safe. "I think you should be cautious. Please work with me on the ATF angle from now on. You're putting yourself at risk by asking questions. Do you have a security system?"

She nodded. "Security system may be overstating it a bit, but I have an alarm. It doesn't have all the bells and whistles like Sophie's, but it's functional, and I use it all the time, especially since I live alone." She took another sip of water. "But I live in a nice neighborhood. Lots of families and young couples and some retirees. It's not exactly a high-crime area, but I realize in Atlanta we have crime everywhere, especially the closer you get to the city."

"You did the right thing by fighting back today."

Her face paled. "We learned in my self-defense class that there are ways to fend off attackers even when they're much stronger." She paused. "You've been a friend to me even though I probably don't deserve it after how I've treated you lately. I'm not sure how I would've made it through this alone. This is the second time now that you've stepped up and helped me."

"Don't give it another thought. Why don't we get you home? I'll make sure everything is fine at your house, and then once you get some sleep, I think you'll feel better."

"Thank you." Mia rose from the couch.

Noah knew one thing. No one else was going to harm her tonight.

—◁◇▷—

The next day, Mia sat in Chase's office, but she couldn't seem to move out of his chair. The events of last night had taken a toll. She believed deep within her gut that the man who had attacked her was the man she'd seen at Chase's place. But she also had to come to grips with the fact that if that was true, then McDonald might not be the killer. Or McDonald could have been working with this man as his accomplice. He'd specifically told her to stop asking questions, and the only questions she'd been asking had been about McDonald's ATF past. Either way, at the end of the day, she wanted the right person to pay for Chase's death.

Noah was so adamant about McDonald's innocence. She'd thought this case was open and shut, but she wondered if it was a bit more complicated after all. Could McDonald be innocent? She had more questions now than ever.

There were loose ends that bothered her greatly. Why were Chase's files in such disarray? It was almost like he'd been looking for something. Or someone else had been looking for something. And then she remembered that Chase's apartment had been turned upside down. At first, she'd assumed that Chase and McDonald had fought in the living room, but could she have been wrong about that?

If her attacker was also Chase's killer, then that meant that he'd been looking for something in Chase's apartment. But what?

She let out a sigh and closed her eyes. Maybe she was grasping at straws, trying to create problems that didn't even exist. There was no doubt in her mind that she was off her game. She had to find a way to push through this. She couldn't wallow in self-pity about the attack. She had a case to run—and win. Chase wouldn't want her to make a mess of it.

She rummaged through his files, planning to pack up all the LCI materials and take them back to her office. It probably wasn't healthy to spend too long in his office, even though she also felt a connection to him while she was here. She still needed to box up all of his other things, but she couldn't bring herself to do it just yet. The finality of that act was just too much to deal with. For now, she'd target the LCI files. Harper had given her time, and she couldn't imagine they were going to put anyone else in this office anytime soon.

As she searched through the desk drawer to gather up all the relevant files, her hand hit something on the bottom of the drawer above. She leaned down and felt around, then grabbed onto the object and pulled it out of the desk.

She stared down at the flash drive that had been taped to the bottom of the drawer. This was weird. She made a mental note to check what documents were on it. It might not have anything to do with the LCI case, but Chase wasn't normally one to tape his office supplies to his desk. A chill shot down her spine. Things were only getting stranger. Could this have anything to do with his files being a mess?

Grabbing a stack of folders, she made her way back down the hall to her office. It was probably better for her to work there, or people would start talking. That was one thing about the firm: people were *always* talking. Just like how Nancy was trying to stir things up.

Mia had lost a bit of sleep wondering if people at the firm really thought about her that way. Chase was the person she had been closest to. She actually didn't consider anyone else at the firm a good friend. But she also didn't think she had a bad relationship with any of the staff or attorneys. There was no one she would have called an enemy, and she tried her best to be cordial to everyone. That was why Nancy's claims had caught her so off guard.

Her phone rang, and she was greeted by the sound of Owen's voice.

"How's it going?" he asked.

"I sent you a summary update last night on where we are with the document review. Did you get that?"

"Yes. And you said nothing harmful had been identified yet, right?"

"Correct. We'll keep searching." She was still learning the personalities of all the LCI executives. She wasn't sure how frank she could be with the business guys, but she felt it was a necessity to be open with Owen. "I know at the meeting everyone said there was nothing to be worried about, but between us, I'd like to ask again. Do you think any of the execs could have anything to hide here?"

"I don't think you'll find anything. And my guys say they're all tidied up." He paused.

She sensed his hesitation. There was always more to the story in these cases. If there weren't, her firm wouldn't have been hired. "You can trust me, Owen. That's what I'm here for. But I can't fix what I don't know about." This was a dance she'd done many times.

"Howard has been a bit shifty lately. That's always been part of his personality, and maybe I'm just paranoid. I worry about what we could possibly find in his email."

She had to push further. "What are you specifically concerned about?"

"I don't know what I don't know. And that's what bothers me. Howard has consistently pushed for settlement since this thing got started, but at the same time, he claims it's a sham lawsuit. I worry that there could be something out there maybe not even related to this case that he doesn't want to come out. He's said some things over the past month about emails and the sensitivity of his work."

"I imagine he does handle the most sensitive matters, given that you're a tech company."

"Yes, Howard and Ed are the two pillars of the technology development that the company does. They're not only the brains, they're also business savvy. Without them, LCI wouldn't be the same company. I've never met anyone as brilliant in the tech space as the two of them." Owen sighed loudly. "I'm probably just spooked, given everything that has happened. I want to make sure we're on top of things the best way we can be. And as far as I'm concerned, there's no way I'm going to take this case to the board to settle unless we get a completely reasonable number. I don't see that happening unless things change significantly. The board would laugh me out of the room right now."

She looped back to the Howard issue. "Don't read too much into anything at this point. Everyone gets antsy when they know their entire hard drive has been swept up and people are rummaging through their emails. Unless you have something concrete, don't worry about it. Leave the worrying to me, and if the team finds anything questionable at all, you'll be the very first to know."

"Thank you, Mia. Keep up the good work."

They ended the call, and Mia was glad that Owen had faith in her. The question was whether she still had faith in herself.

CHAPTER
NINE

The next morning, Mia pulled out the flash drive she'd found in Chase's drawer and placed it into the USB port of her computer. She waited as her computer recognized the external device, then immediately saw a folder named LCI. Well, that answered her question about whether there would be any files relevant to her case on the drive.

There were a lot of documents in the folder, but it wasn't an unmanageable amount for her to flip through. Not wanting to miss anything, she started with the first file and planned to work her way through the folder. Fifteen minutes later, she had made it through about a fourth of the docs when her eyes stopped on one email.

She took a moment and reread the email a couple of times. It had caught her eye because someone was communicating with Baxter Global, asking to set up a meeting. Baxter was LCI's chief competitor. They weren't connected to this lawsuit in any way that she knew of, but they were definitely gunning for LCI.

Staring at the email, thoughts raced through her mind. She looked carefully at the text, rereading it again. The email hadn't come from an LCI account. It was a generic web-based address. She quickly typed the name of the Baxter Global recipient into an internet search engine and watched as the results popped up. According to his professional profile, Jeff McIntosh was listed as being vice president of technology at Baxter.

Mia knew it was a long shot, but she typed in the generic email address and ran a search. Just as she suspected, there were no hits. This had all the makings of a dummy account. Someone had created this web-based email account to protect their identity.

The more pressing question that popped into her head was how Chase had gotten his hands on these emails. If they were included in the data that was collected for the litigation, she should be able to trace back what computer they had come from. But that was a question for her IT people.

She kept reading until she finished all the emails in the folder. There were two additional emails from the mystery account, also setting up in-person meetings between the sender and McIntosh. If someone at LCI was meeting with their biggest competitor, then that could be huge. Bigger than huge. Tech companies like LCI depended on their employees keeping the tech confidential. If there had been a legitimate need for the two competitors to meet, then the email would have come from the actual email account of the person at LCI. No, her gut was telling her this had to be something more sinister. People didn't create dummy accounts to conduct business on the up-and-up.

She thought for a few moments, trying to figure out any plausible connection to the breach of contract lawsuit. What had Chase stumbled upon? Her stomach clenched. Maybe she was letting her imagination get the best of her, but what if there was something else here? What if LCI had a mole?

She contacted her firm's lead IT person through their internal messaging system and told him to come to her office ASAP. She had to find out whose computers these emails had come from.

Mia only had to wait about five minutes before JJ Savine came into her office. JJ didn't look like your typical techie, being more of a gym rat. While most women at the firm swooned over his biceps, Mia hardly paid attention to him—except when it came to IT issues. He knew his stuff better than any other IT person she'd ever known. He was the key to helping her get to the bottom of things.

She explained her issue to him and handed over the emails she'd printed from the USB drive. "I need to know where these came from—like yesterday."

JJ blew out a breath and ran a hand through his wavy dark hair.

"Why aren't you looking me in the eyes?" she asked. "What's wrong, JJ?"

"You don't know?"

"Know what?" She bit her bottom lip as she prepared for the worst.

He looked up, and his brown eyes met hers. "There was a complete system failure, and the data got corrupted during the document pull. We were able to save most of it, but the metadata, including the sourcing of about eighty percent of the docs, got lost completely. All the metadata pre-collection got completely wiped from LCI's system."

"You can't be serious."

"Sadly, I am."

"Eighty percent of the metadata?" The metadata included all the information about the documents—where they came from, who created them, when they were created, and where they were stored.

"Yes," he responded quietly. "I'm sorry, Mia."

"So there's a good chance you can't find out where these emails came from?"

JJ nodded. "That's right."

More questions ripped through her mind. "Were all custodians affected?"

"No. I can give you one piece of good news. Lew's data is pristine, but oddly, he's the only one."

She sighed with relief. At least they wouldn't have to worry about that issue during the trial. Having the CEO's data intact was especially important. That still didn't solve the problem of the eighty percent that had been lost. How would she explain this to the court?

Right now she had plenty of follow-up questions for JJ. "So these documents, where it looks like someone saved the emails from their web-based account, where would they have most likely been found?"

"Probably in the My Documents folder or C Drive, which is each individual's drive space at LCI. They could have stored them on a shared drive, but if they wanted to keep them to themselves, that wouldn't have made any sense. One other possibility is that they were downloaded to a temporary internet file, and when we did the document collection, they got pulled in that way."

"And Chase knew all of this?"

JJ nodded. "We talked about it right after it happened, and Chase told me that he was going to tell Harper, to make sure he was in the loop, given the impact it may have."

"When did this happen?"

"Just a few days before his death," JJ said quietly.

Her pulse thumped. "So there's a chance that Chase never got to tell Harper about this?"

"Yeah, though I hadn't even thought about that. I'm sorry. I'm so busy, this fell completely off my radar, and I was on to putting out the next fire. It never occurred to me that Chase could've been the only attorney who knew what was going on. Again, I'm sorry."

Mia couldn't blame JJ. It wasn't his job to manage all these issues. He'd given the information to Chase and had assumed that Harper was in the know. "So Chase asked you about these specific emails, right?"

JJ looked closely at the printed pages. "Yeah. Chase isolated a handful of emails that he wanted me to segregate and remove from the review database. I think these were them."

"So our team doesn't have access to these, right?"

"Correct. I pulled them out of the database completely and put them on a USB drive for Chase."

That explained where the USB drive had come from, but she still had so many questions. Like how Chase had gotten his hands on these to begin with. "You set up the database and let Chase have access to it first?"

"Yes. He wanted to run some targeted searches to see if anything hot came up. After that, he asked me to pull these emails and segregate them. I didn't think much of it, honestly. We get a lot of requests to do things with certain documents that need further attention."

At least she was getting some answers. "Let's go back to the data corruption. That happened when you pulled the data from the LCI system?"

"Yes. During the document collection process, there was a system failure. After we rebooted, we had documents, but the metadata was completely stripped—both from the documents we pulled and the originals on the LCI system."

"Do you have any theories about how that happened?"

JJ leaned against her desk. "Usually it would be due to some virus or malware that forced the shutdown and enabled the metadata wipe. Whatever it was, it was highly sophisticated, but we haven't determined yet what we're going to do about it. We're dealing with one fire at a time."

It was becoming obvious to her that things were a lot murkier than they had first appeared. "But you can't guarantee that we have all the actual documents?"

JJ shook his head. "No. If you forced me to put a number on it, I'd say I'm confident we got at least ninety percent. And of that ninety percent, the metadata is completely gone for about eighty percent."

Mia sighed and rubbed her temples. "Thanks for your help, JJ."

He stood up. "Need anything else?"

"Not right now, thanks."

She needed to get completely on top of this. And fast. Not only was she dealing with a potential traitor, but when the opposing counsel found out about the data corruption, she was going to be in big trouble. Had Chase kept this information from the client on purpose? Had he just not had time to tell Harper and LCI?

She knew what her next step had to be. She picked up her phone.

—◈—

Owen sat at his desk, still trying to work his way through the stack of emails that had come in overnight. His clients at LCI called, emailed, and texted him 24-7. There was no such thing as downtime. He'd been under the illusion that he would be able to unplug some at this job, but he had been dead wrong.

His cell rang, and he picked it up, seeing that it was Mia calling. At least her phone call wouldn't annoy him.

"Hey there," he answered. "I'm in my office if you want to call my landline."

"I actually think it would be better for you to stay on your cell," Mia said, her voice tight.

"What?" That statement made his head spin. "What's going on?"

"I don't want to alarm you, but I think we have major issues. I'd prefer to talk to you about some of this in person, but there's one thing I want to talk to you about right now."

He wondered what Mia had stumbled onto. "Sure."

"Did Chase say anything to you about data corruption?"

He started racking his brain. "What kind of data corruption?"

"When the documents were pulled from the LCI system for

this case, the metadata of eighty percent of them was corrupted. And there's no way to retrieve it. It's gone forever. Erased from the LCI system. Everything that existed before the data collection."

"How?"

"We don't know. It could be some type of virus or malware, but I take it from your response that Chase hadn't told you about this?"

"No. And I don't know why he would've kept it from me." Chase had been brutally honest about the evaluation of the case.

"I may have an answer for that, but we need to meet. And you can't discuss this with anyone right now. It's important that you keep this between us. Do you understand?"

"Yes. You name the time and place." Owen didn't like the sound of any of this. The last thing he needed was a spoliation issue. The other side could argue that LCI had corrupted the data on purpose.

"I'll text you details soon."

"Did actual documents get corrupted or just the metadata?" he asked.

"I'm still investigating that. It's possible that some docs got caught up in the web too."

Owen groaned loudly.

"Yeah, I share your pain. The other side will have a field day with this."

"One more reason to consider settlement. We have to figure out a way to get their number down."

"Let me work on that. I'll text you meeting details. I have one other thing I need to handle first." Mia hung up.

Owen sat at his desk in shock. A million questions swirled in his head like water going down a drain.

He'd assumed that Chase had told him everything about the case. Why wouldn't he have shared this when it was such a huge deal? Chase was a highly seasoned litigator and knew the implications of something like this. Knew that it could have a major impact on the case.

Judges these days didn't have much patience for this type of thing and could levy monetary sanctions against the company if there was any whiff that this was intentional—or even just negligent.

And then there was Mia's shiftiness. Something bigger was going on. He intended to find out what it was. He picked up the phone to dial LCI's IT guy but then stopped short. Mia had said to keep it to himself.

He should do as she asked and wait for the meeting. Even it if was going to be difficult.

⊲◇▷

"What are we doing here?" Mia asked Noah. He had asked her to meet him at a storage facility up I-285. The traffic had been awful getting there from her office in Midtown. They stood outside in front of the storage facility as a cool breeze blew. She cinched her navy jacket tight at her waist.

"I've got David's code to his storage unit. We're going to go through it."

That got her attention. "Do you think there'll be anything useful in it?"

"According to Ty, David had two units. One official and one off the books. It's customary for deep-cover agents to have places like this to keep information and personal effects related to their cover."

"All right. Let's see what we can find."

Noah punched in the code and opened the unit's door. A musty smell hit her as she walked inside.

"Why don't you start on that side, and I'll start on this one," he said.

"What exactly are we looking for?" she asked.

"I'm not sure, but I think there will be something here that can help us. Ty wouldn't have asked me to come if that wasn't the case."

"But why bring me along?"

"Because I want to show you that I have nothing to hide, and that David is innocent. I believe there's stuff here that can help prove that. Especially given what happened to you."

She nodded and went to work. She couldn't put on blinders. While it was easy to target McDonald, the strange happenings that kept occurring made her willing to look elsewhere.

Taking a methodical approach, she started going through the boxes one by one. They worked in silence for almost an hour, until she started to think they were on a wild goose chase.

She flipped through a large notebook filled with chicken scratch writing. She couldn't make out much of what McDonald had written, but what she could read didn't seem relevant. That didn't stop her from trying to read every page. "Tell me more about what you know about this militia group," she said as she skimmed.

"They're antigovernment, violent, and make their money through a variety of illegal activities. David was trying to get in deep to figure out their weapons network—including shipments and how they moved their money. From what I can tell, it was a lot more complicated than anyone at ATF had suspected. Van Thompson rules with an iron fist."

She kept flipping through the notebook. "Why isn't Thompson in jail?"

"He wasn't there the night of the raid, and the Feds haven't been able to put together an airtight case against him. A lot of evidence was destroyed in the raid. They don't want to bring charges until they think they can get a conviction. He's a master at keeping his hands clean. He just has a bunch of thugs do his dirty work."

"I still don't see how we tie them to the murder." It was a question that kept her up at night. "Why would they want to kill Chase?"

Noah blew out a breath. "Maybe Chase was just caught in the cross fire and proved to be a convenient target to get back at McDonald. Guys like Thompson have long memories, and they want their revenge. In Thompson's mind, David is solely responsible for the death of two of his own, including his own flesh and blood, plus the trashing of his main compound." He looked at her and set down the paper in his hand. "I have to get to the bottom of this. You have to admit something doesn't add up here. You being attacked and warned off is red flag enough for me, and it should be for you too."

She didn't refute that. He had a point. She turned to her next box and started riffling through the contents.

"Hey," Noah said, breaking her out of her thoughts.

"What? Did you find something?" She turned to face him.

"Oh yeah. Look at this." He walked over to her. "This is a picture of Van Thompson and some of his associates. Take a look." He handed her the picture.

She studied the picture, focusing on each man in turn. One face made her drop the picture, and it fluttered to the ground.

Noah placed his hand on her shoulder. "What's wrong?" He leaned down and picked up the picture.

She pointed to the photo. "That man in the background there, turned to the side. Do you know who that is?"

He shook his head. "No. We can try to find out. Why?"

Mia looked up at him. "That's the man who attacked me. The guy I saw at Chase's apartment."

His eyes widened. "Are you sure?"

"I know it's a grainy picture, but yeah. That's him." Her mind raced as she tried to play out what this could mean.

"Mia, this is huge." Noah grabbed her hands. "This is one of Van's men. You can ID him and put him at the murder scene." His expression hardened. "That means you're in danger."

—◁◇▷—

Noah sat in his office with Ty and looked at the forty-something defense attorney. Instead of wearing a suit, Ty just wore a button-down and khakis. Noah had to fill Ty in on what they'd found in the storage unit.

"I have some stuff to tell you too," Ty said. "But why don't you start."

Noah pulled the picture from his bag. "This man." He pointed. "Mia saw him leaving the apartment complex the night she found Chase's body. She also thinks this is the man who attacked her in Piedmont Park." He had already filled Ty in on the attack.

"Do we know who he is?" Ty asked.

"Not yet. We're trying to track down his identity, but we know that he is associated with the militia. Can you show it to David and see if he knows who this is?"

Ty nodded. "Absolutely. We'll make a color copy, and I'll take it to him. This could be a big break in the case. If nothing else, it introduces doubt. It would mean that David was spot-on about being set up."

"I agree. We still have no idea why this guy would've wanted to kill Chase as part of a revenge plot against David, though. I'm hoping that once we get a positive identification, we can put those pieces together."

"That sounds like a plan. I'll let you know as soon as I get David's feedback on the picture."

"What else did you want to talk about?" Noah asked.

"We have an interesting development," Ty said.

"Interesting good or interesting bad?"

Ty rubbed his chin. "Well, that remains to be seen."

"Just spit it out, man."

"One of the evidence bags has gone missing from APD."

That threw Noah for a loop. "What? How?"

Ty cleared his throat. "We're trying to get to the bottom of that."

"What was in the bag?"

"The hair fibers tying McDonald to the scene. And maybe something else. That's also an issue. The labeling of the bags wasn't done to protocol."

"Isn't this good, then?" Noah failed to see how this would be harmful to the case. If anything, it seemed like a positive development.

"When Anna finds out, she's going to blow a gasket, and I think it might make her go for blood. I wouldn't be surprised if she accuses the defense of evidence tampering."

Noah took a breath and looked into Ty's eyes. Would this man have tampered with evidence to help his client?

"And before you even start thinking it, no, I was not behind this. I do everything I can to defend my clients, but I do not and have never broken the law." Ty lifted his chin in defiance.

"I never said you did."

"But you were thinking it," Ty quickly shot back.

"The thought crossed my mind, but you don't seem like the type to get your hands dirty."

"I'm not. The moment I get a reputation for being willing to skirt the law, I lose any moral high ground I have in defending those who are wrongly accused. And in this case, I believe that your friend is innocent."

"What will we do about this latest development?"

"Nothing. Just wait and see if the police can find the missing evidence. If they can't, then this will obviously be a piece of what I present at trial. Anna will go ballistic, but she won't be able to overcome the fact that the evidence went missing from APD—that's more on the prosecution than on us." Ty took a breath. "There's one more request I have."

"Shoot."

"It's about Mia. Can you leverage your relationship with her to try to get any information you can about Chase's life? No detail is too small. She clearly was the closest person to him, and we need to know what she knows. I don't have to remind you that a man's life is on the line."

"You should know that she's out for vengeance. She's hurting over the loss of her friend, and even with this new evidence, she still isn't ready to think that David is innocent."

"Then it will be your job to introduce doubt into her mind. She's an attorney. If she really cared about this guy, she will want the right man caught. I can promise you that."

"Easier said than done."

Ty gave him a sly smile. "I'm sure you'll figure out a way."

CHAPTER TEN

That night Owen waited patiently for Mia to arrive at the Colony Square coffee shop in Midtown they'd agreed on. He'd purposely arrived a few minutes early because that was his usual practice. The anticipation of what Mia had to talk to him about was taking over. He'd run through their conversation over and over in his head. He'd still done as she directed and not talked to anyone at the company about the data issues, but he feared that what Mia was about to drop on him was going to be a lot more.

A few minutes later, Mia walked in the coffee shop and made her way over to the table he'd secured in the corner.

"Hi," she said.

He stood up to greet her with a kind handshake. "Can I get you something to drink?" he asked.

"No, I'm good." She sat down, and he took his seat.

"I admit you have my interest piqued," he said. That was an understatement.

"Sorry about the inconvenience, but once I explain everything to you, I think you'll understand."

"Please, go ahead." Owen steadied himself for whatever was to come.

She frowned, and he knew this was going to be serious.

"I already told you about the data corruption. My IT guy tells me he only has confidence that ninety percent of the documents were recovered, and upward of eighty percent of the metadata is gone. The good news is that Lew's metadata is completely intact."

"That's something." But Owen knew there was more bad news to come.

"The reason I even found out about this is that I discovered a USB drive in Chase's office. That drive had a set of documents from LCI on it. When I reviewed them, I found some emails between a dummy account and the VP of technology at Baxter Global."

"Wait a minute. There were emails pulled from LCI that were sent to the VP of technology at Baxter Global?"

She nodded. "Now you see why I wanted to meet you like this."

He had to hold himself back from releasing a string of curses. This was bad. Really bad. "You think someone on the inside is working with our competitor?"

Mia bit her bottom lip. "I can't be sure. The emails only indicated that meetings were being set up, so I have no idea whether they actually took place or what was discussed if they happened. But given the sensitivity of the type of work you do and the fact that Baxter Global is your biggest competitor, this sent up all sorts of warning signs for me."

His mind swam as he sat in silence for a moment, trying to think through the implications.

"And what's more, I suspect that the malware or virus was put into the system by the person who sent that email. They're trying to cover their tracks. With the metadata gone, there's no way for us to trace where that email came from. The sender probably tried to delete these documents too, but something slipped through the cracks. My IT guy mentioned that they could've gotten pulled as temporary internet files. So there could be more that we aren't seeing because they were wiped from the system."

He was impressed by her level of strategic thinking. "I don't have to tell you how big this is. I think you already know that from the way you've handled everything."

She drummed her fingers on the table. "Now we need to think about next steps. Not just in terms of the case, but even more importantly in terms of finding the mole."

"That's more my problem than yours." And it had just become number one on his priority list. Everything else paled in comparison.

She shook her head. "It's both of our problems. I'm here to help in any way you need it. I think the first step is figuring out who to tell at the company."

He blew out a breath. "I have to let Lew know."

Mia nodded. "I figured as much. And the fact that his data was clean definitely decreases the risk that he's involved. But beyond that, I don't know how much you can trust the rest of the executive team and their direct reports. I would advise you to think long and hard about who you can actually trust, given how high the stakes are here."

He ran his hand through his hair. His day had just gone from bad to worse. He had come up with multiple scenarios in his mind for what Mia was going to reveal, but nothing like this. "I need a little time to think through all of this. Also, Lew is probably going to direct me on who I include once I tell him."

"Do you want to involve me in the conversation with Lew?"

"I think, given the sensitivity here, it might be best to have the initial conversation just between him and me. I imagine it's going to be a very unpleasant conversation. No offense to you, but I think you get it."

"Totally. I realize your top priority has to be the mole, but we also have to figure out a game plan for handling the data issue in the litigation. When the opposing counsel finds out, it's going to get super ugly."

"Yeah. And the scary thing is that isn't even the biggest area of exposure for us. You've laid a lot on me." That might be the understatement of his legal career.

"I know you need time to think. But the sooner we come up with a strategy, the better. The timing of the disclosure of the data problem to the other side may become an issue with the court. EPG is going to move for sanctions as surely as I'm sitting here with you right now."

"And the sad thing is that sanctions might be the least of our problems. We might have to face the fact that sanctions are inevitable and worry about the bigger picture. I know you don't want to hear that, because your firm could get sanctioned as well. But if we have an insider working with Baxter Global, the existence of the company is at stake. The sanctions would be a mere afterthought."

She patted his forearm. "I'm really sorry about this."

"It's not your fault, Mia. I appreciate you bringing it to me so quickly. And speaking of that, don't you think it's strange that Chase didn't tell me?"

"Maybe he just hadn't gotten a chance yet. I bet he was trying to find answers so that he'd have some sort of explanation for you. As outside counsel, we hate to drop something on our clients without understanding the full landscape and scope of possible exposure. Given the timing, it's possible he just didn't get the chance." She paused. "You don't have to answer this, but is there anything the company is working on right now that would be more high profile than normal? Some technology that, if it got in the hands of a competitor, would be devastating?"

"Yes. I can't divulge the details, but I know of a couple of products that would fit that description. In our business, that's just the nature of the game. Our employees sign highly restrictive covenants not to compete and strict confidentiality agreements. The tech space is high-risk like that."

"Someone may be looking to sell out, and this case has just gotten in their way."

That was exactly what he feared.

—◁◇▷—

Mia heard a knock at her door about seven o'clock on Saturday night. She wasn't expecting anyone. A thread of fear pulsed through her, as she was still on edge, especially now that the picture was haunting her dreams. But logic told her the attacker wasn't going to ring her doorbell.

She walked to her front door and looked through the peephole. She frowned as she saw Noah standing on the other side. She opened the door, and he smiled at her.

"Sorry to bother you on a Saturday night," Noah said, "but can I come in and talk for a minute?"

She hesitated.

"If you'd rather come out, that's fine too." He stepped to the side.

"No, no. Come on in." She allowed him through the front door. "Can I get you anything to drink?"

"Don't suppose you have some coffee?"

She laughed. "Coffee is a requirement in my life. Come into the kitchen, and I'll make some. Are you here to check on me?" She wasn't sure what Noah's angle was.

He took a seat at her kitchen table while she put on the coffee. "This is a great kitchen," he said.

The small talk was awkward, so it was better to just cut to the chase. "I know you didn't come over here to talk about my kitchen. What's on your mind?"

"I was hoping we could talk about Chase. I'm trying to put together the puzzle pieces here, and I think it would be helpful."

"I admit I have a lot more questions than answers right now, but I'm still not at the point where I'm completely convinced that McDonald's not guilty. But with each new revelation, I'll admit I'm getting closer to that conclusion."

"Mia." Noah reached out and grabbed her hand. "David McDonald is innocent."

His warm touch startled her. For a moment she couldn't speak, and she didn't want to move her hand away from his grip. As she locked eyes with him, a spark of electricity shot through her. The last thing she needed was a crush on this guy, but there was a magnetic force drawing her to him instead of pushing her away. Finally she broke contact and stood up to pour the coffee.

Would she be betraying Chase by talking to Noah about him? But then, Noah had a point. At the end of the day, this was about seeking the truth and getting justice. "How do I know that you won't use what I tell you to help McDonald, and it turns out he truly is guilty?"

"Mia, I realize you don't know me that well, and I don't expect you to jump into this and give me all of your trust. But I'm asking you—I'm *begging* you—for a chance to let me *earn* your trust."

"And how do we do that?"

He locked eyes with her. "Honest communication and my word that I will not betray you. I take this all very seriously, and the truth matters to me. If I were to find out that David had done this, then I would want him to be punished too."

As his words soaked in, a feeling deep inside urged her to give him a chance. "You'll have to forgive my apprehension, but in my line of work, I don't really trust people."

"My faith demands that I see this through, Mia. That I defend the innocent. And that I do it while searching for the truth."

"I'm learning more and more each day what it means to live your faith. I spent my whole life not believing in anything. To change that has been a challenge, but also eye opening. It's also caused me to have more questions."

"Like what?"

"Why would God let an innocent man be brutally murdered? Chase did absolutely nothing wrong. He was loved by everyone. Kind, caring, funny. It doesn't make sense to me. I don't have the answers, but I'd like them."

Noah shifted in his seat. "This world is a messed up place, Mia. There's no promise that life on earth is good or fair or anything like that. I know our culture tells us that life should be good and fair, but it's not. And God never told us that it would be—in fact, He told us it would be just the opposite. But the thing is that this life here on earth isn't the end of the line. This situation on earth is only temporary."

She sighed. "I've heard those concepts talked about in church, though maybe not exactly the way you're saying them now. But why would God design a world that was so messed up?"

"It's a long story, but I'm happy to try to explain. Do you want to hear?"

"Maybe another time." The gentleness in his eyes was almost more than she could handle.

"You're hurting. I want to help."

"But why? I don't get it. Why do you want to help me?" she whispered.

"Because I do."

—◁◇▷—

Noah looked into Mia's big brown eyes, which were filled with confusion. He could tell that thoughts were flying through her head. He couldn't help wanting to walk with her on her faith journey, but he also didn't want to push. She was going through a traumatic time, and it was natural for her to have questions. He appreciated that she didn't blindly accept doctrines but instead really wanted to understand her newfound beliefs. That made him have a lot of respect for her. But it also made him cautious about how close he was getting.

"I want to help. That's all I'm saying. Help everyone get to the truth," he said.

"You remind me so much of Kate."

"What do you mean?" he asked.

"She's one of those people who is always trying to help people. To do the right thing."

"You say that as if it's bad."

She shook her head. "No, not at all. It's just that I find most people are much more self-interested than they let on. Kate's a rarity, and I was just pointing out that you seem that way too. It's refreshing."

"Tell me about Chase." He thought it best to move on. For now.

Mia raised her floral coffee cup to her lips. "Like I said, everyone liked him. He was the type of guy people wanted at firm events. He could talk to anyone, but he wasn't the least bit pretentious, even if he was incredibly smart."

Watching her talk about him, he wondered again if Mia had feelings for Chase. "You don't know of anyone who would want to hurt him? Anyone he had disagreements with? Friends, coworkers?"

"The only disagreement I know about is his running feud with McDonald."

"What kind of work did he do at the firm?"

"Same as me. We're both in the litigation department, but on the corporate defense side."

"You defend big companies?" Noah asked.

"You don't have to say it with such contempt."

He lifted up his hands. "Wait a minute, I never said there was anything wrong with it."

"You didn't have to say it. It was written all over your face."

"I really didn't mean to give you that idea. In my line of work, I deal with companies of all sizes."

"I have six figures in debt I've been working to pay down from

Emory law school. I had to take out loans because I didn't have any support or money from anywhere else. So my only option is to work in Big Law and get the six-figure salary. As you can tell, I don't live a particularly flashy lifestyle."

He had noticed that her home was nice but not what he would call luxurious. It actually felt very homey and warm to him. "I respect you for all the hard work you've put in. I can't even imagine making it through law school, much less the years you've put in at the firm. I've heard that most lawyers in big law firms get burned out by the five-year mark."

"Yeah, it's really common. Not many stay to try to make partner. Ideally, I'll stay long enough to pay off my debt and then transition into something else. But I'm still a few years away from that."

"Was Chase working on anything high-profile at the time of his death?"

Mia pursed her lips. "He had his normal caseload, which included one high-profile case."

"Can you tell me about that one? Just generally, nothing confidential."

She set down her coffee cup. "I actually took it over."

Now, wasn't that interesting. "How did that happen?"

"Honestly, I think Harper Page, the managing partner, felt sorry for me and wanted to give it to me to help me process the grief."

"What's the case?"

She leaned back in her chair. "We represent LCI."

"The software company?"

"Yeah. It's a breach of contract case brought by a smaller company called Electronics Pursuit Group, or EPG."

"So some type of tech dispute over a contract?" He was no lawyer, but he understood general business terms.

"To simplify it, yes."

Noah shook his head. "I'm just trying to gather the facts.

Understand the landscape. See who Chase was interacting with at the time of his death. Those people could hold the clues to finding how he was connected to this mystery man." He could tell that she hadn't shut him down yet. She was a smart woman, and he was trying to appeal to that side of her. The emotional side of her would still fight for vengeance against David, and he couldn't really blame her.

"You really think so, don't you?" she said.

"I do. I can't say that any of this will matter, but it's worth tracking down every single person he's been in contact with."

She bit her lip. "There is something else."

"What?" He was intrigued by her hesitancy.

"Nancy, an associate at the firm, claimed she was Chase's secret girlfriend."

"You seem very skeptical."

"I think she's crazy. Chase wouldn't have kept me in the dark."

"There sure wasn't any sign of Nancy in the apartment." Noah took a moment and then had to ask, "How did you and Chase get to be so close?"

She didn't immediately answer. "I know you think we had some type of romantic history, but it's actually much different from that."

What did she mean? "I don't understand."

"We had a lot in common. Once we started to get to know each other, we found out that we came from a similar background. We were both raised by single moms who struggled with drug addiction and relationship problems. As you know, his mom is still alive. Mine succumbed to her addiction a few years ago."

So that was where a lot of the pain in Mia's eyes came from. She hadn't had an easy life. That also explained why Mia was helping Chase's mom with the packing. So many pieces were fitting together. "I'm sorry that you had to go through that."

"It is what it is. But that's one of the reasons Chase and I clicked. He took me under his wing and made me a better attorney. Like the big brother I never had. He was fiercely protective of me, threatening to beat up the random guys I dated." She smiled. "And he meant it. He wanted to make sure I was safe." But then her eyes filled with tears. "Like I said, Chase was a great guy." She looked down.

"I didn't mean to upset you." Noah's gut clenched at seeing her in pain. He hated seeing people hurt—and it really bothered him seeing Mia like that. It was almost as if he felt somehow responsible for the hurt she felt, given his connection to David. That was just another motivating factor for him to find the real culprit.

Mia looked up at him. "I live in a constant state of pain right now."

That statement was the final punch to the gut. He couldn't help himself. He rose from his chair and pulled her into his arms.

At first he thought she might pull away, but she rested her head on his chest and returned the hug.

He leaned down, and the smell of peach shampoo filled his senses. What had started as a friendly outreach effort was turning into something more. At least for him.

ELEVEN

M ia walked into work Monday morning still reeling from one simple thing—Noah's hug Saturday night. Yeah, he was gorgeous, and when he'd wrapped his strong arms around her, she couldn't deny the attraction. But the kindness he had extended threatened to melt her. That alone let her know that the lack of sleep and continuing grief she felt was messing with her head.

Mia had never been in a serious relationship—and that was on purpose. She'd learned from her mother's disastrous life-style, and she'd rather be alone than turn over control to a guy who wouldn't have her best interest at heart. She'd seen it happen time and again with her mom. Would it be nice to have a husband one day? Yeah. But she knew her heart was tightly guarded to protect herself from getting hurt. And she wasn't sure Noah would even want someone like her.

They'd had such different life experiences—hers based on rationality and his on belief. But her life had been changing, and she had opened herself in ways that she had never thought possible. If you had told her a year ago that she'd be going to church weekly with Sophie, she would have laughed in your face. But there was no denying God was changing her. She just didn't know how much He could do. Could He fix the damage that her mother had done? There was a ton—instilled during her formative years. She didn't know if anyone or anything was that powerful. In her mind, it was an open question, but one she was at least willing to ask. That was a step in the right direction, or at least she hoped it was.

When she was around Noah, he made her feel more alive. Like she had someone by her side who actually cared about her as a person. But over time, would that change too? Would he become just like any other guy she'd dated? No one she'd gone out with had actually seemed that invested and interested in her as a person.

"Get a grip," she said out loud. It was time to prepare for her first meeting with opposing counsel in the LCI case.

She walked into the conference room where she knew her guest was already waiting. EPG was represented by Kate's firm, Warren McGee. Thankfully Kate wasn't the lawyer, because the last thing Mia needed right now was to go up against her friend. She was glad the attorney was someone she didn't know. Well, she knew *of* her by reputation, but that was only because of what Kate had told her over the years.

Bonnie Olson stood when Mia entered the room. The Warren McGee partner was in her late forties. Her platinum blond hair was styled in a sleek cut that almost hit her shoulders, and she wore a perfectly tailored gray pantsuit with a light lavender blouse. A strand of southern lady pearls adorned her thin, pale neck. She was known as an ice queen who would go for the jugular, and Mia did her best to try to disarm her with an encouraging smile. But Bonnie's cold façade didn't break. She extended her clammy hand and gave Mia a monster shake.

"So you're taking over the LCI case?" Bonnie's cool blue eyes met her own.

They each took their seats at the conference room table. "I am. Thanks for meeting me today. I thought we could start hashing out some of the discovery issues."

"You won't be thanking me when we're done with the meeting." Bonnie smiled, revealing pearly white teeth.

Mia could play this two ways. She could engage in Bonnie's games and tactics, or she could ignore them and just be all business. Frankly, she didn't have the energy to spar with Bonnie, and she knew Bonnie was a pro. Better to just get down to business and get out of there. "Do you want to talk about the document production?"

Bonnie nodded and opened up her laptop. She clicked away for a minute in silence, then made eye contact. "Look, I'm not a heartless woman, unlike what you've probably heard about me."

"All right." Mia wasn't sure what Bonnie's point was going to be, but this was sure a big windup.

"I of course gave generous extensions on discovery deadlines after Chase's untimely death, but I think we now have to get this case back on track. You're a perfectly capable and accomplished attorney, and while I'm sympathetic, I have my client's interests to think about now. And they are starting to get impatient. Highly impatient. It's not their fault all of this occurred. They were injured by your client economically, and it's high time we get a move on."

Mia was tiring of Bonnie's long-winded speech. "What exactly are you suggesting?"

"I want to tie down dates for completing your document production. My client can only wait so long."

Mia bit the inside of her cheek. Her temper was starting to rise. "You realize that the person running this case was brutally murdered?"

"Of course." Bonnie flipped her hair back. "But we're still alive. Life goes on. Right?"

"Are you being serious right now?"

"I've been reasonable," Bonnie shot back.

"You were hounding us about the litigation the day after Chase's murder. The *day after*."

"Once I realized the situation, I backed off. As was appropriate. Don't twist the facts."

"If what you did is backing off, then you really are a piece of work."

Bonnie laughed. "I want to set the record straight. I've laid off for the past few weeks, but now it's time to get down to business. There's no need to get emotional about it. Let's put some new dates on the calendar and proceed."

"Get emotional?" All of Mia's plans to be cool as a cucumber had evaporated, and she felt like she was about to erupt like an angry volcano.

"Getting emotional is so unbecoming in a female attorney. It makes you look weak."

Mia felt her mouth drop open, and her nails dug into the flesh of her hands.

"Are you sure you're going to be able to handle this?" Bonnie asked.

"*You* . . ." Mia stuttered. "You are everything I've heard about you and a million times worse. You will get your documents. And when I crush you in the courtroom and your client wants to fire you because you lost their case, then that will make me happy."

"You're friends with Kate James, right?"

"Yes, but I fail to see what she has to do with this." Why was Bonnie dragging Kate into this?

"You could learn a lot from her. You're still too green to tangle with attorneys like me. Go back to your managing partner and get his assistance on the case. Better to ask than to totally flop."

"You're trying to give me career advice now?"

Bonnie smiled. "You're no threat to me."

It took every bit of strength Mia had not to leap across the table and wring Bonnie's skinny neck. But she had to be the bigger woman here. Bonnie was trying to get inside her head, and Mia was playing right into her game. It was time to toughen up.

"Bonnie, did you come here to grandstand, or are we actually going to talk about the discovery?"

"Sure. Let's talk about the fact that there are still fifty discovery responses unanswered." Bonnie crossed her arms.

"Speaking of that, when should I expect to receive the rest of *your* documents? I've only received a small number at this point. I'm sure you have more, right? I know you want to paint EPG as a small entrepreneurial start-up, but we both know that's not true. You've got more tech power in that company than ninety-nine percent of the tech companies in the world." That might've been overstepping just a bit, but Mia knew she had a point. EPG wasn't a small fish. Compared to LCI, they were much smaller, but they had tremendous power in the tech space. The last thing she wanted was for a jury to believe that this was a David and Goliath type of case. That was the narrative she was going to have to fight. She planned on doing just that. That was why she needed to push Bonnie on documents.

"We're well within the time we have to produce documents. You might not realize this, since you're new on the file, but Chase didn't serve discovery on us until two months after we served him. Therefore our deadlines are not even close to being over, given the extensions each side has granted each other. You will receive more documents, and you probably don't even want the volume that I'm going to give you. You asked for it, so you're going to get it."

Mia needed to push more. "When will I get to depose your key witnesses?"

Bonnie stood and whisked up her laptop in one fluid motion. She walked to the door before finally turning around. "I'll let you know. I think maybe it's best for us to conduct these negotiations via email until you've pulled yourself together a bit more. You're clearly not stable right now. I think the pressure and circumstances have clouded your ability to be rational about this case."

Mia forced a laugh at Bonnie's ridiculous assertion. The gauntlet was thrown, and she couldn't allow herself to back down.

—◁◇▷—

Noah had tapped in to every facial recognition program he had access to and still hadn't found the identity of the man in the picture of Thompson and his militia group. The photo quality made the software less accurate. While computer work was Noah's forte, sometimes the computers couldn't give you all the answers you needed.

Ty had shown the picture to David, but unfortunately, he hadn't been able to identify the mystery man. So here was Noah, with Cooper by his side, about to head into a biker bar south of the city that was a known hangout for some of the militia members. The owner was an old friend of Van Thompson's, and the place was a safe haven for the group.

This wasn't Noah's scene, but he knew that to find the answers they were looking for, they'd have to ask questions of people who might know. When Noah had told Cooper his idea, his friend had insisted on joining him, and Noah was thankful for the backup. Cooper had done undercover work when he was with the APD, so the two of them had the skills to pull it off, but Noah knew that asking questions in crowds like this could be a recipe for disaster.

"You ready to go in?" Cooper asked.

"Roger that."

They had both dressed to try to fit in. Noah wore a black leather jacket and jeans. But he couldn't change his ultimate look—his Latino heritage from his dad's side of the family. He also lacked the requisite tattoos, but the jacket covered his arms anyway.

"I'll take the lead initially," Cooper said. They'd both agreed that Cooper might be more successful than Noah in getting answers.

When they walked through the door, the smell of smoke hit Noah right off. "I hate these places," he mumbled.

"I know. I don't miss this part of my old job," Cooper said.

There was a solid crowd for a Monday night, and they made their way through a group of guys playing pool and up to the bar area.

"Let's start with the bartender," Cooper said.

The two men sat down on some empty stools and waited for the bartender to approach.

Noah sat quietly as Cooper struck up a conversation. They both knew they couldn't just whip out the picture first thing and jump into it. They had to work up to it—or at least that was the plan.

About half an hour later, Cooper pulled out the picture and slid it across the bar. They'd cropped the photo to only include the man in question.

The bartender frowned deeply. "Are you two cops?"

"Absolutely not," Noah said.

"Then why are you here asking questions?" The bartender crossed his large, meaty arms across his body. "I think it might be time for you to get a move on."

A stocky bald man with full body tattoos walked over. "Is there a problem here?"

"No problem," Cooper said. He stood up and turned to face the bald guy, and Noah did the same.

"I don't think you belong here," the bald man said, directing his comment at Noah.

Noah shook it off. They had bigger problems than this man's biases.

"They're asking questions about this picture," the bartender said.

The bald man picked up the photo, and a smile spread across his face. "You two have to be Feds," he said loudly. Too loudly. His words got the attention of other patrons.

This was going south quickly.

"We're not Feds," Cooper said. "We're actually PIs, and this guy owes our client some serious money."

Noah held his breath, hoping this cover story would hold. "We're trying to track him down to make sure he's all squared away with our client."

The bald man laughed. "You punks don't realize what you've gotten into. Whatever your client is paying you, it isn't nearly enough. You're messing with the wrong man. I suggest you walk out of here right now and pretend like you never had this job. Call your client and tell them that if they want to live, they should just let it go."

A tall lanky guy joined the conversation. Noah was acutely aware that he and Cooper were starting to get boxed in. The lanky man picked up the picture. "Who's looking for Liam?"

A first name!

"I think these two gentlemen were just leaving," the bartender said. "Isn't that right?"

"We'd like to maybe play a round of pool, since we're here," Cooper said, trying to stall to get more information.

The bald man took a step closer. "That's not going to happen."

"Then where could we find this Liam?" Noah asked. "Our client is going to want their debt paid."

"You work for the cartel?" the lanky man asked Noah, making assumptions based on the way Noah looked.

"We're PIs," Cooper responded.

"And we need to know where this Liam is," Noah insisted.

The lanky man spoke again. "This isn't the cartel's turf, and Morrow won't appreciate you trying to bother him here. Tell your bosses that."

"I'll ask again—where can we find Liam Morrow?" Noah was glad to have the name, but he quickly realized he'd pushed it too far.

The bald man slammed his fist into Noah's stomach, but Noah was able to block the next attempt.

Another man grabbed him from behind and held him while he took some hits. Cooper was also trying to fend off a couple of attackers. While they were outnumbered, they weren't out-matched. These men were scrappy, but they weren't well trained. After taking a few punches, Noah was able to land a few jabs himself to gain some breathing room.

"Run!" Cooper told him.

They both broke free and turned over chairs as they ran toward the exit to try to keep anyone from following. They were quicker and sober, which helped, and when the fresh air filled Noah's lungs, he had a moment of relief.

That quickly ended when someone tackled him hard from behind. But Cooper was able to pull the man off of Noah and throw him aside.

"Go, go, go!" Cooper yelled.

Noah ran to the passenger side and flung open the door. They jumped into the car, and Cooper floored it.

"That was a close call," Cooper said.

It was, but it was well worth it. "We got the name. Mission accomplished."

—◁◇▷—

On Tuesday afternoon, Ty took a deep breath before walking into the Fulton County courtroom. Just as he had predicted, Anna had immediately started pointing fingers in his direction over the missing evidence.

It was no surprise that she'd filed this motion with the court. The problem for Anna was that she was on the wrong side of this thing, which was what he planned to explain to the judge. He felt Anna was letting her feelings get the best of her and wasn't thinking through this rationally. Once the judge heard the facts, Ty thought he'd be fine, and they could move on.

But first he'd have to get through what would probably be an unpleasant hearing.

This would be their first appearance before their newly assigned judge—Judge Franklin Davenport. Ty knew all of the active judges in Fulton County, and Judge Davenport was no exception. The judge's record skewed pretty heavily toward the prosecution, but Ty thought that under these circumstances, he should be okay, at least for today. Judge Davenport's record, however, was one of the reasons he didn't want this case to go to trial. But unless he found some great exculpatory evidence, he didn't see Anna backing down. She was like a dog with a bone and viewed this case as a résumé builder in addition to doing what she believed was the right thing.

He noticed that Anna was already sitting at her counsel's table. The curly-haired prosecutor might look innocent enough, but he knew her as the type to go to the max in prosecuting her cases. The rumor mill had it that she had her eye on a bigger job one day, and this senior ADA position was just a step on the ladder.

He could only hope he'd be able to come up with another suspect before the trial. The more time he spent with David, the more convinced he was of David's innocence. But he still didn't have a plausible alternative to put forward. He wasn't going to give up, though. He still had time to figure this out.

He walked over to Anna. "Good afternoon."

She looked up at him. "I hope you realize that this motion isn't personal, but I have no other choice."

He couldn't help but laugh. "How can it not be personal? You personally accused *me* of stealing evidence from the storage room of an Atlanta police precinct."

Anna shrugged. "The way I see it, that's the most likely scenario. I certainly didn't take it."

Unbelievable. "Guess we'll leave that up to the judge."

She pushed her shoulders back. "Yes, we will. Judge Davenport will no doubt take my view on this."

"You don't lack confidence, do you?"

A slight smile spread over her rosy lips. "I'm just doing my job. You're a worthy adversary, but I'm on the right side this time."

"That's where you're wrong." He turned and walked to his table to get organized as he waited for the judge to arrive.

He didn't have to wait long, as the judge entered the courtroom a couple of minutes later, and Ty rose from his seat. Davenport was a large fellow, bald and in his late fifties. He'd been on the bench a good twenty years.

"Please take a seat. Ms. Esposito, so nice to see you again in my courtroom."

"Thank you, Your Honor."

That wasn't a good sign. They were already buddy-buddy.

"This is the state's motion, is it not?" the judge asked.

Anna shot up out of her chair. "Yes, Your Honor."

Judge Davenport nodded. "Then let's get started."

Anna adjusted her navy suit jacket. "Let me preface my argument by saying that I realize this is a rather unique motion to be filed at this time, but if Your Honor will allow me to explain, I think it will make sense."

"Go ahead," the judge responded.

Anna glanced over at Ty before continuing. "Last week I received word from Atlanta police that one of the evidence bags that contained hair follicles and possibly other materials had gone missing from the evidence room at the station. While under most circumstances this would be a problem for the prosecution, as I laid out in my motion, I believe the defense tampered with the evidence."

"Let's pause right there for a moment. I did read your motion, Ms. Esposito, and I must say it was very eloquently written."

Uh-oh. Let the love fest begin. Ty tried to keep his facial expression neutral.

"Thank you, Your Honor." Anna's cheeks reddened.

"However, as strong as the writing is, it's a bit thin on facts to support your allegation," the judge said. "I'm wondering if you have more evidence than what you included in your written motion."

"Your Honor, as you know with these matters, getting hard physical evidence to prove tampering is difficult. Even in cases with more evidence than presented here, there isn't a smoking gun like in so many other scenarios we deal with."

Judge Davenport nodded. "Mr. Spencer, I haven't let you speak yet. Let me hear your initial reaction."

Ty stood. He had to play his cards carefully. If he pushed too hard, he might lose any momentum that could go his way. He had to make a strong argument without going over the top and losing the judge. "Your Honor, I think Ms. Esposito is missing the most fundamental point here. The evidence was in *police* custody. Therefore, if there was any tampering or mishandling of any kind, I don't see how that could be put on the defense—or me personally, as Ms. Esposito states in her papers."

The judge nodded. "I tend to be sympathetic to your point, Mr. Spencer. Which is why I'm expecting that Ms. Esposito has something more than what we've heard so far, because she's a seasoned prosecutor and wouldn't have filed this motion based solely on her own conjecture." He gave Anna a look that was half-expectation, half-warning.

Ty had to admit that Davenport was being much more favorable to him than he could've hoped.

"Ms. Esposito?" the judge prompted.

"I do have something, Your Honor. Surveillance tapes at the station showing that Mr. Spencer was at the police station before the evidence went missing."

Ty couldn't hold back a laugh. "Your Honor, I'm a defense attorney. I'm at the police station all the time."

"That's exactly my point!" Anna exclaimed. "Mr. Spencer had both the opportunity and the strong motive to tamper with the evidence. Can I explain exactly how he did it? No. But he has many contacts on the police force, and he could've made it happen. That evidence was absolutely crucial to my case. There is zero reason why anyone associated with the prosecution would take it. It would be directly against the state's interest to remove that evidence. Only someone who wanted to help the defense would've done it."

Ty shrugged. "Your Honor, I'm an officer of this court. And I submit to you right now that I did not tamper with evidence."

"Did you direct anyone to do so?" Anna asked.

"Your Honor, am I being examined by Ms. Esposito right now? Do I need to be sworn in?" He was doing his best to keep his temper and sarcasm in check, but it was proving to be difficult.

"Okay, counselors, let's reel this back in." Judge Davenport leaned forward in his seat. "Ms. Esposito, unless you can present some additional evidence, I have no choice but to deny your motion for sanctions against the defense."

"But, Your Honor, this is critical to the state's case."

"I understand that, but you have no real evidence tying Mr. Spencer to any of this. If you find something more, I'd be happy to entertain it at a later date. But for now, this matter is over."

Ty watched as Anna's shoulders slumped. He was surprised she had been so cavalier with such a serious topic.

After the judge exited the courtroom, Anna approached Ty while he was packing up. "You may think you can get away with this, but this isn't over."

He placed his hand on her shoulder, trying to make a point. "Anna, I promise I had nothing to do with that evidence going missing."

"Maybe it wasn't you personally, or at least I can't prove it yet. But you or someone on your team did have something to do with it. Of that I'm certain."

"You've really gone off the deep end on this one."

"Why should I believe a word you say?"

"Are you that distrustful of defense attorneys? Do you think we're all just a bunch of liars?"

Her eyebrows raised. "You said it, not me."

He shook his head. "You're unbelievable. You sit on your high horse and claim to care about justice, but all you want is another win in your victory column. I've got you figured out now, Anna Esposito. It's not about justice for you. It's just about you."

She gasped. "You have some nerve."

"I think I hit the nail on the head."

"Once a jury hears everything, they will convict your client. Even if I don't have that physical evidence. I don't even need it. All the circumstantial evidence will more than suffice."

"Not after they've heard my defense. There are other possible suspects here."

"Like who?"

He was bluffing, but he'd gone too far to back down now. "You'll find out soon enough." He paused. "And the next time you accuse me of breaking the law in front of a sitting judge, you better have something to back it up."

He'd had enough of Anna's tactics for one day. It only made him more motivated to prove his client was innocent.

―◄◇►―

Mia sat on her living room couch with Sophie by her side. It was at times like these that she was thankful to have her best friend near. Mia was a wreck and felt like she was almost at her breaking point. After the altercation with Bonnie, she was beginning to question not only her people skills, but her abilities as a lawyer.

"Thanks for coming over, Soph."

"Of course. You know I'm always here for you. No matter what. I feel like since I got married that you've backed away." Sophie's blue eyes looked at her with concern.

Mia broke eye contact, feeling a bit guilty. "Yeah, that's probably true. But just because I wanted to give you time with Cooper. I don't want to be selfish. I know I'm the odd woman out, and you're so happy right now. I don't want to bring you down with all of my problems."

"Mia, we're best friends. It doesn't matter what I'm going through or what you're going through. We are with each other through the good and the bad. You've let me cry on your shoulder. You're always so tough. Please let me help you get through this rough time in your life. I'll do whatever I can to help you."

Mia's heart warmed at Sophie's kind words. Sophie was known as the softy in the group, always in touch with her emotions. Unlike Mia, who had built a wall around her heart, refusing to let others see in. "Your friendship means the world to me."

Sophie turned squarely toward her. "So tell me what's going on."

"As much as I wanted Kate to come over too, I'm actually glad she couldn't make it."

"Why is that?"

"Because this has to do with Bonnie Olson."

"Oh!" Sophie rolled her eyes. "You're referring to Kate's partner at Warren McGee, right?"

"Yeah. It turns out she's the lead attorney representing EPG in the case that I took over for Chase. He was working on it before his death, and Harper assigned it to me. I think he did that for a variety of reasons. He wanted to make sure I had something to do, given my grief, but he also knew how close Chase and I were, and he wanted me to be able to honor his memory in some way."

"So you had an encounter with Bonnie?"

"*Encounter* is an interesting way to describe it. Because it was a hot mess."

Sophie patted Mia's knee. "You know you can tell me about it."

Mia took in a deep breath, preparing to tell the story. "I

suggested that we have a meeting to catch up on the discovery schedule and because we're going to be dealing with each other a lot as the case goes forward. I assumed Bonnie would be highly professional, even if she was a pain, but boy, was I wrong." Mia took a breath, trying to decide how much to tell Sophie. It was kind of embarrassing, but she figured it was best to just let it all out instead of keeping it bottled up inside. "Bonnie basically accused me of being unfit to try the case and said I was overly emotional. She just sat there in the conference room, hurling accusations at me like she was on some high horse and I was her underling."

Sophie's blue eyes widened. "You've got to be kidding. That woman is unbelievable. I know she's given Kate fits over the years, but I guess she acts even worse to her opposing counsel."

"Yeah, it's one thing to be a tough lawyer and grind at opposing counsel. There's even something to be said for mind games and tactics. But she was downright mean and rude and exhibited a totally callous attitude toward Chase's death and a hostile attitude toward me. I've never even met her before or done anything against her. I just don't know where it came from. It seemed very odd how she came at me."

"You know, Bonnie was probably just trying to get inside your head. She knows you're very vulnerable right now because your close friend was killed. I don't know that I would take it personally. I think she's just trying to get a leg up in the litigation, and we've all heard that she's a no-holds-barred type of litigator."

Mia considered Sophie's words for a minute and thought there was probably some truth to them. But something else was bothering her. "There's another thing."

"What is it?"

"There's an associate at the firm named Nancy. She came to me and claimed that she and Chase had a secret relationship."

"Are you serious?" Sophie's voice squeaked.

"Yeah. I really don't believe it. I don't think Chase would've hidden it from me. I also don't think he would've dated an associate at his own firm, since he was a partner. That would be a real no-no. And Chase was full of integrity. More than most lawyers I know." Mia paused before revealing the most hurtful part of the conversation. "Nancy also said that I had an awful reputation at the firm. That no one respected me, and that I had no one on my side." As the words came out of her mouth, she felt even worse.

"Mia, that's absolutely ridiculous. You not only have a good reputation at your firm, but you have a strong reputation in the legal community. Everyone at AWA knows how hard you work on the committees. And you always do it with a positive attitude instead of complaining like so many others. I think Nancy might have it out for you. What if she was in love with Chase and saw you as an impediment?"

That thought had crossed Mia's mind. "I considered that. But you should've seen the reaction when I told the team I would be taking over the case and that there would not be a partner on the file."

"Don't you think that's just because they're used to having an ultimate partner authority figure and they don't want to answer to someone on their level? You are a senior associate as opposed to a junior or midlevel, but still."

"Yeah, it's possible. But I just feel like I'm getting beaten while I'm down, if you know what I mean. And you have to remember that all this came on top of me getting jumped in the park. I'm wondering if I can handle everything."

Sophie squeezed her hands. "Mia, you're the rock of our group. You're always strong, independent, and fearless. But you don't always have to be that way. You're human. You've been through a traumatic month. Not just Chase's murder, but like you said, the attack in Piedmont Park and all the upheaval on your cases. It's bound to take a toll. You're not Superwoman, even though I know you try to be. And it's really okay for you to ask your friends for help. Never think that I'm going to be too busy for you just because I got married. We were friends long before my husband came along. You've let me cry on your shoulder a million times."

Mia was overcome with emotion. For the first time in a while, she felt a little peace at being able to talk so openly about her feelings. "How do you think I should handle the team?"

"Give them some time to adjust to you. As long as you're working hard and being fair and reasonable to them, they will learn to respect you. You understand what it's like being an associate in Big Law. It's a really hard lifestyle. Yeah, you get the huge salary and perks, but it's demanding, and it's 24-7. You just act the way I know you do as a lawyer, and once they get to know you better, they'll appreciate all you bring to the table. You'll be a great leader, and I'm sure your team will notice your commitment level." Sophie paused. "I know the last thing on your mind right now is making partner. I get that. I also live in a different world as a prosecutor, so it's easy for me to play career counselor here. But please don't overlook the fact that this is a huge career opportunity for you. If you run with this case, manage it well, and pull off a victory, you will be a superstar at Finley & Hughes."

Mia gave her a wavering smile. "I appreciate the vote of confidence, but right now I'm just trying not to drown."

"Let me help. You don't have to bear this burden alone." Sophie bit her bottom lip and looked directly at her. "The Lord will listen to your prayers, Mia. He's right there by your side and can do more for you than I can. But know that I'm praying for you each day. You're in a dark valley right now, but you will get through this. And you will be stronger in the end."

Mia gained strength from Sophie's words. "Thanks. And I know I can be a pain by always questioning and asking more and more, the deeper I get on this new path I'm taking. There are no simple answers for me. One answer just leads to more seeking and asking."

Sophie nodded. "By asking those questions, you've shown that you care and that you want to live life in a new way. We've known each other since law school, and I can tell that the woman sitting beside me right now is not the same woman I met back then. Back then you were a true skeptic. That's not who I'm talking to anymore. This tragedy may have thrown you for a loop, but sometimes that's just how life works. It doesn't have to define who you are. You're strong, Mia, and the Lord is right there with you, holding you up when you think you can't take another step."

The conviction in Sophie's voice allowed Mia to open up even further. "I still feel restless. You and Kate seem so much more content than me. Maybe it's because you have someone in your life you love, but I think it's deeper than that."

"Faith isn't a magic pill. It's important to understand that. Not to expect the pain to just stop because you've let God into your life." Sophie paused. "But it does allow you to cope with the pain in a different way. There is a peace that God provides that you can't get from anywhere else—even in the darkest of days." Sophie's eyes glistened with tears.

Her friend's words rang true to Mia. "And I do believe that. If this tragedy had happened a few years ago, I honestly don't know if I would've made it through. Thanks, as always, for talking to me and being so open and honest. I don't know what I'd do without you." It was funny, because she'd always assumed Kate and Sophie had gotten it wrong. But seeing how the two of them faced adversity with such strength and grace, and now going through it all herself, she understood that she was the one who had been wrong the entire time.

CHAPTER
TWELVE

Owen sat in the living room of Lew's penthouse in a Midtown high-rise. He'd just finished recounting to Lew everything he knew up to this point.

Lew had interrupted only a couple of times, asking questions, but besides that had let Owen talk. Now Lew sat in silence, and his face had grown noticeably red. Owen thought it best to give him time to process the bombshell he had just dropped.

"I'm going to need a stiffer drink. Do you want anything?" Lew asked.

"No. I'm good." Owen wanted to make sure he was thinking clearly for this important conversation.

Lew returned a couple of minutes later with a drink in his hand. "How in the world did this happen?"

"Unfortunately, there can always be a bad apple out there."

"Bad apple!" Lew uncharacteristically raised his voice. "This could bring down the entire company! Everything I've worked the past decade to build. Everything the rest of the team has worked on. This has been our entire lives."

Owen had to keep Lew calm. "I know. Which is why we need to decide how we want to handle this right away. And the biggest question we have to ask ourselves is who we bring into the circle."

"I don't think we can bring anyone else into the circle. Until we know more, everyone is suspect. And I mean everyone." Lew's face got even redder.

"Mia brought this to me. I think we could use her help."

Lew nodded. "Yes. That's good, she doesn't count. But no one inside the company can know about this. We can't take the risk that we'll tip them off. This has to be completely off the grid."

"I think that's the right call at this juncture." Owen was relieved that Lew didn't want to pull in the rest of the executive team.

"We need someone who can get into our system and figure out what's going on, but it has to be an outside source. Not one of our internal IT people."

"I'm sure Mia has someone who can help." Owen made a mental note to get right on that.

"Good." Lew set down his drink. "And as far as the lawsuit, we just march forward?"

"Yes. We'll take some heat on the missing data, for sure, but I think you'll agree that we just have to face the consequences. The viability of the company is the thing that matters most right now."

"I think we need to focus on the executive leadership first and work our way down."

"Understood. I'll talk with Mia, get an action plan together, and circle back."

"You realize this is all of our jobs on the line?"

All too well. "Yes, sir, I do. I'll do my best to get to the bottom of this as quickly as possible."

"I also want you to be thinking about every legal action we can take against this culprit when we find him or her."

"Will do."

Lew nodded, and Owen got the feeling he was being dismissed. He rose from his chair, and so did Lew.

"Thanks for bringing this to me so quickly," Lew said. "I don't know what I'd do without you in my corner. And please thank Mia for her diligence as well."

As he left the apartment, Owen pulled out his cell. He hated calling his outside counsel this late, but Mia would understand. They had a lot of work ahead of them.

⬦

Noah had been surprised to receive a call from Mia asking to meet at her office. He wasn't sure what was going on, but he happily agreed to the meeting. He'd given her the identity of her attacker once he'd discovered it and wondered if this request for a meeting had something to do with that.

It was ironic that Mia was the first woman he'd been seriously attracted to since the debacle with his ex. But attraction was one thing. Acting on it was another. She was in a vulnerable state right now, and he worried that he might be misreading the signs.

That didn't mean he couldn't continue to work with her as he tried to prove David's innocence. It just meant that he needed to draw a clean line in the sand and know in his own head and heart where he stood with her. He had a feeling that if he did open his heart to her, things could get really messy, really quickly.

As he waited in the reception area on the thirtieth floor, it reminded him what different worlds the two of them lived in. The posh and swanky law firm was a vast departure from his sparsely decorated and practical office a few minutes away downtown.

But he was also reminded of Mia's words about having to pay off her debt. He knew that large firms like this paid top dollar, and he wasn't begrudging her that.

A few minutes later, Mia walked into the lobby to greet him. Today she wasn't wearing a suit but instead a light blue sweater and black pants. She had her long hair pulled back into a bun.

"Thanks for coming down," she said.

145

"No problem. It's just a few minutes from my office."

"Come with me. Do you mind taking the stairs? I'm just one flight up."

"Stairs are good with me." He eyed the long staircase adorned with dark wood. Everything in this office came with a hefty price tag. "This place is pretty spectacular."

"Yeah. When clients pay fees like ours, they expect to be pampered for it. The office upkeep is really important to firm management."

He laughed. "We don't have the same concern at K&R Security."

She smiled at him. "We're in different lines of business." She led him down the hall and into her office, closing the door behind him. "Please sit."

Noah looked out her window. "Great view. I'm guessing there aren't any bad views up here."

"Thanks. Sometimes it's actually depressing having the view because I'm locked in here."

"I get that." He paused. "What did you want to talk about?"

She leaned forward. "First, I want to let you know that I contacted my DOJ friend about getting intel on Morrow. I'll let you know if he knows anything."

"Good. We're working all of our sources too. Now that we have an ID, it's only a matter of time before we figure this whole thing out."

"Figuring this out is what I want to talk to you about. I need to hire you."

He wasn't expecting that. "Hire me? For what?"

"Remember I told you I've taken on a big case of Chase's?"

"Yeah."

"Something has come up that I need your help on. Would you be willing to sign a confidentiality agreement so I can explain in more detail?"

He was definitely intrigued but also a little hesitant. "Sure.

I'll sign one, but, of course, I'd like to hear everything before I commit to taking it on."

Mia nodded. "Of course." She opened up a manila folder on her desk and slid a piece of paper and a pen in front of him.

He took a moment to read the one-page agreement. Seeing nothing out of the ordinary, he picked up his pen and signed before giving the document back to her.

A half hour later, he'd heard what seemed like a pretty crazy story, but he was withholding judgment for now. She had given him enough information to make him agree to take the case.

"You're concerned that there's a mole, and you need me to get into the LCI system and see what I can find?"

"Yes, but you have to do it off the grid. You have the express permission of the CEO, Lew Winston. So whatever you need to get in without the LCI IT guys finding you, you can do."

"You're basically asking me to hack their system."

She shifted in her seat. "Hacking implies something nefarious. This is aboveboard because Lew is the CEO and has signed off. I don't know if you completely understand how high the stakes are here. The company could stand to lose millions if an LCI employee sells their tech to Baxter Global."

"No, I get it."

"We can also use the general counsel, Owen Manley, as a resource. If you need his help to get a door into the system, he can do that. I'm not well-versed in all your tech methods, so you'll just have to let me know what you need from me or LCI."

Noah started processing all of this information. "If we find out who planted the malware, then we find the mole."

Mia tapped her pen on her notepad. "You're the expert. However you think it's best to go about your investigation, I will leave up to you. But needless to say, timing is important. The longer the mole goes undetected, the more damage he can do."

"Is there a priority of suspects?"

"Yes. Glad you asked that. We need to start with the executive team. I can get you a list." She started typing on her computer.

This side of Mia was all business, and it suited her well. He could tell how dedicated she was to this case. But there was something bothering him as he took everything in. "Can we go back for a minute?"

"Sure." She turned her attention away from her computer screen. "I emailed you the list."

"Thanks," he said.

"Tell me what you're thinking."

"I'm concerned about the fact that Chase hid those documents in his desk and didn't tell anyone what he knew. Isn't that odd? Why didn't he tell the general counsel immediately? That seems like it would be the first phone call no matter what, given the high stakes involved here and the potential implications to the viability of the company."

Mia frowned. "I've thought about that a lot, and honestly I'm not sure what happened. You're right that it's very odd. My best guess is that Chase wanted to take the client something concrete and not just speculation."

"Is that what you would've done?" He needed to understand if he was off base here.

She didn't immediately answer. A few beats of silence passed between them. "I don't think so, but it's so hard to say when you're not in the situation. Chase was probably conducting his own investigation, and his life got taken before he could get the answers he needed to feel he could go to the client. It's a lot easier to look back, knowing what we do now, and question it. At the time, he was probably just trying to figure out what in the world was going on." She shook her head. "I'll put you in contact with Owen. It's just Owen and Lew who have any idea about this, and we need to keep it that way."

"Understood. Discretion is a huge part of my job."

"Thanks for working on this. You have a reputation for being one of the best on this tech stuff."

"In my business, half the battle is persistence. And I'm not one to give up."

CHAPTER
THIRTEEN

Mia had agreed to meet Walt at the coffee shop, as he preferred to talk to her in person. She'd given him a call immediately after she had learned the name of the man who had attacked her and asked for Walt's assistance.

She felt a little bad because she knew he was so eager to help her because he had a crush, but she'd been completely up front about how she felt about him. And he still said he wanted to assist.

She waited patiently as she sipped her mocha—a special treat that she felt like she needed today. After a few minutes, Walt arrived, but today he wasn't smiling. Her lanky, blond friend was a good-looking guy, but she couldn't help that she felt zero spark toward him.

He gave her a quick hug and sat across from her.

"Do you want something to drink?" she asked.

He shook his head. "No. We should get right to it."

"What is it?"

His blue eyes honed in on her. "This guy you asked me to run down, Mia. Before I get into what I found, I need to know—are you in some sort of trouble? I can help you if you are, but I need to know."

"No. It's not like that." She explained why she was interested. She had tried her best to keep him out of it, but he needed to understand what this was about.

He ran a hand through his hair. "I'm worried about your safety."

"Tell me what you found out."

"Liam Morrow is bad news. He's a hired mercenary who will do anything for a price. The majority of his business dealings have been with Van Thompson's militia group, but he's also worked for a few different organized crime groups as well. He's known as being ruthless and highly efficient at his job. Simply said, he's a pro. And if you're on his radar, then you're in trouble."

"But if he really wanted to kill me, he could've already done so."

"Sounds like he warned you to drop it, but you've kept digging. His warning may turn into action next time." Walt placed his hand on top of hers. "I'm really worried. I think you need some type of protection until this is sorted out."

She nodded. "I'm working with someone who can help on that front."

He moved his hand away from hers. "My questioning has raised some eyebrows. You know I'd do anything I can to help you, but at some point, people are going to get suspicious as to why I'm trying to get all of this info."

"You've done so much for me already, Walt. And I know you have a ton on your plate right now. I'm forever grateful to you for looking into all of this."

He crossed his arms. "You want to give me the bottom line about what this is really about?"

Mia bit her lip. This would be the first time she'd said the words out loud. "I think Morrow was hired to kill Chase and have McDonald take the fall."

"So whoever put out the hit had to have known about McDonald's past."

"Bingo. But as you've shown me, if you have the right contacts, you can find out these things. I'm guessing the possibilities for this type of knowledge are endless?"

"I wouldn't say endless, but if you're well connected and know the right people, you can get the intel. No question about it. But on this point I don't even have to speculate, because there's something else I need to tell you."

"What?"

"My FBI contact told me that I haven't been the only one asking about McDonald."

"Seriously?"

"Yeah. I can't trace back who was making the ultimate ask, but through a series of contacts, someone got to my guy and asked about McDonald before I started digging around. This is bigger than you think. And much more dangerous."

Owen sat in his office for a closed-door meeting with Noah Ramirez from K&R Security. Thankfully, no one could see into his office, and the closed door gave them privacy.

"Thanks for jumping on this so fast." Owen sized up the man in front of him. Looking at Noah reminded him that he needed to pry himself away from his desk more often and get back to hitting the gym. He guessed Noah was in his thirties, and from the research he'd done, Noah came highly recommended. Mia had also sung his praises, and Owen hoped it would pay off, because they were in dire straits at the moment.

Noah looked at him. "I'm ready when you are."

"What do you need from me?" Owen was generally comfortable around most technology, but he assumed this would be much more complicated.

"Are you logged in to your computer?" Noah's dark eyes questioned him.

"Yeah."

"All right. Can we switch seats? I need to get onto your computer, but I will have some questions as I go."

"Of course."

Owen stood up, and Noah moved to his seat. Noah's hands started pounding away at the keyboard at a crazy rate. Owen considered himself a proficient typist, but this guy was on another level. He was just glad that Noah was on their side and not on the other. Although whoever the sellout was had to be proficient at technology or know someone who was, especially given the data corruption issue. Owen was convinced the mole had done that to try to destroy evidence of his traitorous acts.

"I realize that normally I'd be working with IT, but the situation here is too risky to do that." Noah kept typing as he spoke. "I know you have other things you'd rather be doing."

"Yeah, of course. But there's nothing more important than this. Though I must admit, this is my first time dealing with circumstances like these."

"We'll get to the bottom of what's going on. It just may require more patience than any of us really have."

Noah proceeded to ask him a string of technical questions about their server and how their systems worked. Luckily, Owen had enough knowledge to be able to answer him.

"What exactly will you be looking for?" Owen asked.

"I'll be doing a few things. Right now I'm creating a way to remote into your computer so I can do most of my work offsite. I don't want anyone to get tipped off if they see me here too much. People will start asking questions, and we don't want that. Better to stay under the radar."

"That's a good idea." And one Owen hadn't thought of.

"If anyone asks, just say I'm a friend of yours."

"Will do." Owen paused. "Is this always so spy-like?"

Noah shook his head. "No. Most of my cases aren't like this. But every once in a while, we get a hot one."

"I'd prefer it be cold, but I guess we don't get any control over that. Once you're into the system, what will you do?"

"I'll look for the source of the malware, and then I'll do a sweep to see if I can find any other communication between employees here and Baxter Global. After I complete that, I'm going to do a specific deep dive on the executive team."

"Including me?"

"You got anything to hide?" Noah raised an eyebrow.

Owen laughed. Noah's straight-to-the-point approach was a welcome change of pace. But he didn't have anything to hide. "If only I was so interesting. I'm married to this job, man. I've got nothing exciting going on in my life."

"I can relate to that." Noah continued to type.

"Sometimes I wonder why we put ourselves through all this." He wasn't sure why he was having this conversation with Noah, but the words just came out.

Noah stopped typing and looked over at him. "Don't you like being a lawyer?"

Owen considered the question carefully. "I don't hate it. But I don't love it either. I don't know many people who do have a true passion for it. Especially not on the corporate law side. What about you?"

Noah's fingers resumed flying over the keys. "I love having my own business. It's great. The work is challenging, and I can take on things I really want to do."

Owen didn't know whether this case would be a fun challenge for someone like Noah or a thorn in his side. "So you wanted this case?"

"Yes. And Mia asked me."

"Are you two close?"

"We share mutual friends."

That was a pretty evasive answer, but it wasn't any of Owen's business.

"Aha," Noah said.

"What is it?"

"I'm good to get in the system. Question for you. I need you to answer honestly."

"Shoot."

"How good are your IT guys?"

Owen thought about it for a moment. "Good. Given the sensitive nature of our work, we try to hire highly competent people. But this is coming from someone who is only mildly competent with technology. I can handle the standard gadgets and programs, but that's as far as it goes. Our IT people operate on a different level from that. They've always been able to quickly diagnose and resolve any issues I've had."

"I figured as much. Do you know how aggressive they are at monitoring system intrusions?"

"I've never heard any of them mention any specific protocol or issue surrounding that. If there were a corporate directive to engage in monitoring, I'd be fully in the loop on that, given the legal and compliance implications. Honestly, the biggest issue we have is keeping everyone from chewing up the bandwidth on social media. But Lew refused to use a blocking program to keep people off of it, so IT goes crazy over that. They will seek you out and give you a reprimand if you're streaming too much content, unless you're an executive. The rules of bandwidth don't apply to that level, but everything below the executive team is monitored for usage, since Lew wouldn't go for the blocking software."

"Lew is building up goodwill, huh?"

"He believes it's more important to be a loved CEO than a feared one."

Noah tilted his head. "Sometimes fear is good, though."

Owen let those words sink in. Given the situation they found themselves in, he felt Noah was right. "Well, this thing has rocked Lew, so I imagine there will be changes going forward. I just hope he doesn't get freaked out and swing too far the other direction and get all command-and-control on us."

"Another question."

"I'm ready." Or at least he hoped he was.

Noah locked eyes with him. "I need your best assessment. If your life depended on it and you had to say today who you think the mole is, who would it be?"

Owen cracked his knuckles. "You're putting me in an awkward spot."

"It'll be a lot more awkward if this blows up."

Owen knew Noah was right. "If you held a gun to my head, I'd say Howard Brooks. But that's just because he's been acting a little on edge lately, and he's the top technology officer of the company. He has access to our top-secret projects and wouldn't need to go through anyone to get to them. He has that level of control and autonomy, plus the know-how."

"That would be one bold move, would it not?"

"Yeah, and deep in my gut, I don't really think he would sell out, but you asked for my best guess. That's what I've got."

"I'll start with him."

"Good."

Noah turned. "You know I'll also be looking through all your stuff."

"Yeah. Like I said, knock yourself out. It's as boring as it comes."

"It just seems wrong not to be upfront about my snooping."

"I get it. Whatever you need, any time of day or night, you call my cell."

"Thanks. I'm going to go back to my office and start working."

"Good luck."

―◁◇▷―

As Mia sat in the Fulton County courthouse, she couldn't believe how gutsy Bonnie Olson was. Well, actually she could believe it, because Bonnie was quickly becoming her least favorite person on the planet. Even given all the extenuating circumstances, Bonnie had filed a motion to compel—and a scathing one, at that—claiming that LCI was intentionally withholding key documents.

When the motion had popped up in her inbox, Mia thought she might go through the roof. The little email full of smart comments from Bonnie only pushed her further toward the edge. She was mad at herself for letting Bonnie get so far inside her head. There had to be a way out of Bonnie's nasty web, because right now Mia felt like Bonnie was in control, and she didn't like it one bit.

Hopefully the judge would see how preposterous this motion was and summarily dismiss it. But butterflies jumped through Mia's stomach. This was her first time arguing on this case, and she desperately wanted to make a good impression on the judge. The judge would know the circumstances of the change of counsel, and she hoped he would be reasonable about the timing of the document production.

Mia was also in an impossible position because she wasn't ready to talk to Bonnie about the missing data. She had to be armed with all the information to have that conversation. There was a risk—and a big one—in not bringing it up, but she had to consider the bigger picture here and deal with the fallout later.

Judge Andrews entered the courtroom, and everyone stood.

Mia glanced over at Bonnie, who was wearing a bright red power suit and black heels that were taller than any Mia would ever attempt to wear. Everything about Bonnie was larger than life. Mia preferred a more understated approach, like the dark gray pantsuit and one-inch heels she wore today.

"Please be seated," Judge Andrews said. "This is a specially set hearing on EPG's motion to compel the production of documents. Who do we have here today representing the parties?"

"Bonnie Olson for EPG, Your Honor. Nice to see you again."

"Thank you, Ms. Olson. And for LCI?"

Mia stood and straightened her shoulders. This was no time to let her nerves show. She was no shrinking violet. "Mia Shaw, Your Honor."

"Ms. Shaw, nice to have you here today." He paused. "Although I'm sure we all wish it were under different circumstances."

"Thank you, Your Honor." Hopefully his comment meant he would be sympathetic about the situation. Everyone in the entire Atlanta legal community knew about Chase's murder.

"Ms. Olson, this is your motion, so please, the floor is yours."

Bonnie strode up to the podium, steady as a rock on her monster heels. Mia almost wished she would trip, but knew that wasn't a very nice thought.

Bonnie glanced over her shoulder, giving Mia a cutting look. Mia did her best to remain expressionless and not flinch. This was going to be a battle of wills.

"Your Honor," Bonnie began, "obviously it goes without saying that our hearts and prayers are with everyone at Finley & Hughes over this tragic loss. But on the other hand, this case still has to proceed, and my client's economic and business interests are also important here. They shouldn't be punished because of this tragedy. That's why I've filed the present motion to compel. We served our discovery requests immediately upon filing the complaint, well before Mr. Jackson's tragic death. Therefore, most of LCI's arguments will ring hollow to Your Honor's ears. We've been exceedingly patient, working with the new counsel for LCI. Ms. Shaw is an associate at Finley & Hughes, and I realize this case is a lot for her to take on."

Mia felt her cheeks redden. She couldn't believe Bonnie had called her out like that. She rose from her seat. "Your Honor, I fail to see how Ms. Olson's editorializing about me is relevant here."

"I tend to agree. Get to the point, Ms. Olson."

Bonnie glanced at Mia again with daggers in her eyes. "The

point is that Ms. Shaw is in over her head, but that is not my client's problem. There has been adequate time to review and produce the requested documents, and all I've received so far are hard-copy files that are close to worthless. We're eagerly awaiting the electronic documents and have given two extensions." Bonnie held up two fingers for dramatic flair. "I've still failed to receive anything, nor have I gotten a date certain that we will. So I am urging the court to compel production by a date certain, one week from today. I think that's more than reasonable, given how much time they've had."

"Ms. Shaw?" the judge asked.

Bonnie's little theatrical show was enough to make Mia sick. "Your Honor, Ms. Olson only presents part of the picture. She fails to account for the sheer volume of data we're dealing with. Because Ms. Olson didn't budge on search terms, we are literally having to wade through *terabytes* of data. It's a problem entirely of her own making. If she had been reasonable about search terms, she could've already had the relevant documents."

"Is that true, Ms. Olson?" Judge Andrews asked.

"It's true we didn't agree to their overlimiting search terms that were purely self-serving. They didn't propose a reasonable option, so we declined to engage in further discussions and sought a full production without the usage of search terms. Once again, Ms. Shaw highly simplifies the situation, but of course, I can hardly blame someone of her experience level."

Mia jumped back in. "Your Honor, the lack of reasonableness is clearly apparent here, and it's not on LCI's part. We're working as fast as we can and as diligently as we can to respond and respond quickly. But there are only so many hours in a day."

Judge Andrews looked at her. "You could add more staff, though. Finley & Hughes is the second largest law firm in the city."

Ouch. That wasn't very accommodating. "We could, but it would take those attorneys days to get up to speed. The core team knows all the facts and players, and we are relying on them to efficiently review the documents. Our client shouldn't have to pay for inefficiency caused by the unreasonableness of opposing counsel's document requests."

The judge nodded. "I'm sympathetic to that. What is your best estimate on timing here, Ms. Shaw?"

"A month before we can get a substantial production out the door."

"That's too long," Bonnie interjected. "My client will be severely prejudiced if it takes that long. Then a month turns into two, and the next thing you know, it'll be summertime."

The judge sighed loudly. "Counsel, I'm disappointed that the two of you, two highly competent and seasoned attorneys from sterling law firms, couldn't work this out yourselves. But now you have come here and given me the power to decide. You may or may not like the way I see this."

Neither woman responded, because it wasn't smart to spar with the judge after that dressing down. But Mia knew this was ultimately Bonnie's doing, and hopefully that would play in her favor.

"Very well." The judge removed his glasses and rubbed his eyes. "I have great sympathy for the position you're in, Ms. Shaw."

She let out a breath.

"But I also want to make sure we move this along so both sides can get their fair hearing. The motion to compel is granted in part and denied in part. The date for production shall be three weeks from today. That's it." The judge stood.

Mia couldn't help but smile as she looked over at Bonnie. She'd said a month to give herself a cushion.

Bonnie scowled and walked over to her. "You can only play the sympathy card for so long, Mia. The judge will get tired of it and see through your poor, sad routine."

"You know, you don't have to be so nasty to me. I've never done anything to you."

"You don't have to have done anything to me." Bonnie's eyes narrowed. "You're opposing counsel. That's all that matters."

"You and I practice law very differently."

Bonnie crossed her arms. "Watch and learn."

Mia didn't want to engage any longer and turned to pack up. This was a victory. Sometimes the good guys won, and today was one of those days.

FOURTEEN

N oah had been working long hours for the past two days, but he had made good progress. Although the progress he'd made led him to have more questions than answers. As he pulled up into Mia's driveway, he went over in his head how best to present his findings to her.

He'd had previous experience in corporate espionage cases on a smaller scale, and in his opinion, they were some of the most challenging work—but also the most exciting. The stakes were exponentially increased when you were talking about a tech company's secrets. Those secrets could make the difference between record profits and going under.

Noah walked up to Mia's door and rang the bell. A few moments later, she opened the door, wearing a casual pink sweater and jeans. He'd texted her that he was going to swing by because he didn't think he should drop in unannounced a second time.

"Come on in." She gave him a warm smile that made his stomach clench. A simple smile from this woman was making him feel like a goofy teenager.

He followed her into the living room and took a seat on the couch beside her. He made sure not to get too close. There was no point in that.

"So you've got something for me?" She was in business mode. Somewhere he needed to get ASAP.

"Yeah. Not the answers you're looking for yet, but some stuff I want to go through."

"I'm listening."

He launched into what he had found so far. "You can rest easy on one thing. Lew and Owen are clean as whistles. I didn't even find a lot of the junk I normally do when I go snooping through people's computers. They are professional and on the up-and-up. No sign of any activities or contacts with the competition. Nothing that set off even a small red flag."

"And you're sure?"

Noah nodded. "I specialize in finding things people don't want to be found. As far as the two of them go, they're in the clear. I can say that with confidence."

She raised an eyebrow. "What about the other members of the executive team?"

This wouldn't be so clear-cut. "That's where it gets trickier. Because Ed and Howard's data was corrupted, I don't have confidence at this point that either of them are clean. I found a lot more deleted files on their servers, and that fact raises my antenna a bit. I'm not saying that either of them are dirty, but that it's too soon to make any final decision. As far as I'm concerned, you cannot rule them out and need to actively consider the possibility that either one of them could be your mole."

"What's your timeline like?"

"I can't give you a hard date except to say that I'm pulling long hours and hope to get you answers soon. I don't have to tell you that being right is more important than being quick. I wouldn't tell either of those guys what's going on right now. Keep the circle tight. That's the best chance of success here."

"So what are our next steps?" Mia asked.

"For now, I'm hoping that as you continue to look at the

documents, you might be able to connect the dots on your side while I'm doing my part of the work." Noah looked into Mia's discerning gaze and wondered what was going on in her head. "You look concerned."

"Shouldn't I be concerned? We're talking about some pretty big stuff here. And Bonnie will explode when she finds out what happened to our document data."

"Do you have to tell her about that?" He wasn't sure how that worked from the legal perspective.

Mia nodded. "Unfortunately. The longer I wait, the worse it is for us. At least if I disclose it now, there will be a colorable argument that I just recently found out, did my investigation, and am now disclosing."

"What about Harper?"

"I was hoping to keep him out of it, but we're at the point where I probably can't. I don't think Chase got around to telling Harper about the data. JJ thought Chase was going to, but there's no guarantee he did, and I'm certain Harper would've told me if he knew. That's not something you leave out when you assign a case to someone."

"Why didn't you go to Harper immediately?"

"I didn't want him to think I can't handle things. I needed to make sure I fully understood the landscape so I can explain to him how I'm handling it. Obviously, if he has different ideas, I'll be open to them. But if he did know about it, I'm concerned why he didn't tell me when we had our first meeting about me taking over the case."

"Maybe he was trying to protect you, or he was trying to give you time to settle in and some plausible deniability."

"Yeah, but it doesn't work that way. The judge will still hold the firm accountable if he knew. He probably won't hold us accountable if only Chase knew, but if Harper knew, the judge is not going to be very happy."

"Sounds like you need to talk to Harper ASAP. You have

enough information now to make an informed decision and have a good discussion with him."

"Yeah, I'm planning to do that tomorrow. I wanted to hear what your survey had to say first. It seems from your initial research that we have at least two client contacts who are clean, and I can tell Harper that as well. He'll have concerns about the firm's liability and potential exposure. I know that sounds bad, but we always have to worry about how these cases will impact the firm's reputation. These are very unique circumstances. And very trying ones."

Noah looked at Mia and felt the pain she was going through. Not only was she dealing with the loss of her friend, but also now the questionable antics of her own client. "You're not alone."

"I appreciate all your help, I really do. Between you, Sophie, and realizing that God is actually willing to be there for me, it's helped a lot."

"He is there. And always will be." Noah believed that with all of his heart.

She paused for a moment. "Can I ask you something?"

"Yeah, go ahead."

Mia hesitated for a second before continuing. "How can you be so sure? You have a level of certainty that I don't know if I'll ever get to."

He decided to share with her how he had gotten to this place. "My life experience has made me certain. My journey is not like yours, because we come from different places and circumstances, and that's completely okay. That's the way it's supposed to be. We're not all the same."

"You've always believed?" Mia asked.

"Well, I was raised as a preacher's kid." But that was only the beginning of the story.

She smiled. "I can't even begin to fathom that. I was raised the opposite of that. Meaning no sense of religion or faith or anything. It would be a stretch to say that my mom taught me basic principles of morality. She struggled to make it through each day, so that type of thing wasn't a priority. It was more like survival. I'm sure your life was very different from that."

It was, but he wanted to share the fuller picture with her. "Faith was instilled in me from day one, but I had to find my own path as an adult. And that path had many twists and turns and valleys. Really dark valleys that I don't ever want to go back to again. But even in those valleys, God was with me, even if I didn't believe it every day at the time."

"Did you go through something traumatic?"

"It was traumatic for me. I found out that my girlfriend was cheating on me." He put his head down. He dreaded talking about this, but he felt that maybe if he did, it would show Mia something that he couldn't otherwise show. "It wasn't just the fact that she cheated on me. It was who she cheated on me with."

"Someone you knew?"

"Landon."

Mia sucked in a breath. "Are you serious?"

"Unfortunately, yes." Noah took a deep breath himself, trying to settle his nerves. "Landon went through a really dark time when he returned from his final army deployment. I've gotten past it, but it took a long time. It hurt so badly because it was the woman I loved and my best friend. But that part of my life made me wonder why God had left me high and dry like that. I was always trying to do the right thing in life, Mia. I was trying to live life the best way I knew how. Trying to follow God. And I thought to myself, this is what I get? The harsh betrayal of my best friend and my girlfriend? A woman I had hoped to marry. It really shook me to the core. It made me question my beliefs. Question whether God really loved me. Even to the point of asking if He really existed."

She placed her hand on his. "Seriously? You really had those doubts?"

Oh yeah, he had. "Yes. I had never had those thoughts before, because it had been so ingrained in me that there was a God and that He was there for me. That trial in my life made me reexamine things, and I even went through a time when I didn't talk to God that much. Which for me was a departure from what I had been like the rest of my life."

"Based on things you've said to me, you obviously aren't that way now, so what changed?"

He looked down into her eyes. "When my father died suddenly, things shifted. At first my dad's death was just another thing that made me question everything. I thought I had hit rock bottom over the cheating, but his death really pushed me down another level. Once I actually processed my grief, I found myself at a fork in the road. All these trials and obstacles could make my faith stronger, or I could just walk away from it all, wash my hands, and be done with it."

"And you didn't walk away," she said softly.

"No. I chose the first path, but it was far from easy and didn't happen overnight. But as I reflected back over my father's life and the things he taught me, I found myself yearning for the closeness I had once felt with the Lord. The foundation of truth that I knew as a young person was still there. I did still believe. Even after all the questioning and angry moments. It took time, and I'm still working my way through it all. If I didn't have my faith to hold me up, I never would've come out on the other side."

"If I was put in your shoes, I would've probably taken the easy way out. Cut and run."

He shook his head. "I don't believe that about you at all."

"Maybe I'm afraid," she replied, her voice shaky.

Noah hoped she understood that her feelings mattered to him. And to God. "It's okay to be afraid, but the more you grow, the more confidence you'll have. God has an interesting way of tugging at our hearts and opening up our minds. Using the dark and painful challenges of life to speak into our hearts."

"I was raised by a single mom who didn't believe in anything—except her own reckless behavior. While your foundation was faith, mine was learning the hard lesson of not being like my mother—a struggling addict with a revolving door for men. That's the lens through which I have seen the world, and in that world there was no God. I've had to get to the place I am today through the back roads and a lot of uphill climbing."

"It doesn't matter how you got there, Mia. All that matters is that you're there now." He laced his fingers through hers and figured he'd deal with the consequences of his feelings later.

—◆—

The next afternoon, Mia sat in Harper's office. For the past hour, she had debriefed him on the secret files Chase had hidden and the data corruption issues that she'd uncovered.

The more she talked, the paler Harper became.

"Mia, I had no idea." He rubbed his chin. "Chase didn't tell me anything about this."

She had to push him on this point. "Are you sure? I know you're super busy. Maybe you could've forgotten?"

His eyes widened. "About a bombshell revelation like this? No way. I know I'm not young anymore, but my memory is still good. Especially about something with a large impact like this." He paused. "Why didn't you come to me sooner?"

"Honestly, sir, I wanted to make sure I had a good plan in place to move forward, and then I could tell you about everything at once."

Harper nodded. "I know you're under pressure to perform on this case on top of everything else. How do you think Lew is handling things?"

"Both he and Owen are rock solid."

"Do you want me to take a hands-on role? I can jump in and do whatever it is you need."

She wanted to immediately answer no, but she figured she

needed to be more diplomatic than that. "I'd really like to continue managing the case myself, but I understand if you feel like you have to be involved." She needed to give him the option because of the huge implications.

"No. You're doing everything right, as far as I can tell. As long as Lew is both innocent and happy, that helps us a lot. At the end of the day, this is wrongdoing at LCI. It's not on us at the firm. If we can help them ferret out the mole and get out of this lawsuit relatively unscathed, it will be a huge victory for the firm, and more importantly, for you. This type of situation would go a long way in a partnership discussion meeting. This case and the facts we're facing are unique. I know you'll say the politically correct thing, that it's all about the client, so I'm saying this for you, because your future and career aspirations at the firm matter." He smiled. "You're very talented, Mia. The only thing I see you lacking is a drive for power, but I think that can be developed with time."

She wasn't sure how to respond to that, so she took the easy way out. "Thank you."

"I'm here if you need me. Please keep me posted on any major developments. I don't need to know the day-to-day, but given the larger picture here, I know you get it."

"Of course." She rose from her seat. "Thank you for letting me continue to run with this."

He stood up and walked over to her. "Don't let me down." He patted her shoulder.

She nodded and exited his office. When she got back to her desk, she picked up the phone and called Owen.

He answered on the second ring. "Hey, you got anything for me?"

They'd had so many calls lately that they had quickly dispensed with the usual pleasantries. "Noah is still hard at work, but nothing concrete yet. He's good, though. He'll find it. And I'm doing a separate review of documents that my team has gone through to see if by chance anything could help me figure out what's going on."

"Everything here is business as usual. I keep expecting something crazy to happen, but frankly, it's boring. Nothing out of the ordinary. Everyone just going about their daily business."

"And the other executive team members?" Mia asked.

"No change in behavior. Howard is his usual needy and paranoid self, Ed does his own thing and only comes to me on major issues, and the other two team members are in Switzerland, working on some large projects. I don't expect them back for two months."

She jotted down a note about the whereabouts of the team. "Once we clear everyone on the executive team, we'll move to the next level below them. I've got that list ready to go. Thanks for your help in compiling it."

"Of course."

"Have you talked to Lew?"

"Yeah. He's definitely down but doing his best to put on a bright and smiling face. Frankly, I think I'm probably the same way. Keeping the game face on is something we lawyers have to be good at, but it doesn't mean it's easy."

Mia empathized with the difficult position Owen was in. "I'm sorry you're in the middle of this and having to walk a fine line."

"It's not your fault. Lew and I appreciate how on top of everything you've been. We're going to catch the culprit. It might not be as fast as we want, but we also have the upper hand, because he doesn't know we're on to him." Owen paused. "I'm calling him a guy because we're a very male-heavy company, especially at the higher levels. I would be surprised if we were dealing with one of our female employees."

She didn't want to put on any blinders. "I understand, but right now everyone is suspect except you and Lew."

"You're always the voice of reason."

She smiled. "That's my job. I'll keep you posted. Let me know if you need anything else from me."

"Will do."

Mia ended the call and spent the next two hours reviewing email from Ed's and Howard's files. There was nothing suspicious at all, but she had to put her eyes on the pages to make sure she wasn't missing anything. Out of context, an email might seem benign, but knowing what she knew now, she could look at everything through a different lens from the rest of her team.

She threw her head back and groaned, thinking about the conversation she needed to have with Bonnie. She had to prepare herself for the firestorm she was about to unleash. Looking at the time on her computer, she saw it was almost eight o'clock and decided to call it a day.

As she walked down the hall to the elevator, Harper's words rang through her mind. He thought she lacked the desire for power. Wasn't he right? Power wasn't what she wanted, stability was. Given her tumultuous childhood, what she wanted the most was a stable job where she knew she could support herself and not have to depend on anyone else to get by.

Her mom had taught her that lesson the hard way. Her mother's addictions were one of the reasons Mia had never touched drugs and rarely drank alcohol. She feared that she would end up hooked like her mom, and that nightmare was too much for her. She didn't even like taking over-the-counter meds for headaches. It might seem irrational to most people, but to Mia it made perfect sense.

She made it to the main lobby of the large high-rise and walked to the elevator bay for the underground garage. One of the perks of working at Finley & Hughes was the parking. She never had to face the elements to get to her car, and she always felt safer leaving in the evening than if she had to walk outside to get to her car.

As she started her vehicle, her conversation with Noah came back to her mind. They had come from such different places in life and had been raised in completely opposite ways. But she would be in denial if she didn't admit they were forming a bond. Not just on a physical level—that part was easy—but on a deeper emotional level. It was so strange to her, because initially she had assumed they would be incompatible. That he'd never be able to understand her because she wasn't like him.

Now that they'd spent more time together, she was beginning to see that they were connecting in a special way. To hear that he had faced struggles in his past about faith and life made her realize that while their experiences were different, they did have some common ground. Maybe the stress of Chase's murder and the kindness Noah had shown her were clouding her judgment. She would have never assumed before that she and Noah could have anything together, but maybe she was wrong. He was opening her eyes and heart to feelings she wasn't sure existed before.

If what her heart was telling her was any indication, then she needed to stay open-minded where he was concerned. What she didn't know was whether he had romantic feelings toward her. She thought she felt that spark between them, but she'd been wrong before. Her romantic radar wasn't the best, mainly because she rarely used it. One thing she did feel sure about was that Noah wasn't a bad guy—he wasn't like the men she'd grown up around. There was something special about him.

She turned on her blinker and pulled out into the street to start her drive home. Maybe she'd get a good night's sleep and tomorrow would be a less hectic day. Every day lately had been intense. She breezed through Midtown, making every light, and turned left down Piedmont, taking her normal route home. She couldn't wait to turn on some mindless TV and decompress. Everything in her life right now seemed like a serious decision, so watching a TV show where she didn't have to think about life was just what she needed. She debated which show would be the best for her current mood.

As the light in front of her turned yellow, she figured it

was better not to push her luck, so she tapped the brakes. She didn't slow down much, so she tried again. But she didn't slow down at all. Something was wrong.

She tapped the brakes again, but still nothing. Panicking, she pushed the brakes down hard, and still the car kept moving. The light turned red, and she laid on her horn and sped through the red light. There was no other choice. She fought the urge to close her eyes.

She tried the brakes again to no avail. She needed to stop before she got into an even more crowded area. Making another attempt, she tapped the pedal softly before pushing down all the way, but nothing worked.

Something was horribly wrong. Getting off the road was key. She didn't want to hurt anyone, and the farther she got down Piedmont, the more crowded it would become as she approached Buckhead, and the fewer options she would have to get into the grass and force the car to a stop.

She surveyed her surroundings and saw houses coming up on her right. It was now or never. She took a deep breath and got ready. For a moment, she considered that she might get really hurt.

"Lord, please, I could really use your help right now!"

Turning the wheel to the right, she went into the first yard, and the grass slowed her down a notch. But not enough. She could only hope that her airbag would deploy on contact.

The car propelled forward through another yard and didn't stop until she ran straight into a big tree.

FIFTEEN

Noah rushed into the hospital, frantically looking for Mia's room. Supposedly she was in stable condition, but he needed to see it with his own eyes. When he'd gotten the call from Cooper that Mia had been in a car accident, his thoughts immediately went to the worst-case scenario.

But then he found out that Mia had been well enough to call Sophie, and that gave him some reassurance. Surely she couldn't be too badly off if she was conscious and making phone calls. Still, he wanted to see her for himself and make his own determination.

His reaction to all of this told him that he was really starting to have feelings for Mia. He could tell himself that it was just friendly and professional, but he hated lying—especially to himself. Mia was unlike the other women he'd dated, but in a way that might be just what he needed. After being burned so badly, feeling her honesty shine through meant a lot to him. But dating was the last thing he should be thinking of right now. He should be focusing on whether she was okay and whether she needed help.

He found Mia's room and walked in to find Sophie sitting beside her. He'd learned that these two women were extremely close. Mia was awake, and her big brown eyes met his own. He sucked in a breath at the sight of her lying in a hospital bed, but he didn't want to show his reaction and worry her further.

"Noah." Sophie stood and gave him a quick hug. "Glad you're here. I'm going to go get some coffee and let you two talk. I'll be back in a bit to check on you, Mia, but I know you're in good hands with Noah."

"Thanks, Sophie," Noah said.

Sophie grabbed her purse and left the room. Noah approached Mia and studied her closely. She had an IV in her left arm and bandages on her cheek and forehead. There were also red splotches on her face and bruising on her arms.

He couldn't help taking her hand as he sat beside the bed. "Are you all right?"

She gave a weak smile. "It looks a lot worse than it is. I fought a tree and the tree won. Total knockout."

His mind started going haywire. "How did you hit a tree? Did you fall asleep at the wheel? You've been working so much."

"No. It's nothing like that. It would be easier it if were, actually. I'm glad you're here, because we need to talk." All the levity in her smile had vanished.

His stomach clenched. "What happened? Tell me everything." He had a feeling she was about to drop a big bomb.

"I left work just like a normal night and started the drive home. I didn't notice until I was on Piedmont that my brakes weren't working."

"What?" Her brakes had failed? There couldn't be a good explanation for this.

"Yeah. Everything was normal at first. Then I reached a red light that I needed to stop for just past Piedmont Park. I tapped the brakes and only slowed a little. So I tried again, but the car kept going. I ended up running the red. I knew that if I kept going toward Buckhead, the traffic would only get heavier, and I didn't want to go downhill and run into someone and hurt them. So I did the only thing I could think of in that moment, and that was to turn off into someone's yard to get off the street and into the grass, and that's when I hit the tree. It seemed like the safer alternative, because I couldn't drive into the house. That might've hurt people. The tree was my only hope."

So many questions floated through his mind. "When was the last time you had your car serviced?"

"Less than six months ago. And the car is only two years old."

That confirmed his worst suspicion. "Did you talk to the police?"

"Yes. They left just a few minutes before you got here. I think they thought I was driving under the influence or something, but I voluntarily submitted to multiple tests, and they were all clear. They seemed to believe me after I passed the tests, and they're going to investigate. Cooper said he would follow up, since he's former APD."

His first priority was making sure she felt okay. "Are you in pain?"

"A little, but it could've been a lot worse. Thankfully, the airbag deployed, but I also got some burns on my face. I've got a mild case of whiplash, but they don't think it's anything too severe. Right now I have a pounding headache, but that should pass." She took a breath. "This was intentional, right?"

He wasn't surprised that Mia had connected all of these dots, but he was worried about her. "That's the most rational explanation. Morrow has stepped up his game."

"There's someone else to consider."

"Who?"

"The mole," she said quietly. "He could know that we're on to him."

"That's possible. He might've detected something, or he just got spooked and paranoid. He knows you're new to the case and snooping around. It might make him jumpy."

Mia squeezed his hand. "Noah."

"Yes?"

"I could've been seriously injured or worse tonight."

"Yeah. I'm so thankful that you weren't."

She closed her eyes. He could tell she needed to rest.

"Go ahead and sleep. I'm not going anywhere." There was no way he was leaving her side.

—◁◇▷—

Mia awoke from a nightmare. Beads of sweat were on her brow. For a second she was confused, and then it all came rushing back to her. She looked over and saw Noah dozing in a chair beside her bed.

The doctor had wanted to keep her overnight for observation. She glanced at the clock and saw it was three in the morning. The last time she remembered the nurse checking on her was about two hours ago.

She smiled as she looked at Noah sleeping so peacefully. Fear also struck her as she realized how much she was starting to care for this guy. It was totally uncharacteristic of her. So much in her life right now felt different. She was questioning things, acting in ways that were not normally like her. Were these changes because of Noah in her life? Or something else?

The trauma she'd suffered over Chase's loss had changed her. Maybe it was time to face the facts—she was never going to be the same woman she was before she'd found him murdered that night. Her life had been altered, and now it was up to her to determine how she wanted to move forward.

Looking at Noah, a piece of her longed to move forward with a man like him. No—with *him*. It wasn't his type that she was drawn to. It was Noah the man. He'd shown her only kindness when she'd shown him just the opposite over his accused friend. She wasn't used to being treated that way by a guy. No man in her mother's life had ever been even remotely like Noah. Mia truly cared for him.

His eyes flickered open and honed in on her. "Why didn't you wake me up?"

"You looked so peaceful sleeping." She hated that he had woken up, but now that he was awake, they could talk about something that was weighing heavily on her mind.

He sat up in his chair and stretched his arms above his head. "How are you feeling?"

"The headache isn't as bad now. Sleeping it off helped some."

"Good."

"There's something I wanted to talk to you about. Maybe I'm making a leap." She wasn't sure what he would think of her theory, but she had to ask.

"What? Tell me what's on your mind."

"We were talking earlier about the mole and how he might be the one who did this."

"Yeah?"

"What if the mole also knew that Chase was on to him?" She took a deep breath. "What if he is behind Chase's murder? What if he's the one who hired Liam Morrow?"

Noah's dark eyes suddenly didn't look so sleepy anymore. But there also wasn't the shock she had expected. "That's a possibility."

"Wait a minute, did you already suspect that?" She didn't have to wait for him to speak to know the answer was yes.

He ran a hand through his hair. "I didn't want to say anything prematurely and then be wrong about it and end up hurting you in the process. I know how important it is for Chase's murderer to be held to account for what he did. If the mole was behind this, it shows he is willing to take action to harm people. Before, all we knew was that he had sold out to Baxter Global. This would be a game changer."

Waves of thought floated through her mind. "Let's start at square one. What's the connection between what's happening at LCI and Chase's murder?"

"Chase uncovers the existence of a traitor at his client. Days later he ends up murdered."

She processed this. "We were assuming Chase hadn't told anyone at LCI about what he'd found. But what if he figured out who the mole was and confronted him?"

"Or the mole determined that Chase had found him out. What if he asked to meet Chase to talk it through?"

"To explain everything, and Chase said yes, hoping it was all a mistake." Her heart pounded as they played out the nightmare scenario.

Noah leaned forward in his seat. "But the mole never had any intention of explaining anything. Instead, he hired Morrow and had Chase killed to silence him, and then framed David for it using his ATF baggage. And he knew David could be the fall guy because Chase had gotten into the fight and had a black eye. Maybe the mole started looking into David and found out about his ATF past. He makes some calls and finds Morrow."

"My DOJ contact did say that someone else had been inquiring about David before he even asked. All of this is starting to fall into place. And now I'm a target." She shuddered at the thought. The traitor had brutally murdered her friend. He probably wouldn't give a second thought to taking her out too. "He's not going to stop, is he?"

Noah gave her hand a reassuring squeeze. "I'm worried that he won't. Not until he thinks he's in the clear. As long as you're looking into this, he's at risk." He paused. "He made a big move here with the brakes. And since you can identify Morrow, you're a loose end to him too. So you have it from both sides. For all we know, the mole sent Morrow to mess with your brakes."

A chill shot down her back. "Why not just kill me?"

"Because another murder within the same law firm in such a short time would draw a lot of attention. But if the mole feels cornered or threatened enough, then all bets are off."

"This isn't just a cover-up of him selling out to a competitor. Now it's a murder cover-up as well."

Her head started to pound again, and she closed her eyes for a moment.

"I think you need to get some more rest. There's nothing we can do about it right now. You're safe in this hospital with me by your side. Get some sleep, and we'll regroup in the morning."

She felt like she needed to act, but she knew he was right. Rest. That was what she needed now. Then she could live to fight another day.

◄◇►

When Ty's cell started ringing at six o'clock, he knew that was never a good sign. He hated mornings, and the loud ringing was extra annoying because he'd stayed up late working. But when he picked up his phone and saw it was Noah calling, he immediately perked up.

"What's up, man?" he answered.

"Sorry to call you this early."

"I figure you have a good reason." He'd better.

"Yeah. I'm actually at the hospital with Mia."

"What happened?"

"Someone tampered with her brakes, and she hit a tree."

"Ouch. You're sure it was intentional?"

"Yes."

"I'm sorry, man." Ty was sympathetic, but he still wasn't sure why this warranted calling *him* at six in the morning.

"Here's the thing," Noah said. "I think this is all connected to Chase's murder."

Now Ty was wide awake. "You've got to connect some dots for me. I'm not following you. I haven't had my coffee yet."

"I think Mia has uncovered a conspiracy involving one of her clients, and I think Chase uncovered that same conspiracy—and was killed for it by Liam Morrow."

Ty rubbed his sleep-filled eyes. "Whoa. That's a big statement. What do you have to back it up?"

"I have some evidence, but I can't go into it because of client confidentiality. All I can say right now is that there is a really good chance someone wrapped up in this is responsible either directly or indirectly for Chase's murder."

"Man, I get confidentiality, but I need more here." Noah couldn't just drop that on him and expect him to take it at face value with no details. His client's life was on the line.

"I'm sorry. Right now that's all I can tell you. But this means we have to push even harder. We can't let this case go to trial."

"You realize the trial date is right around the corner."

"Then we need to act fast. I'll do everything I can on my end and give you all the information I can while maintaining confidences. Unfortunately, the rest will have to be up to you, but I know you're up for the challenge."

"This is huge. This could change a man's life."

"I know. His life is in your hands right now."

"Believe me, it's a feeling I know all too well. Keep me posted."

Ty hung up the phone and threw back the covers. It was time to get to work. He'd gotten just what he needed—reasonable doubt.

SIXTEEN

Mia walked slowly toward Harper's office late the next day. She had to talk to him in person about what had happened. Noah hadn't wanted her to go to work, but it was more important than ever now that she did.

The fact that someone had tried to hurt her told her that she was onto something big. And the idea that Chase had been murdered for it made her sick. What people would do for money and power was truly mind-boggling.

She was still in pain from the accident, but she would push through it. The more she thought about what that man had done to Chase, the angrier she got. And all over a stupid business deal.

When she reached Harper's office door, it was closed. She knocked and heard him tell her to come in.

Harper looked up from the stack of papers in front of him. His eyes grew large. "Mia, what happened to you? Are you all right?"

Her facial burns from the airbag were evident to anyone looking. "That's what I want to talk to you about." She shut the door, wanting them to have some privacy. Then she took a seat across from him.

He looked directly at her. "Please tell me what's going on."

Where did she even begin? "I told you about my fears that there is a traitor at LCI."

He nodded fervently. "Yes. Did you get more information on that?"

"Not yet. This guy is really good. We aren't any closer to finding out who it is, we just know who it's not. We're working as fast as we can, but we have come up empty. In the meantime, though, something happened to me."

"I can see that," he said softly.

He needed to know how dangerous this had become. "Someone tampered with my brakes."

"What?" he said loudly. "You mean intentionally?"

"Unfortunately so. The police are investigating it as a criminal act. I ran into a tree on the way home from work last night. That's why I look like this." She lifted a hand to her face.

"Thank goodness you weren't more seriously injured. I can get our firm security person on this right away. They'll work with you and the police to catch whoever did this."

"Harper, I think it's a lot bigger than what happened to me last night."

"That's pretty big in and of itself, isn't it?" His eyes narrowed. "You could've been killed."

"Yes. Definitely. But in the grand scheme of things, I think I'm on the trail of corporate espionage. Major corporate espionage." She paused, gathering her thoughts.

"Are you saying that you think the LCI mole is the person who cut your brakes?"

"It's more than that."

"What?"

She realized Harper would likely be skeptical, but she had to put it out there. "I think the person who is selling out LCI is the same person who is responsible for Chase's murder." There, she'd said it.

"What?" His voice boomed. "I thought the maintenance man was a sure thing. All the evidence was so clear against him."

"I believed that too. But not anymore. Things have changed. I really think there's a good chance that Chase found out who the mole was, decided to confront him, and then was killed for it. That's why Chase never brought the issue to you or anyone else. He went to the mole first. Which was just like Chase, always seeing the good in people. He probably thought it was a big mistake. Hoped that there was a completely innocent explanation. That decision probably cost him his life."

Harper's eyes got wider. "Have you told the police?"

She shook her head. "No, because I don't have any evidence yet, just a theory. So I thought the cops wouldn't believe me. Like you said, everything lines up squarely that McDonald did this. I need more than just my gut feeling to prove otherwise. But if you connect all the dots, it really does start to make sense—in a sick way. Now I'm being targeted because I'm working on the case." She decided not to bring up the Liam Morrow angle right now. This was enough to lay on Harper.

Harper stood, walked over to where she sat, and pulled up another chair beside her. "Mia, you've been through the unthinkable, and I'm sure you're very shaken up by your car accident."

"Yeah. It was scary when I pushed the brakes and nothing happened." Fear rolled through her as she relived the events of the night before.

Harper placed his hand gently on her shoulder. "But I want you to consider that you may be trying to construct a scenario that might not exist. The maintenance man explanation seems so pointless. But if you create this alternate scenario that links to the LCI case, then it makes everything come together in your mind. It becomes a coping mechanism."

"You think I'm crazy?" She didn't even have to ask. The look on Harper's face told her that he thought she was out of it. That she was really stretching to put all the pieces together. She couldn't blame him for being skeptical, since they didn't have any hard proof. But she was going to keep looking.

Harper shook his head. "I don't think you're crazy, but I do think you're in pain. A lot of pain. And I feel partially responsible for giving you this case so soon. I thought it would help you to be fully occupied with work, but now I see that it might have been too much too soon, and the stress and pressure is mounting. First the whole data issue, and now this."

"You really don't believe me, do you?"

"I believe that you believe it. But it's a far stretch to say that just because someone from LCI might have been meeting with Baxter Global, they must also have murdered Chase. I'm not saying that there's no corporate espionage happening here, but murder is obviously something on a different plane."

"Sir, don't you think it's odd, though? The timing of everything. Chase discovers these emails about the meetings with Baxter Global, and then he's killed. Can the timing really be that coincidental? How can you explain that?"

"You can't. Senseless killing is just that, Mia—senseless. I'm not telling you to stop looking into this, but I want you to be smart about it. You can quickly become obsessed with something like this. Let the police and the prosecutor do their jobs. You absolutely do not have to take on the burden of getting justice for Chase. That's not your place, and he would've never expected you to do that. You've already done so much by picking up his major case and running with it."

"I can't just sit back and do nothing." She refused to do that.

"But you also can't allow yourself to lose sight of the fact that you still have a major litigation to run, and you are not a criminal prosecutor. You're way out of your depth."

That seemed a bit cold, but Harper's job was to be all about the bottom line. That was why he was a managing partner at one of the most successful law firms in the nation. He didn't share her extreme emotional connection to this case. She felt that he mourned Chase's loss, but he had moved on. She had not.

"I do plan to work as hard as I can on this case, but now this is all getting intertwined," she said.

"Your opposing counsel won't have sympathy for any of this. They think LCI breached, and they want their monetary damages. They have no part in this supposed espionage, and they want to be compensated for the alleged breach. You can't expect to get any breathing room from Bonnie Olson."

"I get that." Mia didn't know how to make him believe her. He was clearly skeptical about her theory. If she stepped back and listened to all she was saying, then she knew it did seem a bit much, but then again, she was actually having to live through this.

Harper frowned and leaned forward. "I'm worried about you. Like I said, I'm going to have corporate investigations get involved. They'll be reaching out to you. I want you to be extra cautious. I don't know what happened to your car, but I don't want to take any chances. If I'm wrong and you're right, then you could be in jeopardy. I refuse to lose another person at this law firm on my watch. I'd rather be safe than sorry."

His words made her cringe in fear. "Don't worry. I'm going to be watching my back. You should know that I'm meeting with Bonnie tomorrow, and it's not going to go well. I suspect she'll file all sorts of motions with the court afterward."

"Yeah, we knew she would. It's not a reflection on you or how you're handling things. We can't help that the data was corrupted and we didn't know about it. She'll just do what she always does, and we have to stay focused."

"I don't know if the judge will hold that same level of sympathy." Mia had a bad feeling about how that would go, but she had no choice but to face the music. Part of being a senior-level attorney was handling the fallout from situations like this.

"Let me know if you need my help with Bonnie. I know she can be quite a challenge."

"Thanks. I need to deal with her on my own. The last thing she needs to think is that I can't handle this. That would give her exactly what she wants, and I refuse to give in to her aggressive tactics."

Harper smiled. "That's the fire I like to see, Mia. Maybe something good will come out of this after all. You're becoming a much stronger attorney."

"Thank you." She rose from her seat and considered his comment. It should have been a compliment, but it didn't feel right.

―――◁◇▷―――

Noah sat in the coffee shop in Colony Square and stared at Mia as he took a sip of coffee. They were waiting for Owen to arrive so they could regroup.

He'd done a lot of thinking about how they should move forward, and he was worried this was getting too dangerous. If they were right, then the mole had hired Morrow to kill Chase—and he had done so in a brutal manner. But Mia didn't show any signs of backing down.

A few minutes later, Owen joined them with a steaming latte in his hand. Noah wouldn't touch that stuff. It was simple coffee or nothing for him. But then again, he wasn't a lawyer. Maybe being an attorney drove you to fancy froufrou coffee.

"Mia, it's so good to see you. Your message had me really concerned." Owen sat across from Noah and beside Mia at the four-top table.

"I didn't mean to alarm you," she said.

"He should be alarmed," Noah retorted.

Owen looked at Mia and then back to Noah. "What do we know?"

"Every indication is that someone tampered with her brakes,"

Noah said. "It was intentional. Definitely not wear and tear or breakdown."

"What did you tell the police?" Owen asked.

"Nothing about any of this mess," Mia said. "I did fill in Harper."

Owen took a sip of his latte. "How did he take it?"

"He thinks I'm grasping at straws and that all the emotional turmoil has gotten to me. But he said if there was evidence, he'd be happy to look at it. I didn't push it because the last thing I need is Harper trying to pull me off the case because he thinks I can't handle it. I need to stick as close to this thing as possible."

"I take it that you two really think the mole is behind the murder?" Owen asked.

"I do," Mia answered.

Noah nodded. "Same here. We at least have to consider it as a strong possibility. The coincidences are just too many."

"Selling out to a competitor for high dollar is a long shot from murder, don't you think?" Owen asked.

Mia shifted in her seat. "I've thought a lot about that too, but you're the one who said a couple of the things being worked on now by LCI could be worth millions and millions of dollars. People have killed for less—a lot less."

Owen leaned in. "Noah, any updates on checking into Ed and Howard?"

"Nothing yet that would point the finger at either of them, but I still can't say they're clean either. Sorry. I know it's not ideal, but nothing is right now."

"I've started cross-referencing their calendar appointments with the purported meeting times with Baxter Global," Mia said.

"Anything?" Owen asked.

She shook her head. "No. But I assume they would've covered their tracks. If they were smart enough to plan all of this out, I don't think they would've been sloppy on the electronic paper trail."

"We can look at the meetings they do have on their calendars and try to verify if they actually happened. Sometimes people block their calendars or put dummy meetings on there to avoid having to go to other meetings." Owen pulled out a notebook and jotted something down. "Just send me what you have, and I can handle that part."

"Great," Mia said.

Owen placed a hand on her arm. "I'm sorry you got put right in the crosshairs, Mia. We're going to get this guy, shut him down, and then make sure he's prosecuted to the fullest extent of the law."

"Thanks, Owen."

Noah felt a twinge of jealousy as he watched their bond grow. He tried to push those feelings aside. They had a lot bigger problems than his petty jealousy.

"If you guys don't need anything else, I'm going to head back to work," Owen said.

"We're good," Mia said.

"Noah, can you walk me out?" Owen stood.

"I'll be right back," Noah told Mia. He wondered what this was all about.

As the two men walked away from the table, Owen started talking. "Do you really think Mia is in danger?"

Was Owen asking out of friendly concern or something more? "Yeah. I wish I could say otherwise," Noah answered.

"I may be totally overstepping my place here, but I get the feeling the two of you might be more than just professional colleagues."

Noah sucked in a breath. "Not exactly."

"Sorry to pry. I thought I got that vibe from you two. I was hoping you were going to say yes and that you'll be by her side."

"I do plan to stick close. Really close. Until we get this all straightened out."

Owen let out a breath. "Good. Because I couldn't deal with something happening to her and knowing that I somehow had a part in it. Do you think LCI needs to hire her some special security?"

Noah shook his head. "No. I've got that covered."

"Good. I'll be in touch."

Owen walked away, and Noah considered for a moment the conversation they'd just had. He made his way back to the table and sat down.

"What was that all about?" Mia asked.

"Owen is worried about your safety."

She nodded. "What did you tell him?"

"That I was going to keep you safe."

"That isn't part of your job description," she said softly.

"This isn't my job. It's me being your friend and looking out for you." And it was more than that—at least to him.

"I don't even know how to thank you for all you've done. All you're doing."

"Just saying 'thank you' is more than enough." He smiled.

"Noah, I'm scared."

Hearing those words tore him up. He grabbed her hands and held them tightly. "I'm not going to let anything happen to you, Mia. I promise."

"Can you really make that promise?"

"I'm going to do everything in my power."

They sat in silence for a few moments. He didn't feel the need to say anything more. He was just letting it all sink in.

Mia took a sip of her coffee and then looked up at him. "What exactly did you have in mind, as far as keeping me safe?"

"We need to talk about that. I'm not comfortable with you going about your daily routine without any security."

"It's really come to that, huh?"

"I think you know the answer. You'll be sick of me soon."

"I doubt that." She smiled.

"We'll figure out something that works for both of us. But for now, get used to the company."

Mia dreaded what was about to happen. She walked into the lobby of Warren McGee and tried to remain calm. It helped that Kate was meeting with her first before the inevitable beatdown from Bonnie.

When Kate got off the elevator and gave Mia a warm smile, she instantly felt better. That was Kate. She could put anyone at ease.

Kate walked over and gave Mia a big hug. "It's great to see you here, but I'm guessing you'd rather it be under different circumstances."

"Yeah, that's for sure." She hadn't told Kate any details, just that she had to meet with Bonnie over a thorny issue.

"Bonnie is all bark and no bite," Kate said in a low voice. "Don't let her get into your head. She's a master at it. I know I let her do it for too many years, and the last thing I want is for her to do it to you. Underneath it all, she has a steady head on her shoulders."

"She's your partner."

Kate laughed. "Yes, but we'll never be close friends. We co-exist and work together when needed—usually butting heads along the way. We have diametrically opposed views as to how we should practice law, but she is a highly skilled lawyer."

Mia didn't want to put Kate in an awkward position of divided loyalties between the firm and her, so she didn't ask for any further advice on dealing with the monster known as Bonnie. "Thanks for dropping down and saying hello before my meeting."

"Of course. I'm always happy to see you. I heard about your car accident. How are you feeling?"

Kate didn't know the sordid details. "I'm feeling better."

"I'm glad to hear that."

Mia heard the loud clicking of heels behind her and knew

if she turned, she would see Bonnie. She took a deep breath in mental preparation.

"Hello," Bonnie said.

Mia rolled her eyes at Kate before she turned to face Bonnie. "Hi. Thanks for meeting in person."

Bonnie crossed her thin arms. "You said it was important."

"Yes, it is."

"Then let's go to the conference room." Bonnie shifted. "Kate, are you going to join us?"

"No. I'll let you two discuss business." Kate gave Mia's arm a squeeze. "I'm so glad you're all right. Let me know if you need anything."

"Thanks, Kate."

Mia followed Bonnie down the hallway and into a spacious conference room.

"What was Kate talking about?" Bonnie asked.

"I had a car accident." There was no way Mia was going to divulge the actual details.

"Oh. Well, I'm glad you're okay."

"Thanks." Mia didn't know whether Bonnie was being sincere but thought it best just to say thank you and move on. "There's a matter I need to discuss with you."

"By all means." Bonnie took a seat, and Mia did the same. Bonnie was the type of woman never to have a hair out of place. Mia couldn't imagine trying to live like that.

Mia had given a lot of thought to how to approach this with Bonnie. There was no good way, but being direct seemed better than a long buildup. "An issue has arisen with the LCI data."

Bonnie raised a perfectly arched eyebrow. "What type of issue?"

"Some type of virus or malware infected LCI's system when we were doing the document collection. As a result, we lost the metadata for about eighty percent of the collected documents."

"What?" Bonnie asked in a high-pitched voice. "You've got to be kidding me."

"There's more. Let me get it all out there first." Mia paused. "We also lost approximately ten percent of the documents. We can't say for certain the exact amount, but we feel it wasn't more than ten. It could've been less."

Bonnie frowned. "And when exactly were you planning on telling me this?"

"I just recently found out myself."

"And you expect me to believe that? Is this just another ploy to get more time to turn over documents?"

Mia shook her head. "This isn't a ploy. We are still in position to meet the court-ordered deadline."

"But you won't have all the documents we requested, because you're telling me they don't exist."

"I didn't say that. I said that a small percentage don't exist. And that the metadata is really the largest issue. You'll still have the documents."

Bonnie said a few choice words. "I hope you don't expect me to just smile and say this is all okay."

"I obviously know that you won't do that, but I wanted to come here and tell you this face-to-face as opposed to sending an email." Mia held her breath, waiting for the dragon to breathe fire.

But Bonnie just sat there. Not saying a word. Until finally a minute later, she stood. "You'll be seeing some filings on this very soon."

"I figured as much." Mia knew Bonnie would run right to the judge.

"And if I determine that you've cooked up this nonsense to throw off the case, I will come after Finley & Hughes even harder for sanctions than I already am."

There was no point in arguing. It was better to just tuck her tail between her legs and get out of there.

CHAPTER
SEVENTEEN

The next morning Ty sat in his office, typing away at his keyboard. His caseload was high right now, and he had promised himself that no matter what, if he took on a case, he would give it all the attention it needed.

Unfortunately for him, that meant a lot of late nights. And right now he didn't have the luxury of sleeping in. He was burning the candle at both ends.

"Ty, I'm sorry to interrupt."

He turned to face the front of his office. Angie, his secretary, stood with the mail in her hands. The forty-something single mom kept him in line and ran a tight ship. He couldn't imagine running his firm without her.

"What is it?"

"I was going through today's mail." Her voice started to shake.

Instinctively, he got out of his seat and walked over to her. "Talk to me."

"You need to see this." She held up an envelope.

Angie opened his mail daily. He got so much junk that she sorted it into different categories for his review. Nowadays, so much was done via email that the snail mail was mostly stuff he didn't need to spend his time on.

He took the envelope from Angie.

"I didn't even finish reading the whole thing because I knew something was really wrong," she said.

"You did the right thing, Ang." He opened the envelope and pulled out a piece of quality, high-end paper. His eyes skimmed down the page. He'd seen a lot over his years of being a defense attorney, but this was a new one. "Thanks for bringing this to me. I need to make some calls."

"Of course. Let me know if I can help you." Angie left, shutting the door behind her.

Ty knew what his first phone call needed to be. He dialed Noah's number from his desk phone and waited.

A couple of rings later, Noah picked up. "Ty, what's up?"

"I just got a special delivery in the mail."

"What kind of special delivery?"

"A note offering me five hundred thousand dollars to drop David's case."

"What?" Noah said loudly.

"Yeah. My thoughts exactly."

"Did it give any further details?"

"It says I have forty-eight hours to drop the case. If I do, then I get further instructions on how to get paid."

"What about the return address?"

"He put my home address as the return."

"That's smart," Noah said.

"What are we dealing with here?" Ty asked.

"You know I can't reveal all of that to you."

Ty was getting frustrated very quickly with this. "I get that, but this just came to my doorstep. I've still got a trial to get through. How am I supposed to handle that?"

"If you withdraw as David's attorney, what would happen?"

"He'd get assigned a public defender just like before. Unless he could find another lawyer to take his case pro bono."

Noah cleared his throat. "They're worried about you being on this case. That means we're getting close."

"Close to uncovering this conspiracy you referenced?"

"Yeah. We're playing in the big leagues here." Noah paused. "I guess I should've asked first. Are you considering this offer?"

Noah's question offended Ty. "Are you kidding me?"

"Sorry, I had to ask. That's half a million dollars."

"If money was my driver, I wouldn't be taking cases pro bono on a regular basis." Ty tried to keep his temper in check. They both had jobs to do.

"I hear you. The key question is what happens after you don't withdraw. Will they contact you again, upping the offer?"

"Or something else?"

"Like what?"

"I don't think I want to know."

"You need to watch your back," Noah said.

For the first time, it occurred to Ty that he might be in danger too. But he couldn't let that stop him. Not when the stakes were this high. "While I have you on the line, I've got another piece of bad news."

"Really?" Noah sounded exasperated.

"Yeah. Remember the evidence bag that went missing?"

"Of course."

"It was found. It was misfiled with the evidence for another case. I'll still argue that it should be excluded, as the chain of custody is highly questionable, given that it went completely missing. But if it does get let in, it is physical evidence that specifically ties David to the crime scene. On the flip side, if the judge lets it in, that would be a solid basis for me to appeal. But we have to be ready for anything."

Noah sighed. "We really need to catch a break here. Everything is mounting against us."

-◅◇▻-

True to her word, Bonnie hadn't wasted any time filing scathing emergency motions with the court, and now Mia had to face the music. Judge Andrews wasn't going to be happy, and Mia couldn't blame him. The motion read like a textbook spoliation motion, but with all of Bonnie's added flair and pizzazz. Mia had to give it to her, Bonnie was a very effective writer. Her advocacy skills came through loud and clear. Mia had no idea how she was going to get out of this one, because Bonnie had some very solid points both from a factual and legal perspective. While Mia didn't back down from challenges, the importance of the whole picture was weighing heavily on her. This was so much bigger than Bonnie realized, but Mia couldn't dare say that. Not now, with so much hanging in the balance.

When Judge Andrews walked into the courtroom, Mia knew she was toast. His eyes zoomed in on her, and his face reddened. He was ticked. And that was the last thing you ever wanted the judge to be.

"Ms. Olson, your motion speaks for itself. I'd really like to hear what Ms. Shaw has to say for her client—and for herself."

Mia stood, but before she could answer, the judge kept talking.

"And, Ms. Shaw, I think you should cover the fact that I believe you knew about this precise issue the last time you were in front of me, and yet you didn't say a word. Not a *single word* about it."

She waited a moment to see if he was going to say anything else before she launched into her explanation. She feared nothing she could say would shield her from the judge's ire.

Here goes nothing.

She stood as tall as her five foot five inches could get her. "Your Honor, it is a complicated situation."

"Well, you better start trying to *un*-complicate it, Ms. Shaw, before I run out of the scant amount of patience I still have."

"Your Honor, I was alerted to the fact that we had two issues. First, a lack of metadata for about eighty percent of our data, and second, that we are only certain that we have about ninety percent of the data that existed. I was informed that these issues were due to some type of malware or virus that attacked the LCI system during our collection process." She let a beat pass to see if Judge Andrews was going to pounce, but he remained silent, so she kept going.

"I was told by firm IT personnel that Chase Jackson had been notified about the issue. The IT employee thought that Chase was going to inform our managing partner about the findings." She took a breath. "But a couple of days later, as you know, Chase was murdered." She wasn't trying to play the sympathy card, but explain to the judge why this mattered.

"When I found out about this, I immediately started an investigation to better understand the facts, since I couldn't talk to Chase to figure out what he knew. The client didn't know about this either until I told them."

"And, Ms. Shaw, were you conducting that investigation when you were in my courtroom last time?" the judge asked.

"I was, but I had only just begun, Your Honor. I was still trying to figure out what in the world I was dealing with."

"And you didn't think it was important to raise the issue, considering we were discussing a motion to compel the production of documents?" His voice got louder with each word. "I would think that you would have realized that it wasn't just relevant but *highly* relevant to the issues at hand."

"In hindsight, I realize that it might have been a good idea to air out the issue then, but at the time, Your Honor, I was still trying to get my hands around what was going on and thought it best not to speak with incomplete information or out of ignorance."

"And standing here today, do you have your hands around it, Ms. Shaw?"

The last thing she wanted to do was mislead the court, especially since she was already on thin ice that could break at any second. "Not completely, Your Honor, but I can definitely tell you there was a malicious virus involved."

"And who do you think planted that?" he asked.

"I don't know. That's one of the things we're working on."

"And did your managing partner know about this?"

She shook her head. "He had no idea. I don't know why Chase didn't tell him, but my best guess is that he was doing what I am doing now—trying to determine what happened—and before he could get answers to tell the client and others at the firm, he was killed." She took another breath and made the decision to put one more thing out there. "Brutally murdered, Your Honor, and I realize I may be throwing myself on the mercy of this court right now, but these are highly unusual circumstances, and I am asking for some extension of leniency here."

The judge muttered something under his breath that she couldn't understand, then said, "Ms. Shaw, I am trying my best to be sympathetic to the plight you're in right now. I wouldn't wish it on anyone. But I also have a duty to uphold the law and ensure that justice is done in this courtroom. I don't think you did anything particularly nefarious, but I do think you used bad judgment by not raising this issue earlier."

"And I'm sorry about that, Your Honor." Better to just fall on her sword. "This is obviously the first time I've dealt with a situation quite like this."

"Your Honor, if I may?" Bonnie gracefully rose from her seat like a swan rising out of a lake.

Mia wanted to groan because now Bonnie was going to go for blood.

"As I argued last time on the motion to compel, everyone is sympathetic with what Ms. Shaw and her colleagues are going through." Bonnie's face hardened. "But that doesn't excuse this behavior. Very bad behavior, at that. At best this shows that the firm was grossly incompetent, and at worst they were trying to cover up the misdeeds of their client."

"Is it your position, Ms. Olson, that LCI purposely destroyed data?" Judge Andrews asked.

Bonnie nodded. "It is. There had to be something damaging in the documents, so they installed that virus and hoped it would give them cover. They, of course, would have no idea about all of the intervening events. But someone at LCI has wrongfully destroyed evidence, and while I don't know who, it doesn't matter. The result is still the same, and any employee's action at LCI should be imputed to the company, and the company must be held responsible. If you let this slide, then it incentivizes companies to destroy evidence that could be harmful to their case. In my humble opinion, that is absolutely unacceptable."

"What are you seeking?" he asked.

"Sanctions in the amount of half a million against LCI, one hundred thousand against Finley & Hughes, and an adverse inference instruction for the jury."

"Your Honor, that's excessive," Mia pleaded. She wasn't above begging right now. That penalty was extreme.

"I'm not finished," Bonnie said. "I'd also like to depose CEO Lew Winston within the next week. I'd like to hear it from the horse's mouth. If he really is innocent, then I should be able to put him under oath and ask him directly. I deserve that chance. And what's more, my client deserves that chance."

"Your Honor, I say again that the sanctions Ms. Olson is asking for are excessive, as is the jury instruction for an adverse inference," Mia said. "You'd basically be handing the case to them. I ask that you give me more time to fully investigate what happened. It would be highly prejudicial to allow that instruction. Ms. Olson can't even say for certain that LCI is at fault here. I'm asking the court for more time."

"What about the deposition of the CEO and accelerating the timing of that?" Judge Andrews asked.

The last thing Mia needed right now was for Lew to get deposed, but she didn't have much choice. She had to pick her battles. If she pushed back on this, the judge might just give Bonnie everything and more. "We would consent to that."

The judge rubbed his eyes. "I'm highly troubled by the facts here, and I'm even more troubled by wondering what we don't know. And for that very reason, Ms. Shaw, you have two weeks to get to the bottom of this. File your findings with this court, and then I will rule on the pending motion for sanctions." He took a breath. "And don't even think about filing for an extension. Two weeks is me being generous, given everything that has happened, but do not push me on this point. I will not be as generous next time around, and I think you will not be happy with the outcome."

Mia blew out a breath. Two weeks wasn't long enough, but it was something. She'd have to make it work. "Thank you, Your Honor. I appreciate it."

"In the meantime, work with Ms. Olson to get this deposition scheduled. I do not want to see the two of you back in this courtroom over that deposition. That will make for an unpleasant hearing for everyone involved. Is that understood?"

"Yes, Your Honor," they responded.

"That's it. I've heard far too much for today already." The judge stood and exited the courtroom. He was ticked off with Mia, but this was completely out of her control.

She dreaded the impending conversation with Bonnie that was bound to happen in three, two, one . . .

"I'll email you some dates for next week for the deposition," Bonnie said.

"I look forward to it."

Bonnie arched her brow. "I can't quite figure you out, Mia. I don't know whether you're a brilliant mastermind or a complete and utter disaster."

Mia couldn't help but laugh. "Somewhere in the middle."

"You won't be laughing when I win the sanctions motion. I told you to bring in a partner, and you ignored my advice."

"Bonnie, some problems aren't solved by bringing in a partner. Sometimes you just have to deal with what's in front of you."

"Your naïveté is both sad and refreshing at the same time. Once you've been around the block a few times, you'll see things differently."

"Or I could see it exactly the same." She turned away from Bonnie and finished packing up. This was a battle she couldn't afford to lose.

CHAPTER
EIGHTEEN

N oah's fingers quickly pounded the keyboard. He was deep in the dark web, a place he preferred not to go for a lot of reasons. But at least he had state-of-the-art security protections. Because when you started nosing around the dark web, it was highly likely that your computer could be hijacked and locked down and a ransom demanded. He was confident, however, that his firewalls would hold.

He had a few sources on the dark web he relied upon. He wasn't naïve. He knew they weren't completely on the up-and-up, but he had also worked with them enough to know that they weren't bad guys. And he needed them to open a few virtual doors for him to walk through.

He'd been at it for three hours straight when a new window popped open. He had received a message from one of his sources.

This might be what you're looking for.

Noah cracked his knuckles and then opened the attachment. He knew he was taking a risk by opening the file, but he had to trust that his source wouldn't start burning him now.

What he found as his eyes scanned the document were two cash deposits made by Morrow. One before and one after

Chase's death—totaling one million dollars. Noah whistled. That was a pricey hit. But this confirmed their suspicions. Morrow had definitely been hired to kill Chase and make it look like David did it. Whoever hired him had to have known about Chase's uneasy relationship with David. The circle of potential perpetrators continued to shrink.

He logged out and drove over to Mia's. She would want to know what he'd found. About half an hour later, he was sitting in Mia's living room.

"What have you got?" she asked.

He explained the payments he'd found.

She looked at him. "Proof that Morrow killed Chase. Now we just have to find out where those payments came from. Is that something you can do?"

"I'll try my best, but this guy covered his tracks pretty well. I had to go pretty deep to find what I did, and I called in favors from some less-than-savory characters."

"Isn't that dangerous?"

He shook his head. "These guys are no threat to me, but they don't like law enforcement. They work with me because I'm private now. And I pay them like I say I will. At the end of the day, many of these hacker types are just capitalists at heart, trying to make bank."

She took a deep breath. "I guess I owe you a big apology."

"For what?"

"For ever pointing the finger at McDonald. I was so hurt and upset, and it seemed like a slam-dunk case. I immediately jumped to the easiest conclusion and refused to consider other alternatives, even when you told me I was wrong. I let my grief and anger get the best of me."

"Mia, from the very beginning, you and I were both after the same thing—the truth. Making sure that the person who did this to Chase was brought to justice. You had every reason to believe that David was guilty. I don't hold that against you.

You were fighting for your friend the same way I was fighting for mine."

She hung her head. "But I was wrong."

He placed his hand under her chin and tilted her head back up. "You always told me that if you were presented with evidence of David's innocence, that you'd consider it. That's exactly what you have done. Now, in the face of all of this new evidence, I think we're both on the same page."

"I've been trying to think through everything. I believe Chase must have told the mole what happened with David. That's the only way this could've worked out like this. Which means Chase saw him after the fight."

Noah had come to a similar conclusion. "But he didn't necessarily have to tell the mole. He could've told someone else at LCI who then told him, or he was in the same room during the conversation."

"That's a good point. We need to talk to Owen about it and see if we can figure out if Chase talked to any of them about the altercation."

She twisted her hair and pulled it back. The dark circles under her eyes told Noah that she was struggling. But she hadn't complained one time—not about the situation or the pain or everything she'd been through.

He placed his hand gently on her knee. "How are you feeling?"

She looked up at him. "I look awful, don't I?"

He shook his head. "I don't think that's possible. But you've been through a lot, and I know you have to be exhausted."

Mia gave him a weak smile. "I haven't been sleeping well. I guess that isn't surprising. I keep waking up and thinking someone is in the house."

He didn't like the sound of that. "Since you brought it up, I'm working on upgrading your security system."

"That's not necessary."

He really wanted to do this for her. He also wanted to pull her into his arms and hold her. But that wasn't going to happen. "Let me do it. I have the extra equipment. I can install it at no charge. Maybe it will help you sleep better at night."

"All right. I guess at this point I'm not turning away any help. Also, the police called today. The culprit had wiped his prints clean, so we have no leads on who was responsible for cutting my brakes."

"Yeah, but you already expected that."

She pushed a stray hair behind her ear. "I guess I was holding out some hope, but that's been shot down. And time is not on our side. This trial is about to start."

"I understand. Let's just take it one day at a time and deal with each day's problems, then move on to the next. Ty is one of the best. He'll get David out of this. I have confidence in the justice system. When all the facts are put on the table, a jury won't convict. There will be reasonable doubt. We have to make sure of that."

"I need to have a conversation with Anna ASAP."

"Do you think it's too soon? We don't have anything concrete to present." Given how hard-nosed the prosecutor was, he wasn't optimistic that she would receive this information well.

"I need to get her thinking that this is a possibility. I was so hardline that she'll be shocked that I've changed course, and hopefully that will make her rethink things." She started to yawn.

Noah stood. "You're beat. Let me get out of your hair. Lock up behind me and set the alarm. I should have the new security upgrade done in a few days."

"Thanks again, Noah. For everything."

He took both her hands in his. "I'm just glad that I'm here by your side."

A moment passed between them as their eyes locked. He really wanted to lean in closer and kiss her, but he didn't have the courage yet to do so.

"I don't know what I would do without you," Mia said.

He thought the exact same thing about her.

—◁◇▷—

On Monday morning, Mia walked into the DA's office to talk to Anna. She'd left Anna a message that it was urgent. Hopefully Anna wouldn't flip out on her, but Mia had tried to prepare herself for the potential fallout that might occur.

Noah had stuck close during the weekend, which was nice. Not only because of her fear of being targeted again, but because she really enjoyed his company. The craziest part of the weekend was going to church with him on Sunday. She'd only ever been to church with Sophie before, and Noah went to a different church. Mia had been incredibly nervous about the whole thing, but he'd put her at ease. Everyone was super friendly, and the pastor spoke in a way she could understand and that made her think. That hour and a half had been a welcome respite from the craziness that surrounded her.

Being with Noah felt so natural. They were falling into a rhythm with each other, but they hadn't spoken at all about their feelings. She was sure that he felt something too. The way he would touch her or look at her—there was no way she could be so wrong about that. It was no longer just a friendly touch or glance. It had crossed over into something more. A lot more, where she was concerned. But she wasn't in any hurry to have "the talk" about feelings or what their status was. She was fine with letting their relationship grow slowly and organically.

Anna walked into the lobby to greet Mia. She looked confident in her black power suit. "Come on back."

Mia followed Anna down the hallway, making the now-familiar walk to Anna's office.

Anna shut the door, and they took their seats. Anna leaned forward at her desk. "You said it was urgent."

Time to put it out there front and center. "I don't think David McDonald is guilty."

Anna blinked. "What? What do you mean?"

"Some things have happened to me to make me believe that someone else is responsible for Chase's death."

Anna raised an eyebrow. "You have to do better than that. I need details."

And that was exactly what Mia couldn't give her. "I'm sorry that I can't tell you everything I know. I'm restricted by attorney-client privilege."

Anna threw up her hands. "Okay. You have completely lost me. We need to rewind and start from the beginning."

Mia had to engage in a delicate dance here. "I have a thorny issue with one of my clients—a case that Chase worked on. I think Chase discovered what was going on, and I believe that someone related to that issue is who murdered Chase."

"Are you serious?" Anna asked, clearly trying to follow the leap in logic.

"Deadly."

"Let me get this straight. What type of *issue* are you referring to?"

"I can't get into that." She couldn't breach the attorney-client privilege. That was nonnegotiable.

"Because it's your client and you're worried about maintaining the privilege?"

"Yes. I can't reveal that information. You understand how important preserving that privilege is and what ethical duties I have." She was banking on Anna getting how critical this was.

Anna studied the corner of her notepad. "I fully get the ethical obligations you have to live by," she started slowly. "I'm going to do the best I can to read between the lines here. There's something shady going on at your client. This client was also a client of Chase's. So far so good?"

"Yes."

"All right. Whatever it is that you can't tell me is bad. Chase discovered whatever it is. And what?"

"I think he was killed for what he found out."

Anna pushed further. "You're saying someone at your client is a killer?"

Mia couldn't respond to that, so she sat silently without making any facial gestures. While she needed Anna to understand, she did take her ethical duties seriously.

Anna started nodding again. "Sounds like you might need to withdraw from your case under those circumstances."

"It's a lot more complicated than that." If only Mia could explain how complicated. "There is something I can tell you about."

"Go on."

"While jogging in Piedmont Park, I was attacked by a man who I believe is the same man I saw at Chase's apartment the night of his murder."

Anna's eyes widened. "Did you tell the police?"

Mia nodded. "Yes."

"And what did they say?"

"They aren't convinced it's the same guy, but I know in my gut that it was. All of these connections, Anna. I know I can't tell you all the pieces in play, but I know enough to question my original position. That's why it's so important that you don't go through with McDonald's trial right now."

"What do you want me to do?" Anna asked.

"Give me some time to dig into this. Can't you ask for a continuance? The trial doesn't have to go forward as scheduled."

"I've been pushing my luck by speeding this thing along and keeping everyone's feet to the fire—largely because of you and your passion about this case. Now you come in here and want me to do a full stop with no evidence to support your theory? I'm not buying it. Sorry. Something sounds fishy here, Mia. I'm not sure what it is, but I have to trust my gut."

Mia had expected pushback, but this was even worse than she'd expected. "It's your job as a prosecutor to make sure justice is served. You're right that I was all about McDonald being the one who did this, but now I have facts that tell me otherwise."

"And I don't have those facts," Anna shot back.

"My brakes were cut."

"Huh?"

"I'm on to something. I think Chase was too. They tried to hurt me, but they killed him. I ran off the road and into a tree, but I could've wound up dead too."

A frown pulled at Anna's glossy red lips. "I'm beginning to be concerned about you, Mia. Are you sure you're really okay? Do you need to talk to someone about your grief?"

Great, now Anna thought Mia was having a nervous breakdown. "You can talk to APD yourself if you don't believe me. They're investigating what happened to my car. I'm not making this up or delusional. Unfortunately, this is all too real. Another reason I'm more determined than ever to make the right person pay."

Anna sat there, not saying a word.

Mia was convinced that Anna thought she was crazy. But she had to ask. "I'll take any time you can give me to try to get answers. Right now the trial is only a week away."

"Let me think on it and get back to you. Okay?"

Anna was probably going to talk to APD. It would actually help if she did. "Thanks. I appreciate it. I want justice for Chase, and I need to make sure it's actually the right person who did it. The last thing I want is for an innocent man to be convicted." She couldn't allow that to happen.

CHAPTER
NINETEEN

Howard and Ed walked into Owen's office before he'd even finished his first cup of morning coffee. "What can I do for you two?" he asked.

Ed shut the door behind him, and the two men sat in the large chairs opposite Owen's desk.

"Something is wrong with Lew," Howard said.

Owen's stomach clenched, but he showed no outward emotional reaction. "What do you mean?"

"He's not himself," Ed said. "I've known him for years, and he's always so level, even under pressure. But lately he'll bite your head off."

Howard nodded. "He's yelling at staff, stomping around the halls. The senior managers are starting to talk. Ed and I are doing the best we can to keep things in check, but we can only contain this for so long."

"How have you not noticed?" Ed asked.

"I've been tied up so much on this case and other matters that I've been a hermit. Sorry I haven't been more in tune with what's going on." Owen paused. "But that raises the ultimate question. Has anyone talked to him? Do we have any idea what's up?"

Howard cleared his throat. "That's why we're here. We want to know if you know anything."

Ed shifted in his seat. "Has Lew said anything to you? Anything at all?"

"No. We actually haven't talked much lately." Owen hoped he was being convincing, but he wasn't sure. He hated lying to them, but right now there was no other way.

"Owen, if you know something, you owe it to us to tell us. You represent the company, not Lew individually," Howard said.

"Believe me, I take my role as LCI's general counsel very seriously. I always have the best interest of the company at the top of my mind. I'm not holding out on you guys."

"Are you sure? Is Lew in some type of trouble?" Ed asked. "Is the company in trouble? Are there government investigations?"

"Why would your mind jump to government investigations?" Owen thought that was an odd leap.

Ed and Howard exchanged a look. "Because we've both worked at companies where the government started a criminal investigation, and one of the first things that happened was odd behavior among the senior leaders."

Howard nodded. "This is your time to come clean. We can handle it. But we need to know the truth."

Owen was in an impossible position. How could he tell them the truth when he wasn't sure if one of them was a traitor? He would just have to try to push them off . . . for now. Buy some time. "I don't know anything, but I'm more concerned with what you guys know that I don't. What could we possibly be under investigation for?"

Ed and Howard exchanged another tense glance.

Owen began to worry that there was something else going on. "You guys need to start talking. Whatever it is, I need to know about it."

"We don't know of anything specific," Howard said. "But Ed and I have been talking, and the paranoia took over."

Owen took in a breath. "So you don't have knowledge of any criminal wrongdoing at the company?"

"No," both men said in unison.

Owen let out a breath in relief. "That's good. Let me put your mind at ease. If there was an active government investigation, I would know about it. The government would've involved me as the lawyer for the company. Don't let all of this get to you."

"That still doesn't explain Lew's odd behavior," Ed said.

"I'll talk to him and see if I can get any insight into what is bothering him. Has it ever occurred to you that he's just stressed out about this case and the workload? I know he's a great guy, but he's not perfect. Maybe you just need to cut him some slack."

Howard scoffed. "No way. I've known Lew for almost twenty years and worked with him for half of that. Something is off. I'm telling you."

"Okay, okay. I'll go talk to him." Owen stopped to gather his thoughts. "But I need the two of you to look me in the eyes and tell me again that you don't know of anything else going on that I need to know about."

"No," Ed said. "That's why we're talking to you. We're letting our imaginations run wild, and it's making us go crazy."

"Thanks for coming to me. Let me see what I can find out."

"One more thing." Howard stood. "If Lew is having a mental breakdown or something that impacts his ability to run LCI, we need to report it to the board and institute our succession plan."

Now wasn't that interesting. Because Owen knew that Howard would be the one to take over under the current LCI succession plan. "Let's not get ahead of ourselves. I'll talk to Lew today, and we'll figure things out. I'll keep you guys posted."

Ed and Howard thanked him and then left him alone in his office.

This was worse than Owen could've expected. And now

his suspicions of the two men were only greater. He needed to track Lew down right away.

─◁◇▷─

It took some effort, but Ty had gotten Anna to agree to meet him for coffee in Midtown. He thought it best that he look her in the eyes as he tried to convince her to put on the brakes. The last thing he wanted was for the trial against David to commence.

He sat in the coffee shop, patiently waiting for her to arrive. He had already downed an espresso and was now on to a regular cup. It wasn't much longer before the prosecutor arrived.

Today she wore a bright red top and black slacks. If she wasn't the enemy right now, he might even consider her attractive. But he had bigger fish to fry. Much bigger.

"Hello, Ty." She took a seat across from him.

"Don't you want to grab some coffee?"

"You tell me. Is this going to be a short and pointless meeting?"

Her question made him smile. "I certainly hope not."

She smiled too. "Then I'll give you the benefit of the doubt." She stood and went to the counter to place her order.

He'd gone over strategy in his mind, including whether he was going to tell her about the demand he'd gotten in the mail. He wasn't sure how she would take that, so he would have to feel her out.

A couple of minutes later, she rejoined him at the table with a steaming cup in hand. "All right. You have my attention."

"I don't know what all you've heard, but I think we have a situation on our hands."

She blew on her coffee to try to cool it. "You're being cryptic."

"I'm hoping you know more than I do." He wasn't sure what Anna knew, but he was going to push as hard as he could to have this discussion. "I want to have a frank conversation with you."

"You haven't said anything yet."

"I think there's some information out there that will prove my client's innocence. The problem is that I don't have access to it at this point. But if things proceed as I think they will, this whole case is going to blow wide open, and we're going to find out that David McDonald is completely blameless."

"I need to know what you know first," Anna said quietly.

"Did you hear about Mia Shaw's brakes being intentionally tampered with? Or her being attacked in the park?"

Her neutral expression, showing no sign of surprise, told him that she had heard. "Yes. My contacts at APD characterize both incidents as active investigations, but from what I understand, they don't have any solid leads on the culprit or culprits."

"Did you talk to Mia about it?"

Anna tucked a dark curl behind her ear. "I did, and frankly she had a far-out conspiracy theory she tried to pitch me. I have the feeling that's why you're here too."

This was going to be even more challenging than he had expected. "Anna, why are you so unwilling to consider that my client is innocent? I'm sure over your career you've had situations where you've changed your mind about whether your suspect was actually guilty of the charged crime, right?"

She didn't immediately respond, just looked down at her coffee cup. "Yes, that has happened, but this situation isn't like that. I really think Mia is struggling with Chase's death, and that this is an emotional reaction. My job isn't about emotion. Someone has to be level-headed here, and I take my job seriously. I understand why it would be to your and your client's benefit to buy in to whatever Mia is peddling right now, but you have to understand that she may not be in the best frame of mind. She went from being a fierce advocate of this prosecution to trying to get me to put on the brakes. That kind of one-eighty greatly disturbs me, especially knowing everything she has gone through."

"Okay, let's play this out. If you're right, then all well and good. But if you're wrong, Anna, the stakes are incredibly high. If there's some larger conspiracy at the root of why Chase was killed, don't you want to know it? Explore that option and see where it takes you?"

"But what evidence of this larger conspiracy do you have? Because I sure don't have any. Just the rampant speculation of the victim's best friend."

He rubbed the back of his neck. This next move could seriously backfire, but he felt he had no choice. "There is something else you need to know."

Her dark eyes narrowed. "Go on."

"I got a letter in the mail offering me half a million dollars if I withdrew from the case within forty-eight hours."

"Are you joking?"

"Unfortunately not."

She leaned forward in her seat. "You think this is all connected, then?"

"I do."

"And I also take it that you're not going to withdraw?"

"Of course not."

"How do you know that the letter is even legitimate?"

"I've never gotten anything like this before. Given what else I believe could be going on, I think there's a much deeper plot here that we haven't even begun to grasp. And I'm saying all of this to you because I'm hoping that you will reconsider and allow for a continuance of the trial. Just until we get all of this stuff worked out. If you're still right, it won't matter. The outcome will be the same. Just a little delay. And David's already locked up, so you shouldn't have any concern about him being a threat to anyone."

Anna bit her bottom lip. "I'll think about it. But I'm not making you any promises. I still think this sounds farfetched."

"I'm not asking for promises or commitments. Just that you'll take a hard look at the big picture and consider my request."

"I can do that."

"That's all I ask." He just hoped she would come to the right conclusion.

Later that night, Owen arrived at Lew's penthouse. He'd told the CEO they needed to talk in private, and Lew suggested he come over to his place.

Owen had thought long and hard that afternoon about how to handle the situation. He didn't know whether Ed and Howard were overreacting, or worse, playing some type of game. He hadn't even considered the possibility until this afternoon that Ed and Howard could *both* be involved. The thing was that they both could also be innocent.

When Lew opened the door for him, Owen knew immediately that something was off. Lew's face was red, and Owen could smell the alcohol on his breath.

"Come in," Lew said.

Owen followed him down the hallway and into a large living room. "Lew, what's going on? Talk to me."

"Everything is falling apart." Lew sat in one of the large ivory chairs.

"What do you mean?" Owen asked.

Lew's gaze darted around the room. "The traitor, the lawsuit, everything. All of it. I'll lose my job and be a washed-up has-been."

So maybe Ed and Howard hadn't been exaggerating. Lew was clearly losing it, and right now Owen felt like Lew needed some tough love. "Lew, you need to get ahold of yourself. The only way all those awful things will happen is if you give up and roll over. You need to sober up, get with the program, and stop having a pity party."

Lew stood and started pacing back and forth. "Have you talked to Mia today?"

"Not since first thing this morning. She called, but I haven't had a chance to call her back yet."

Lew stopped and looked at him. "Do you know why she was calling?"

"No." Owen didn't know where Lew was going with this.

"Well, let me tell you." Lew sat back down and dropped his head into his hands.

This was much worse than Owen could have imagined. "I'm listening, Lew. Whatever it is, we'll tackle it together."

"I have to be deposed next week."

Owen released the breath he was holding. "Lew, you've been deposed multiple times, and you've done just fine."

"But not under these circumstances. What will I do when they ask about the missing documents? Say, 'oh yeah, we figured out we have a mole who's probably selling the company out to Baxter Global'?"

"It does present a unique challenge, but it's something we can deal with." Owen wasn't quite sure yet *how* they would deal with it, but it didn't warrant Lew's behavior. "The guys told me that you've been acting out in the office, but that was before today. I think there's more at play here than this deposition. People are starting to talk, and it's not looking good for you right now."

"My entire life is tied up with LCI. If it goes down, I go down. I've worked my whole life to get to this level. I can't lose it."

"If you keep acting this way, you'll ensure that you do lose it. You have to pull it together. Face one problem at a time. You have a reputation for being one of the most level-headed CEOs in the business. Be that guy. Not the one sitting here right now. Not the one throwing little tantrums in front of the staff."

"And if I fail?" Lew's words came out as a whisper.

"Then at least you know that you gave it your all, and that you didn't collapse. But if you keep going down the path you're on right now, I guarantee that you'll fail. You've spooked Howard and Ed, and I don't think you want them running to the board and arguing that you're unfit. That will kick off the succession plan, and I don't have to tell you how that will end for you."

"Is this your way of encouraging me? If so, it's not working."

"I'm being straight with you." Lew needed to understand that Owen wasn't blowing smoke. This was serious.

"I have to meet Mia for deposition prep tomorrow. Will you come?" Lew asked.

"Yes, I'll clear my schedule." He had to warn Mia. She probably didn't realize that Lew had gone off the deep end.

"Good." Lew stared off to the side, not making eye contact.

Owen was at a loss for what to say next. Was there anything left to do? He rose from his seat. "I'll see you tomorrow, Lew. Please take some time tonight to try to get your head right."

Lew nodded.

As Owen left the penthouse, he felt like things were starting to slip away. This wasn't going to end well.

―◁◇▷―

The next day Mia waited for Owen and Lew to arrive at the firm. She'd gotten a strange call from Owen late last night warning her that Lew was on the brink of losing it. She'd had the sense when she spoke to Lew that he was feeling the pressure, but nothing as extreme as what Owen said he had experienced. An unstable Lew was the last thing she needed right now. It was just one more obstacle thrown in her way.

Her stomach clenched as she thought about how this could play out. Having the CEO deposed was already a huge deal and something they tried to avoid in litigation at all costs. But given the document debacle, she wasn't surprised that the judge was willing to give Bonnie pretty much anything she asked for. Mia had no idea how they were going to have Lew answer truthfully and still not let slip the fact that they were worried about a mole. Hopefully Bonnie would ask questions in such a way that allowed Lew not to reveal that fact. Bonnie would have no reason to think of that line of questioning, since she had no idea the other ordeal they were facing even existed.

Instead, Bonnie would be more focused on a how the documents got destroyed in the first place, because she was convinced LCI intentionally wanted to get rid of damaging documents. The only good news was that Lew had absolutely nothing to do with any data corruption, and he could truthfully answer questions on that subject all day long.

Mia had her files in front of her and her laptop open to her prep outline. This was going to be unlike any prep session she'd done before. She had never defended a CEO deposition before, and the circumstances here meant she was up for a challenge. Her nerves were also amplified because Owen was going to be there, and no doubt he'd be judging her skills.

After a few more minutes, a receptionist brought Owen and Lew into the conference room. They exchanged pleasantries, and she offered them coffee before they took their seats.

She carefully examined Lew. He didn't appear disheveled or distraught—just the opposite. Impeccably dressed in a tailored navy suit. Owen, on the other hand, was showing distinct signs of stress. He had dark circles under his eyes, and his hair was a bit unruly today.

She hoped this meant that Lew was going to be able to pull it together. But today was the first test. *Here goes nothing. . . .*

"Lew, first I want to apologize for you having to be deposed. As you know, normally we would fight tooth and nail to stop a CEO-level deposition. But the judge isn't sympathetic to us right now. In fact, he's downright hostile to our position, given the fact that it looks like we might have purposely destroyed documents."

"But we didn't," Lew interjected.

"Yes. Here's the problem, though. Our best defense to the document issue is the mole, and I don't think anyone wants to bring that up in a deposition setting. So we'll just have to go with the fact that you didn't have anything to do with it and knew absolutely nothing about it."

Owen cleared his throat. "I've been doing a lot of thinking about this. What if we pushed for an in-camera hearing with the judge? We explain what happened there."

"That's a good idea, but that would mean Bonnie would also know. Even if we got the judge to restrict what she could tell her client on that issue, it would still impact her litigation strategy, including her settlement number."

"Do we really have that luxury right now, to make those types of choices?" Owen asked.

She doodled a note on her legal pad. "It all depends on what LCI's appetite is for settlement."

Lew took a sip of coffee. "It hasn't changed unless the number goes down."

"All right. Let's take this one step at a time. Do the deposition. If it starts to go off the rails, I'll tell Bonnie that we have to get the judge on the phone and have an in-camera discussion."

"And you think she'll go for that?" Owen asked.

"I won't give her a choice. I won't put Lew in a position where he has to perjure himself. That's the absolute last thing we can allow to happen. Hopefully this is just a worst-case scenario and the deposition will be largely uneventful, but at least we have an escape plan if we need one."

"Agreed," Owen said. "Lew, you good?"

Lew nodded. "Have we gotten any closer to tracking down the mole through the forensic examination we're doing?"

Mia knew that question was coming. "Unfortunately not. This guy was good—or whoever he hired to do it was good. Noah is hitting up against a lot of brick walls, but thankfully he is also as good as it gets on this stuff. If there's any way to find the mole, he will. And he thinks he'll be done vetting Ed and Howard within a couple of days. He'll give us the full report on what he finds."

"I talked to him last night," Owen said. "No one else has popped up on his radar so far, and he's been able to clear some of Ed and Howard's direct reports. So that's one silver lining."

Lew ran a hand through his hair. "And if everyone turns up clean, then what?"

"Then we're nowhere," Mia said.

"Lew, there is one more thing," Owen said. "I'd like full access going forward to everyone's system. If there is a traitor, he might be doing things right now. We need visibility on that."

"That's highly intrusive," Lew responded.

Owen nodded. "Yeah, but everyone knows that what they do on the company server is fair game for monitoring."

"All right. Do it. But find me something. We've been spinning in circles for days with no progress."

Lew's frustration was building, and Mia feared things were going to get a lot worse before they got better. They were running out of time.

TWENTY

Owen's stomach was in knots as he entered the conference room at Warren McGee, flanked by Lew on one side and Mia on the other. The past few days had gone by quickly as they scrambled to prepare Lew and to push as hard as they could on the internal investigation. Noah claimed they were making progress and that he'd have a definitive report within the next forty-eight hours. Owen could only imagine what he was finding.

Today would be Owen's first direct interaction with the infamous ice queen, Bonnie Olson. When she sashayed into the conference room, Owen sized her up. She looked very similar to what he had imagined. Probably a little older than him, she commanded the room from the moment her black, insanely high-heeled shoe crossed over the threshold. He wasn't into fashion, but even he could tell that her gray skirt suit was tailored and probably more expensive than five of his suits combined.

Bonnie shook hands with Mia first while Mia made introductions. When Bonnie got to Owen, she gave him a shake that showed she meant business. It almost hurt. He felt like she had to be overcompensating. He realized it was hard for women to make it to the very top of big law firms, and she'd started that climb when it was even harder.

He didn't have anything against her personally, but right now she was enemy number one because she wanted to take down his client.

"I'd like to get started," Bonnie said. "I don't want to waste anyone's time."

Owen took a seat beside Mia, who was seated next to Lew. Mia's role would be to defend the deposition—which meant listening intently to every single question and making the proper objections to preserve the record and protect LCI. Owen was there to watch and to intervene with Mia if he needed to. His goal was for that not to happen, because he didn't want Bonnie to think they were worried about anything. It was totally standard that the GC would be present at the CEO deposition, so she wouldn't have any reason to be suspicious of his presence. Mia couldn't afford to let down her guard, and he was glad to be there as a second set of eyes and ears to make sure nothing got past either of them. He'd spent enough time with Mia to tell that she was on edge, but she was doing an admirable job of playing it cool.

The first hour of the deposition went off without a hitch as Bonnie marched through Lew's background and general questions. Bonnie's approach was highly methodical. She was not going to let anything slip by and was trying to build a very solid record even on the most mundane of questions. Owen had to give it to her, she was very patient and persistent in her approach.

Owen had started to zone out when a question caught his attention.

"Can you repeat the question, please?" Lew said.

"Certainly." Bonnie smiled. But it wasn't a friendly smile. It was an *I'm about to cut your throat* kind of smile. "Mr. Winston, did you destroy documents in the custody of LCI?"

Where had that come from? She'd just jumped to the conclu-

226

sion without any buildup. It was out of character after the first hour of the deposition.

"No," Lew answered. "I did not."

"Mr. Winston, did you direct anyone to destroy documents in the custody of LCI?"

Lew shook his head.

"You need to give a verbal response for the court reporter, Mr. Winston," Bonnie said.

"I did not," Lew said.

"Did you directly or indirectly ask anyone to destroy documents in the custody of LCI?"

"No," Lew answered.

Owen noticed that Mia wasn't objecting. He actually agreed with her silence. Lew could truthfully answer these questions in the negative. It was best to get that on record. There was no point in making legal objections that would be worthless at the end of the day anyway.

A frown pulled at Bonnie's shiny pink lips. She asked Lew the same question multiple ways, trying to get him to break, but he didn't. Lew kept calm and answered in the negative each time.

"Let's take a break," Bonnie said. She took off the microphone that was used for the videotaped deposition and walked out of the room.

They waited a moment to let Bonnie get a head start, and then the three of them exited to go to their breakout room. Each side got their own small conference room to huddle up in during breaks and to have lunch.

Once Owen shut the door to their breakout room, Lew flopped down in one of the chairs and let out a huge sigh. "That woman will not give up," Lew said.

"She really believes with all her being that we're hiding something," Mia said. "She won't let it go. I imagine she could go like this for hours."

"Lew, you're doing great," Owen said. And he really meant

it. This wasn't the same man who had been having a nervous breakdown in his penthouse the other night. "Keep it up, and we'll come out of this unscathed. If she wants to spend the whole day asking you every which way if you destroyed documents, we can live with that."

"It's like she doesn't even care about the actual breach of contract," Lew said, frowning.

"Oh, don't worry. She'll get there," Mia said. "She plans to take the entire day to depose you. We haven't even hit the lunch break yet. It's going to be a very long afternoon."

"I'm going to take this opportunity to run to the restroom." Lew excused himself from the room.

Owen looked at Mia. "How are you holding up?"

She gave a weak smile. "Honestly, I'm a mess of nerves, but who wouldn't be in this situation?"

He placed his hand on her shoulder and gave it a reassuring squeeze. "We'll all get through this. Like you said before, we have bigger problems than this case."

—◁◊▷—

Noah walked into the Fulton County jail, eager to see his friend. David's visiting privileges were limited, but Ty had been able to get Noah in for half an hour.

Noah and Ty had talked, and Ty strongly urged against telling David anything about trying to get the trial delayed. Noah understood Ty's point—not wanting to get David's hopes up, among other things—but it would be hard to look him in the eyes and not tell him anything.

He'd just have to play it by ear. Once he got into the visiting room and the officer brought David into the room in handcuffs, Noah's stomach clenched. *Dear Lord, please find a way to get this innocent man out of prison.*

David's eyes got misty when they met Noah's. "It's good to see you, man. I can't thank you enough."

"There's no need for that. I'm just doing what any friend would do."

"You and I both know that's not true. You're the only friend I have who has stuck by me, and you hooked me up with Ty. He's been amazing. It's like night and day between him and the public defender—and the best part about all of it is that Ty actually believes I'm innocent."

"Well, that definitely makes two of us. We're doing everything we can and then some to get you out of here."

David looked down. "I know you are, but I've also accepted the fact that I could be convicted for this. Ty said the prosecutor may even seek the death penalty. She wants to send a message, since the victim was a lawyer."

Noah nodded. "The prosecutor is tough." He weighed his response. "But we're doing all we can to make her see the error of her ways. To convince her that you're not the one who should be on trial here."

"So you really believe me? This isn't something you're doing purely out of loyalty because of our past history?"

"I do believe you. You're not a murderer, David. I know that as surely as I sit here."

"I have killed people."

"As have many federal agents."

"Have you been able to track down Morrow?"

Noah shook his head. "Not yet. I think he's lying low right now. But I realize we're on the clock."

"Yeah, trial's next week. Ty doesn't want me to testify."

Noah imagined that wasn't how his friend wanted to play it. "Let me guess. You want to take the stand?"

"You better believe it. I want to be able to tell the truth. I want to look into the eyes of the jury and let them know that I'm not a cold-blooded killer. No one else can tell them that. I'm the only one who can vouch for myself. I'm sure the prosecutor is going to bring up all the dirty laundry at the ATF, and I need to be able to combat that by telling my side of the story and letting the jury know that I'm not a monster. I may not have much left in this life, but if I don't have my reputation, then I really have nothing."

"I get it."

"I know you, Ramirez. If you were in my spot, I guarantee you'd be up on that stand, defending yourself and putting the truth out there."

"But you also have to trust Ty. There can be a lot of legal reasons why you don't need to take the stand, and that's a lot different than you just wanting to tell your side of the story. Ty's job is to protect you and make sure he gets a not-guilty verdict—keeping you out of prison, or worse. That's what Ty's trying to do every step of the way, and I'm trying to do the same thing."

David looked at him. "You know how much I appreciate all you both have done for me, but there's something to say about the truth. About the jury being able to evaluate whether I'm a liar, whether I'm a murderer, whether I could've gone to that man's apartment and butchered him."

"You know how the legal system works. The prosecutor will push it to the max. She will try to put your dirty laundry on trial."

"Isn't it better that I be there to combat it? And not just let innuendo or testimony from other witnesses tell the story?"

"Ultimately I think that's a decision you and Ty will have to make. I would love to be able to see you defend yourself. But I'm not a lawyer, and I'd hate to give you advice that could end up harming your case from a legal perspective. At the end of the day, I just want you to be a free man, because that's what you deserve. The right man needs to pay for this." Noah had to be careful not to say too much. He didn't want to start down a path and then have to backtrack.

"Are you any closer to figuring out who hired Morrow?"

"Closer, yes. But not close enough, and I fear the trial will start and we won't have someone to offer up." Time wasn't on their side.

"Just keep at it, man. You never know when something will break your way."

If only. But Noah wasn't going to put a damper on things. He wanted to stay at least somewhat upbeat for David's sake. The last thing he wanted David to know was just how crazy things had become.

--◁◇▷--

Owen had received a very strange phone call from Ed asking to meet at Owen's favorite diner downtown. There'd been a troubling tone to his voice. Owen wondered whether Ed had had another altercation with Lew. Hopefully not.

After the deposition, Owen had hoped that Lew had his head on straight again. Much to Owen's surprise, but also to his relief, the deposition hadn't yielded any fodder for the opposing side. Lew had held it together, and Bonnie's frustration had become evident as the day wore on. The fact that they came out of it unscathed was a big victory in his book, and they had needed one badly.

Owen arrived at the diner and saw Ed seated near the back exit on the left. His eyes were bloodshot, and immediately Owen assumed the worst—something really bad had happened.

Owen took a seat and tried to remain calm. "Ed, what's going on?"

"Thanks for meeting me. I didn't want to talk in the office. It's too much. It's too dangerous." Ed clenched his fists on the table.

"Dangerous?"

"Yes. You're going to think I'm crazy." Ed's gaze darted back and forth and then shifted beyond Owen's shoulder.

Owen turned but didn't recognize anyone else in the diner. "I don't think you're crazy. Just talk to me, tell me what is wrong. Is this about Lew?"

Ed shook his head. "No. Lew doesn't have anything to do with this. And yeah, Lew was acting a little weird, and I know we got freaked out about it, but now things look very different to me."

"I'm so lost, Ed." Owen was clearly missing something, and he hoped Ed would get to the point soon. Owen felt his blood pressure rising higher the longer he sat there not knowing what was happening.

"I'm not even sure where I should start, but I'll do the best I can." Ed took a big dramatic breath before continuing. "Howard and I have been spending a lot of time together, especially once we thought Lew was acting strangely. Howard came to me first with his concerns about Lew, and it all seemed to play out. Everything has been so uncertain that I started questioning my own sanity, my own instincts."

"About what?" Owen was still perplexed about Ed's strange behavior.

"Something's been going on at LCI. I'm sure of it." Ed wiped his brow.

Uh-oh. Did Ed somehow find out there was a mole? How would he have ever known? It was best for Owen to be patient and let Ed work through this in his own time, even if it was driving Owen crazy. "I'm listening."

"I'm an executive in a tech company. I know our IT systems inside and out. I can recognize when something is happening with the servers. I noticed weird things happening on my computer. So I started doing some digging on my own. I didn't want to bring it to anyone until I had something specific, because there's already been enough problems in the office as it is."

Owen's heartbeat thumped rapidly. "What did you find?"

"There's no easy way to say this, Owen." Ed turned and looked around the diner before continuing. "We have a traitor in our midst."

"What are you talking about?"

"Someone at LCI is working with our biggest competitor. More specifically, someone at LCI is selling our top-secret technology, the secrets we work so hard on, the tech we pour our blood, sweat, and tears into. And they're selling it to Baxter Global."

"Do you know who it is? Who's selling us out?" Owen felt like the room was slowly closing in on him, and his vision blurred a bit. Did Ed really hold the secret to this entire ordeal? Could this be the key to everything they had been working on? More questions than answers flooded through his mind, but what he really wanted to know was *who*.

"That's why I wanted to meet you off-site." Ed paused and looked away before making eye contact again. "It's Howard."

"Are you certain?"

Ed nodded vigorously. "Yes. I found evidence. Hard evidence."

"What type of evidence?" How could Ed have found something that Noah and his team didn't?

"I know it's a complete invasion of privacy, but I snooped through Howard's office. We had the strangest conversation last week, and something just seemed off to me. The way he was so eager to get Lew booted out as CEO and take his job. I know most guys want to be at the top by the time you get to be our vintage. I would like to be CEO one day and would prefer LCI than somewhere else, but Howard almost had an obsession lately, something I hadn't noticed previously. Howard's the one who got me all riled up about Lew. Howard had never been so fixated on taking Lew's job before. Now it all makes sense to me. If Howard became CEO, then he could really play both sides of the fence for a pretty penny, and we'd all be unaware, just going about our business. Until our best cutting-edge tech was put on the market by Baxter Global. And we would never suspect Howard. Ever."

Ed was on a roll, but Owen had some questions. As a lawyer,

he needed to cover the legal angle. He couldn't just blindly accept Ed's stories and convict Howard on the spot. "Let's go back to the evidence. What exactly did you find in Howard's office?"

Ed shifted in his seat. "Howard had an encrypted file on his desktop that I was able to crack."

"It was just on his desktop? Nowhere else?" If so, that would explain why Noah hadn't found it yet. He was first working on everything that was on the company's server. But each person's desktop was local to that specific computer.

"Yes. Just on the desktop, and it was hidden in one of his personal folders. I knew something was up when the file was encrypted. There's no need to encrypt personal stuff that is benign. I broke the encryption, and that's when I found it. Howard had set up some type of dummy account on a web-based email and was communicating and meeting with Baxter Global. He'd saved copies of the communications in the encrypted file. Can you believe that?"

"No. I really can't." It was too soon for Owen to fully trust Ed and tell him everything, so Owen thought it best to just let Ed open up completely to him. Ed would understand later when all the facts got put on the table. For now, Owen only needed more information, and fast. "Do you know exactly what he was doing with Baxter? Do you know if he was selling or providing them any of our technology? Do we have any evidence of that?" Owen heard his voice cracking as it rose.

"I don't know what all Howard sold them or gave to them, but from the looks of it, I think this is huge, Owen. You don't just have meetings with your biggest competitor and not tell anyone at the company about it if it was innocent. No way. He had to have been doing something he didn't want any of us to know about. Couple that with how he's been acting about Lew, trying to oust him, and you have an unmitigated disaster. Just imagine if we hadn't figured this out and Howard had gotten his way and kicked Lew to the curb? Then our CEO would basically have been working as a double agent. We're talking about millions upon millions of dollars on the line." Ed's face continued to redden.

Owen needed to know how far this news had spread. "Am I the first person you've told?"

"Yes. Given that you're the company's lawyer, I thought it was most important to come to you first and foremost. I knew you'd know what to do. How we need to attack this thing. I have no idea what to do. I'm in totally over my head right now."

"You did the right thing, Ed, and now we need to figure out how to manage this crisis. I need to think about that."

"Yeah, it's a lot to take in. I considered confronting Howard right when I found out what had happened. I was actually on my way to his house to confront him directly in person, and then I thought better of it. I'm assuming that was the right call?"

"Most definitely. I need to loop Lew in, though. This even goes beyond Lew. This will have to go all the way up to the board. This is above all of our pay grades. The actual existence of the company is at stake."

"Oh yes, I realize that. I just didn't want this completely on my conscience." Ed laughed. "I know it's not funny, but if I'm not laughing, I would be crying right now. I really thought I knew him."

"Don't be so hard on yourself. I think I'm in shock too." That was actually true. Owen had considered the possibility that Howard or Ed could be guilty, but thinking about it and it actually coming true were two totally different things.

"Do you think Howard will try to explain his way out of this?"

"Believe me, Ed, I hope and pray that there might actually be an innocent explanation, but I fear that is an unrealistic goal for all of us. But I would love to hear what Howard has to say for himself."

Ed pursed his lips. "You don't really think there could be a benign explanation, do you?"

"Probably not." Owen took a moment to gather his thoughts. "I think we need to circle the wagons. I need to make some calls. Did you find anything else that I should know about?"

"Isn't that enough?"

"Certainly. And I appreciate you trusting me and bringing this to me. We'll get through this and come out stronger for it. I'll also make sure that Howard is fully held to account for what he has done to LCI. There won't be a lawyer in town who will be able to win his case when it's all said and done."

Ed nodded. "Good. Howard should pay."

Maybe this nightmare could finally come to an end.

―◁◇▷―

Mia opened the door of her house to Noah. He had rushed over because there was breaking news.

"Thanks for coming so quickly." Mia ushered him into the kitchen and took a seat at the table.

"I need you to walk me through everything again," Noah said. "So Ed got suspicious of Howard and decided to break into his computer?"

"That's how Owen told me the story. He's already spoken to Lew once. They were going to meet to go over it further. I think they're trying to decide how to present this to the board, because that will be a huge deal."

Noah ran his fingers through his hair. "It's possible that Howard could have had something on his desktop that I didn't see. We hadn't gotten to the point where we were physically going onto people's desktops in the office to look for things. I'd like to hear more, though, about why Ed felt so suspicious and took such drastic action. What if he was wrong? What if Howard had found him snooping around on his computer?"

"I don't have any of those answers. I'm telling you literally everything I know, and all of that is what Owen told me." She was just as confused about the whole thing as Noah was.

"You know what this means, right?"

Unfortunately Mia knew exactly what it meant, and it made her sick to her stomach. "That Howard Brooks hired Morrow to kill Chase."

Noah nodded. "Did Owen give you any direction as to what we should be doing in the meantime?"

"Yes. He wants you to look at everything now from a fresh perspective, knowing that Howard is the target of the investigation."

"I'll get on it right away. I'll see if I can tie any of Howard's activities to Morrow."

"Maybe this means we can get Anna to drop the charges against David before the trial starts." Mia's cell rang. "It's Owen." She answered the phone. "Owen, what's going on?"

"Mia." Owen's voice was hoarse.

Fear shot through her. "What's wrong?"

"It's Howard," he said softly.

Her stomach clenched. "What? What happened?"

"Howard's dead."

CHAPTER
TWENTY-ONE

Noah sat in a conference room at LCI, surrounded by Mia, Lew, and Owen. They were all still in shock.

"We were going over to his house to confront him. Man-to-man," Lew said. "When we got there, he didn't answer." His face was noticeably pale.

"The front door was locked, but his back door wasn't. We went inside, and that's when we found him." Owen's voice shook.

"What are the police saying?" Noah asked.

Owen turned to him. "They believe he killed himself. There was no sign of forced entry."

"How?" Mia asked.

"Overdose," Lew said. "Looks like he took a whole bottle of pills."

Noah had a million questions. "Had anyone talked to him before the two of you got there?"

"Ed should be here any minute. We don't know whether he did or not," Owen said.

It wasn't long before Ed arrived. He looked awful. His eyes were puffy, and his face was red and blotchy.

"This is all my fault." Ed took a seat to join the others. "I called him." He looked down at his hands. "I couldn't help myself. I was so angry. The longer I thought about what he did, the madder I got. I needed him to understand that what he did was wrong."

"What did you say to him?" Lew asked.

"I said a few choice words, called him some awful names, and talked about him getting prosecuted." Ed's face got redder. "But I had no idea he would do something like this! That wasn't my intention. I really didn't know."

"It's not your fault," Owen said. "You were upset at what he'd done, but Howard was the one who made the decision to take his life."

Noah sat back and listened as they talked. He was annoyed that he hadn't been able to independently find evidence of Howard's wrongdoing. He was also worried that Ed might not be able to take the guilt weighing on his shoulders. "I'd like to examine Howard's desktop computer."

"I'd be happy to let you do that, but I think the police might be taking it," Owen said. "They're just covering all their bases."

"Ed, you didn't happen to copy the files you found on Howard's computer, did you?" Noah knew it was a long shot, but he had to ask.

Ed placed his head in his hands. "No. Honestly, at the time, it didn't even occur to me. All I was thinking about was getting to Howard for answers. I'm sorry. It seems like I'm messing up on all fronts right now."

"Did Howard tell you why when you confronted him?" Lew asked.

Ed nodded. "He said they offered him a deal that was too good to refuse. That he could retire early and be set. Get away from all the nonsense here."

"Did he mention anything about Chase Jackson?" Noah needed to know.

"Chase?" Ed's nose scrunched. "No. But I'm not sure why he would have."

Noah exchanged glances with Mia, and she gave him a nod.

"What am I missing?" Ed asked.

"We believe he put a hit out on Chase."

"What?" Ed's voice got ten times louder. "Are you serious? Are you saying that Howard is also a killer?"

"Yes," Mia said. "And we believe he must have figured out that we were on to him, and had started to try to get us off the case. We believe he hired a man named Liam Morrow to do all his dirty work, including the murder. Morrow's a hired gun who has done a lot of work for the militia group that McDonald infiltrated when he was with the ATF."

"So you see, the suicide makes a lot more sense when you think of all the bad things he did," Owen chimed in. "As if the betrayal wasn't enough, but this goes far beyond that."

Ed stared off into the distance, dazed. "I don't even know what to say. Howard, a killer? Selling our secrets for top dollar is one thing, but murder?" His voice cracked. "The man I know wasn't a murderer."

Mia looked at Ed. "His entire scheme could've collapsed if Chase had talked. We think Chase confronted him, and Howard had him killed."

"I'm at a loss." Ed leaned back in his chair. "Did you tell the police?"

Owen shook his head. "We haven't brought them in yet, but given the circumstances, now we will."

"Why haven't you already told the cops?" Ed asked.

"Because we didn't have any actual evidence. The evidence you found on Howard's computer is the only thing we have," Mia said. "But we have to act, or an innocent man is going to be put on trial."

Ed stood up. "I'm sorry. I think I need to get some air." He walked out of the room and shut the door behind him.

"He feels responsible for this," Owen said.

"It's not his fault. He didn't even realize the bigger picture," Mia said.

Noah nodded. "And speaking of bigger picture, we've got to tell the police everything we know."

"And we have to talk to Anna," Mia said. "Hopefully this will be enough to get her to stop the trial."

Noah wasn't so sure. "We'll see about that."

—◄◇►—

"How did your meeting with Anna go?" Noah looked into Mia's eyes as they sat on the couch in her living room.

"Much better than the last one. She's receptive and is going to be working with APD. If all goes well, I think the trial date will get pushed."

"That's good news," he said quietly as he looked away.

"There's something else, isn't there?" she asked.

He ran a hand through his hair. "Yeah. How everything came together. Something feels off to me."

"Like what?"

He hesitated. "Humor me."

She leaned in closer to him. "All right. Go ahead."

"Howard Brooks was conniving enough to sell out LCI and order Chase's death for finding out his secret, right?"

"Yes."

"But then after Ed confronts him, he just gives up and kills himself? Why not fight? Why not flee the country? He had the means and ability. Suicide as the first option just seems strange to me."

Mia's eyes widened. "What exactly are you saying?"

"I think you know." He studied her carefully. She was smart enough to follow his train of thought. "What if Howard didn't commit suicide? What if he was murdered?"

"By who? Howard was the mole. We know that now," Mia said.

"Maybe Morrow turned on him. I don't think we can just assume this is all tied up with a bow."

"Are you going to talk to the detective about this?"

"I already have. I talked to him while you were with Anna."

"What did he think?"

"He was a little skeptical." All right, more than a little. "But he listened. Normally hit men don't turn on their employers. It's bad for business. I get that. I just can't believe this was a suicide."

"Something has to have led you in this direction. What was it?"

"I know you probably won't like this answer, but it's just a gut feeling. Sometimes it's all about instincts, and mine are telling me that this isn't over."

She shivered. "I just want it to end."

He placed his hand on her arm. "I want that for you too."

She leaned her head against his shoulder. While everything else seemed off, sitting there with Mia seemed completely right.

"The medical examiner's report is inconclusive," Mia said.

Owen looked out Mia's large office window and hoped that they'd be able to figure this out. "So they can't say for certain that it was suicide."

"No, they can't," Noah responded.

The three of them were huddled in Mia's office, trying to determine what they needed to do.

"I've also got Bonnie breathing down my neck," Mia said.

Owen did have some news on that front. "The board's appetite for settlement has greatly increased. They don't want any more negative publicity for LCI. They fear that word of all this is going to get out. It's already public that an LCI executive most likely committed suicide. Lew and Ed are pushing the board hard to put up the cash and end this thing. Can you reach out to Bonnie and see what her current settlement number is?"

"Will do," Mia said. "But she's not stupid. She's been following all of this and will realize that she's in a strong negotiating position. It may only increase her demand."

"I get it, but we're willing to counter. The game has changed. This is no longer a normal case, and the rules don't apply. I think EPG will cave and take the sure thing, because they have to factor in the distinct possibility that LCI will be irreparably harmed from this and may not be in the financial position in the future to put this type of money on the table. We'll just have to see how long EPG takes to think it over. The board wants to do a full internal investigation from top to bottom to ensure that we don't have any more traitors."

"That's a good idea," Noah said.

"I'm glad you think so, because we're hiring you. You're most familiar with the entire set of facts. You can make sure we're covered."

"Even though I didn't figure out Howard was the mole?"

Owen didn't hold that against Noah in the least. "How could you? The only evidence appears to be on his computer, which you never had access to."

"I still want to find some corroborating evidence," Noah said.

"Maybe the police will," Mia added.

"Noah, can you get started right away tearing up our systems? I know you were already going down that path, but now that everything is out in the open, you'll have free rein. Leave no stone unturned and do whatever you have to do."

Noah stood. "Absolutely. I can start right now."

"Good. Let's go." Owen was ready to push things as quickly as possible. "Mia, let me know once you've connected with Bonnie."

Mia nodded. "Of course."

Owen left with Noah, and they headed to the LCI office. When they arrived, they were met by Lew and Ed. The two executives had become even closer after Howard's death. Lew felt badly about Ed's continuing guilt. He wanted to make sure Ed knew that no one was holding him responsible.

Owen wanted to update them on what was happening. "Guys, Noah is about to dig into the system."

"That's great news," Lew said. Ed nodded in agreement.

"I hope I can find the answers that you guys are looking for," Noah said. "Or at least provide some level of comfort that there isn't anyone else trying to sell out."

"Anything you need, just let us know. Our IT staff is here and can assist you in any way," Lew said. "The sooner we can put this behind us, the better, but before we can move on, we have to be absolutely certain that Howard was acting on his own. The company can't withstand another hit. If there's more dirty laundry, I want it aired out now. Not a few months from now."

And wasn't that the truth. Owen feared that he was watching LCI implode right in front of him.

TWENTY-TWO

Mia's nightmares kept getting worse. First there was Chase's dead body. There was even more blood than she remembered. And then the next thing she knew, she was having a hard time breathing. With each belabored breath, the world became darker.

She awoke with a start. For a brief moment, relief washed over her that she was awake, but that feeling quickly subsided. Her room was pitch black, and she started to cough. She realized the bedroom was filled with thick smoke. *Dear Lord, help me.*

It wasn't a nightmare. This was real life. Her house was on fire. She threw the covers back, and smoke burned her eyes and lungs as she tried to take in air. She had to get out of there now, or she'd suffocate from the smoke.

She didn't know where the fire had started and whether she'd be running into the flames. Figuring she was as good as dead if she stayed in her bedroom, she ran out of her room and toward the stairs. Smoke filled the air from below, but the flames were definitely worse on the second floor.

Rushing down the stairs as fast as her wobbly legs could take her, she ran toward the front door and unlocked the dead bolt. She pulled the door, but it didn't budge. What in the world?

More smoke from upstairs wafted down the steps. She turned and saw flames starting to envelop the top of the staircase.

She tried the door again, pulling with all of her might, but nothing happened. Something wasn't right. The door should open. Had someone locked her in her house? There could only be a sinister explanation for that, and her mind went to the worst scenario. But she could analyze the situation later. First she had to make it out of there alive.

Running as fast as she could, she tried her porch door, but the handle was broken off—deliberately. It wasn't like that when she'd gone to sleep.

Her survival instincts were kicking in. She ran into the kitchen and grabbed the heaviest pot she had. Coughing, she tried not to take big breaths because of the smoke and forced herself not to hyperventilate. Time was running out on her.

With all of her strength, she hurled the pot through the living room window, smashing it open, sending glass flying everywhere. She was barefoot and knew her feet would get cut, but that was better than dying. *Lord, I need you.* She grimaced as the glass cut into the bottoms of her feet, and then she dove out the window, landing in one of the bushes with a thud. She knew she couldn't just lie there. She had to get farther away from the fire.

When her lungs filled with cool, fresh air, a burst of energy shot through her, and she pushed herself to get up and move across the street. She stumbled into a neighbor's yard. She heard voices around her, and the blaring of fire trucks filled the air. She couldn't hold on any longer, knowing she was safely away from the fire, and she lay down in her neighbor's yard and closed her eyes.

—◁◇▷—

"Where's Mia?" Noah asked Cooper.

"She's in the den with Sophie," Cooper responded.

Noah had gotten a frantic call from Cooper and hightailed it over to his house. "What do we know?"

"They're investigating, but it looks like the fire might have been set deliberately."

"How is she doing?"

"Shaken up pretty badly." Cooper's eyes told him how serious the situation was.

"And her house?"

"It's not good. It might be a total loss," Cooper said quietly.

"This has gotten completely out of control," Noah said. He wanted to rush to Mia's side, but he needed to talk this through with Cooper first.

"What're you thinking?" Cooper asked.

"That we've got to track down Liam Morrow. I think he was behind this. Now that Howard is dead, the only risk he faces is that Mia will testify against him in Chase's murder."

"Landon and I will put all our resources behind it."

"We made the wrong move when we took everything at face value. Nothing is as it seems, and we have to start operating like that. Morrow is the most likely suspect here, and this time he was trying to finish the job. I'm going to take Mia to my place. From here on out, it's around-the-clock security detail until we get this sorted out."

Cooper nodded. "How do you think Mia's going to take that?"

"She needs a place to stay. It makes sense, as I can keep her safe." Or at least that was what he was going to convince her of.

"I'll call Landon, debrief him, and we'll get on it." Cooper paused. "I'm not crazy, right? Your protection of Mia goes beyond work, doesn't it?"

"Far beyond."

Cooper nodded. "Let me make that call."

Noah went to the den. When he saw Mia seated on the sofa with Sophie's arm wrapped around her, his heart broke. The woman's life had been threatened and her home virtually destroyed.

Sophie made eye contact with him. "Mia, I'm going to make some tea. I'll be back in a bit." She excused herself.

"Noah." Mia jumped up from the couch and threw her arms around him. He held her just as tightly.

He pulled back for a second and pushed the hair out of her face, looking deeply into her eyes. "I'm so glad you're okay."

"By the grace of God." She looked down. "I can't even describe what happened. Not just yet."

"It's okay. We don't have to talk about it." He continued holding her, not wanting to let go.

"I thought I might die." She shook in his arms. And that only made him more motivated to put a stop to this.

"Mia, I failed you, but I won't let that happen again."

"I don't even have a place to live." Her voice wobbled.

"You're going to stay at my place. I've got plenty of extra room, and that way I can provide around-the-clock protection. You're not going to be alone again. Not until this mess is over."

"Will it ever be over?"

"Yes," he answered definitively. And he believed that. "Please, sit."

They sat next to each other on the couch, and he put his arm around her. He was being openly affectionate with her, and that was the only thing that felt good about the current situation. He couldn't even imagine the pain and trauma she was going through right now. All he knew was that the house was on fire, and somehow she had made it out. But beyond that, details were sketchy, and she'd already said she didn't want to talk about it right now. He would have to wait for her to open up. In the meantime, though, he planned to talk to someone at the fire department to get more information.

"I assume you also talked to the police?" He hated to ask but felt it was necessary.

"Yes. They're focused on Morrow, but the trail is cold. The working theory is that he was able to disarm my alarm system and set the fire from the inside. But he also bolted my front door shut from the outside so I couldn't get out and broke the handle off my porch door."

Noah sucked in a breath.

"Yes, my thought exactly." She sighed and rested her head on his shoulder.

Morrow was going in for the kill.

"Are you ready to come with me to my place?" Noah asked, needing to get her somewhere safe as soon as possible. "Do you want to stay here longer with Sophie?"

"I'll come with you. She's had to deal with me for the past few hours, and it wasn't pretty."

"Sorry I didn't get here sooner. I came as soon as I heard."

"I don't even have my phone. Nothing. I've got nothing." Tears filled her eyes. "Sophie is giving me a bag of toiletries, and I'm borrowing some of her clothes. Although she doesn't have much that fits me, given she's a little bit of nothing."

"Just let me know what you need, and I'll make it happen."

"Oh, Noah," she said softly. She looked up into his eyes.

He so badly wanted to pull her to him and kiss her, but he didn't want their first kiss to be like this. "I'm not going to let anything else happen to you, Mia."

―◁◇▷―

Owen had just gotten off the phone with Noah. He couldn't believe what he'd been told. Someone had tried to burn Mia's house down with her in it. He had an awful feeling in the pit of his stomach. If Morrow was the culprit, he was probably trying to cover his own hide.

How could Owen have been so blind about Howard? How didn't he see the signs? His thoughts went back to Lew and his erratic behavior. While they didn't have any evidence tying him to this, something made Owen go back through the past few weeks and question whether Lew could have had some role in this mess. At the same time playing Owen like a fiddle.

Lew and Howard went back many years, and Owen started to jump to the worst conclusions. But why would Lew sabotage his own company? The company he was running? That was what Owen struggled with the most. The motivation just didn't seem clear, but he also didn't have a good explanation for Lew's strange behavior. The drinking, the hot temper, the emotional outbursts.

Owen was in a predicament because, at the end of the day, he was LCI's attorney—not Lew's personal attorney or the attorney of any single executive. His job and ethical responsibility was to protect the company, not the men or women who worked there.

He waited patiently for Lew to come to his office. He wanted to be the one to tell him about Mia and see if he could read any physical cues.

When Lew walked in a few minutes later, his face was red. "You said it was urgent," he said as he took a seat.

The whiff of alcohol on Lew's breath was undeniable. It was only three in the afternoon. Lew had absolutely no reason to be drinking at that time of day. Owen wondered if Lew had been sitting in his office, throwing them back. That was a bad sign for how this conversation might go.

"It is urgent. Someone burned Mia's house down, and she barely escaped with her life."

Lew's red face suddenly lost its color. "They're coming after all of us, aren't they?"

"What do you mean?"

Lew gripped the arms of his chair. "I could've sworn that someone followed me home from the office last night. They were watching me."

This was worse than Owen could have imagined. Lew was

252

acting paranoid, maybe even delusional. "Lew, let's focus on the threat to Mia right now. One step at a time."

Lew nodded. "What do we know?"

"Not much. The police and fire department are investigating, but I'm told by Noah that they're pretty certain it was arson—along with attempted murder. They think it was a man named Liam Morrow, but he's nowhere to be found."

"What are you not telling me, Owen? You have an awful poker face. There's something else going on. I need you to spit it out."

First Owen needed to address the elephant in the room. "You've been drinking, Lew. It's a bit early for that. And in the office?"

Lew scoffed. "This has been a very stressful time for me. You can't fault me for having an afternoon cocktail. Not after everything I've been through. There's a lot riding on my shoulders. Ultimately, as the CEO, I'm the one held to account. No one else."

"I just want to make sure there's not something else going on that I need to know about." Owen was going to push. He had to.

"Like what?"

"Some type of guilt?"

Lew's eyes grew wide. "You can't seriously think that I have anything to do with this mess. That doesn't make any sense. I'm the CEO!"

"Believe me, I've thought the same thing, but none of this makes any sense, Lew. I'm just as frustrated as you are." Owen stared Lew down, hoping that he would break if he had something to hide. But the man sitting in front of him right now didn't seem guilty—just disturbed, like he was battling some personal demons. But Owen found it difficult to believe Lew was working with Howard. Unless he was missing something big—no, something huge—he felt like Lew was innocent.

"Do you believe me? You have to believe me. I would never sell out my company, my people. Thousands of people's jobs depend on the economic viability of this company. That burden is on *my* shoulders. You wonder why I'm having a drink after lunch? It's because of that pressure. If this entire thing implodes on us and LCI goes under, I'll have to try to sleep at night knowing that I failed all of those people and their families. They depend on their jobs to sustain their lives. That is my chief concern."

The empathy Lew was showing seemed completely sincere to Owen. "I do believe you, Lew," he said softly. "But if you and I are innocent, then let's just make sure this thing stopped with Howard's death."

-◁◇▷-

Later that night, Mia curled up on Noah's couch beside him. She didn't want to be the clingy type, but she was scared to death. The thought of closing her eyes and being enveloped in smoke and flames was just too much. But with his strong arms around her, she felt safe. She never thought she'd feel safe around a man—just the opposite. It was one of the reasons she preferred to be alone.

But pretty much everything was different with Noah. He treated her with a respect and kindness that she'd never experienced before. Chase had been good to her, but it was always more like a big brother, joking and giving her a hard time. There was never a thread of romance there. Noah was a completely different story.

The guys she had dated in the past had all let her down. They'd start out seemingly okay, but then their selfishness always came through. Noah didn't have a selfish bone in his body.

"I can almost hear you thinking," Noah said quietly.

"Maybe because I was thinking of you."

He lifted her chin. "Hopefully good?"

"Absolutely. Going through all of this has been horrendous, but having you beside me has really opened my eyes." She had to be careful. It was far too soon to express everything she felt to him, but at the same time, she couldn't completely hold back.

"Whatever it is you're feeling right now, Mia, I guarantee I feel the same way."

She heard herself sigh as he placed his hand on her cheek. He leaned closer, their lips almost touching, looking into each other's eyes. Was this what it meant to love someone? They lingered there for what seemed like an eternity, the looks they exchanged saying more than their words ever could. A silent understanding passed between them.

When his lips finally touched hers, she wasn't apprehensive. There was no doubt in her mind that Noah was the guy for her. The warmth of his lips on hers made her stomach do cartwheels. The kiss deepened and then softened again.

He finally pulled back. "You're smiling."

"Sorry, I couldn't help it."

He grinned. "Nothing makes me happier than to see you smile."

She snuggled up next to him, and for that moment she didn't think about all the danger she faced. She just wanted to be with the man who had stolen her heart.

When Noah's phone buzzed, she was annoyed at the intrusion into their private moment. But given the circumstances, she knew he had to answer.

"I'm sorry, I should get this," he told her.

She nodded.

"Hello," he said.

She listened to the one side of the conversation, unable to make out what was going on.

"Are you sure?" he asked.

She waited for him to end the call. "What's going on?"

Noah looked at her. "That was an APD detective. They found Liam Morrow early this afternoon."

"That's good news. Are they questioning him?" Finally, maybe they'd get definitive answers. Or at the very least, he could now be put on trial for Chase's murder.

"Yes, but he's lawyered up and isn't saying a word. But the good news is that he can't hurt you anymore."

CHAPTER
TWENTY-THREE

N oah waited until Mia fell asleep, and then he went back to work. He was still in search of concrete evidence that Howard had hired Morrow, and he refused to stop until he found it. The news of Morrow's capture gave him a little peace, but he'd feel better if this case was completely put to bed.

He logged on to the K&R system remotely to make sure he had all the necessary firewall protections. After three security validations, he was in.

He'd been working for over an hour when something came up. As part of the mandated internal investigation at LCI, he'd been monitoring the activities of all the executives and had set up a flagging system to alert him to certain actions. That included any web-based financial activity. Noah scoured the re-cords and saw that Ed had been checking the hours of the bank by LCI's office. After some additional digging that forced him to go back to his dark web sources, he found out that Ed had paid a visit to his safety deposit box downtown right before the bank had closed today and then purchased a ticket to Morocco within the past hour. That timing couldn't be a coincidence.

Noah did some quick research to confirm that Morocco didn't have an extradition treaty with the US. If it had only been the bank, then maybe he could've overlooked it. But plans to leave the country made Noah highly suspicious. What if they'd had the wrong man the entire time?

The next morning Noah called everyone in for a meeting. He sat in the K&R Security conference room surrounded by Mia, Owen, Landon, and Cooper. He hadn't wanted to meet at LCI, so he'd insisted they all meet at K&R.

"All right, what do you have?" Cooper asked. "Sounded like it was important."

Noah told the group about his findings from late last night. They'd also been told about Morrow's capture.

Cooper cleared his throat. "I think I know where you're going with this, Noah. You think Howard was always clean, and Ed set him up to take the fall?"

Mia's eyes widened. "Does that mean Ed also killed Howard?"

The room was silent for a moment as everyone thought through this newest theory.

Noah finally spoke up. "Ed realizes that we're hot on his trail. He sets up Howard to try to close the loop once and for all. But when the top-down internal investigation was ordered, he probably got spooked. Then he finds out Morrow is arrested and fears that Morrow will flip on him. He gets some cash and plans to flee. His flight leaves tonight."

"Where is Ed now?" Mia asked.

Owen looked at his watch. "He should be in the office."

"I think we tell the police everything, and they can take him in for questioning," Landon said.

"What if they don't believe us?" Mia asked.

Noah looked at her. "K&R has a good working relationship with APD, especially because Cooper used to be one of them. I think they'll listen to us."

"Maybe I should go back to the office and try to keep him there," Owen said.

"That's a good idea," Noah responded. "If Ed flees the country to Morocco tonight, we might never be able to get to him. And we can't let that happen."

—◄◇►—

Owen's nervousness grew as he entered the LCI building. He had to act as though this was business as usual but at the same time keep Ed occupied long enough for the guys at K&R to convince the police to take Ed into custody.

How did I get myself into this? I need hazard pay.

He was only half joking, because things had gotten out of control. If they were right, Ed was responsible for the deaths of two people! It was beyond his comprehension. This was a man he worked side by side with on a daily basis. And now he was seriously considering that Ed had killed two people in cold blood. Owen didn't think he was naïve, but he also wasn't prepared to face these facts. The problem was that he had no choice. It was all on him right now.

It was then that he realized he was actually afraid, but he owed it to Chase and Howard to buck up and get the job done.

As he exited the elevator on the executive floor, he almost ran straight into Lew.

"I thought you were working from home today," Owen said.

Lew shook his head. "I needed to be here."

"Have you seen Ed?"

"Yeah. He's in his office on a conference call. Why?"

Owen didn't want to tip Lew off. He wasn't sure Lew was sturdy enough to handle this right now. "Oh, I just needed to ask him a question."

Lew looked at him for a moment, then seemed to accept this answer. "I'm just running to get some coffee. Need some fresh air. Do you want anything?"

"No. I'm good." The last thing Owen needed was caffeine, but he was glad Lew was leaving the office.

"See you in a few." Lew pushed the elevator button.

Owen took a moment to gather his thoughts before walking down the hallway. He poked his head into Ed's office. He was no longer on the phone.

"Hey," Owen said.

"What's up?" Ed asked.

"Can I have a seat?"

"Sure." Ed smiled. "But you'll need to make it quick. I'm about to run out."

Was Owen looking into the eyes of a calculated killer? Or were they still off base? "I just needed a break." That sounded weak, but it was the best he could come up with off the top of his head.

Ed shuffled some papers on his desk. "You look like you haven't been sleeping."

"Can you blame me?" Owen could answer that honestly.

Ed looked down. "I'm in the same boat. I know everyone says that Howard's suicide wasn't my fault, but I can't help but feel responsible."

Owen had to hand it to Ed. He was a good actor. But now that Owen knew the truth, he thought he could see something in Ed's eyes that held the true story. A story of murder and deceit. It made Owen sick to think about it, but he had to push through.

He did his best to make small talk for the next few minutes and hoped the police would get there soon.

Ed leaned forward in his chair. "Owen, I really do need to go. I have a flight to catch to London. I'm doing some investor meetings that Howard was originally going to cover."

Uh-oh. This wasn't the plan. Owen knew good and well that Ed's final destination was not London but Morocco. "I just got back to the office. I should probably get some work done anyway." He looked away and felt sweat start to form on his brow. He was not cut out for this.

Ed stood up. "You look like you could use some fresh air. Why don't you walk out with me?"

Owen panicked. He couldn't let Ed leave the building, but if Owen went with him, he might be putting himself in danger. "No. I'll just hang back here." The words shook as they came out of his mouth.

"Owen, if I didn't know better, I'd say you have something on your mind. Want to share?" Ed asked pointedly.

Owen wiped his brow, sensing that this entire plan was unraveling quickly. "It's nothing." He tried to straighten up in the chair and make eye contact. "Just under a bit of stress."

Ed shook his head. "We've worked together very closely for quite a while, Owen. You have an awful poker face."

Owen's stomach dropped as Ed pulled a revolver out of his suit jacket.

"Now, how about that walk?" Ed pointed the gun at him. "No one else has to get hurt around here. Just do as I say."

Owen had to stall. He sat there unmoving. "You had Chase killed, didn't you?"

A scowl spread across Ed's face. "Chase left me no other choice. He thought he could ruin my life, every single thing I had built for myself. He was going to blow the whistle—loudly."

"You're a monster," Owen couldn't help but say. "You also put the virus into the LCI system." He had to keep Ed there for as long as he could.

Ed shrugged. "Yeah, and my first mistake was not taking out the entire system. I wasn't aggressive enough. A couple of emails slipped through in the temporary files, and Chase found them. He confronted me with those emails. He believed he could prove that I sent them to Baxter Global, and he was right. If those had been wiped, then all of this could've been avoided."

Owen couldn't believe how cool and calculated Ed seemed about all of this. "Ed, you're not well."

Ed ignored his comment and kept talking. "I thought you might not buy my story about Howard, but you did. Everything would've been fine if Lew hadn't been so insistent on continuing to search. I knew it was only a matter of time, with full access to our systems, before Noah figured out what I had done or that rat Morrow decided to turn on me."

Owen was at a loss for words. He didn't even know how to respond. Ed wasn't the man Owen had thought he'd known and worked with each day.

"Stand up," Ed barked.

Owen knew that if he left with Ed, that would be the end. But he also didn't want to put anyone else in the office at risk. At the end of the day, he'd rather die than see his colleagues shot down. There had already been far too much bloodshed at this madman's hands.

Owen did the only thing he could do. He slowly rose from his seat, ready to face whatever came and feeling certain that he was nearing the end of his life. He never would have thought he could go out like this.

Then a loud voice sounded behind him, forcing him out of his momentary pity party. He turned and saw a few police officers with guns drawn—all pointed in Ed's direction.

"Put down the weapon," the lead officer yelled.

Owen held his breath and stood as still as a statue. Fear overtook him and he barely heard the continued barks of the officers telling Ed to put down the gun.

It seemed like everything was moving in slow motion. When Ed turned the weapon on himself, placing the gun under his chin, Owen heard the officers shout out, trying to stop him, but it was too late. Ed's bloody body hit the floor, the life no longer there. Most of the officers swarmed around Ed's body, and Owen was grabbed by another.

"Let's get you out of here," the officer said.

Finally. Owen exhaled. This nightmare was over.

—◁◇▷—

Mia looked at Noah. "Thanks for letting me come with you."

"Of course." He wanted to spend as much time with Mia as he could—especially on happier things.

The charges against David had been dropped, and Morrow had been charged with Chase's murder. Noah was picking David up from the detention center, and Mia had asked to come along.

"I want to apologize to him in person for ever going after him as the guilty party," Mia said.

"David's a good guy. He'll understand."

"I would get it if he hated me, but I have to make an effort."

Noah turned to her. "Wait here in the car for a minute, and we'll be right out."

After finishing up some paperwork, David McDonald walked out of the Fulton County jail as a free man.

Once they got out of the building, David gave Noah a huge hug. "Thank you, man. I know you're a big part of why I'm out."

"I also brought someone to meet you. She insisted."

"She?" David raised an eyebrow.

"Chase Jackson's friend. She initially believed you were guilty, but then she worked tirelessly on your behalf to get to the truth."

A slow smile took over David's face. "She's a special one to you though, huh?"

"How did you know?" Noah asked.

"Because your eyes lit up like a Christmas tree."

"Don't get any ideas, buddy," Noah joked. It was so great to have his friend standing there a free man, his name cleared, justice served.

When they got to the car, Mia jumped out. "David, I'm Mia Shaw."

"Yeah, I've already heard about you." David smiled. "And I recognize you from a picture that was in Chase's apartment." He paused and looked off into the distance for a moment. "Chase cared a great deal for you."

"Thank you. I cared for him too," she said quietly. "He was like family."

David took a step toward Mia. "I hear that I owe you a thank-you."

Mia shook her head. "Completely unnecessary. I should apologize to you for ever thinking you were responsible for Chase's death."

"You were doing what any good friend would do."

Mia gave David a hug. "I'm sorry for what you had to go through."

"It's over now." David took a deep breath. "I know it won't do any good now, but I never should've treated Chase so badly. I let my issues get the best of me, and unfortunately he was an easy target. I can't tell him that now, but at least I can tell you."

"Chase would've forgiven you too, especially if he knew your story like I do."

"You're too kind," David said.

"Well, I'm sure you want to get out of here," Mia said.

"Most definitely," David said. "I'd really love some lunch. Anything would beat what I've been eating."

Mia smiled. "Noah, just drop me off at work, and you two guys can get lunch."

"You sure you don't want to come with us?" Noah asked.

"I'd love to, but I need to meet with Bonnie."

"Call me when you're done." Noah knew this would be a tough meeting for Mia, but she had made it this far.

◦─◇─◦

Mia looked at Bonnie from across the conference room table. She dreaded this conversation because it felt like defeat. But ultimately, it wasn't her call. It was the client's.

"LCI is in complete disarray," Bonnie said. "Why should I negotiate with you now?"

"Because of what you just said. What if LCI goes under? Your client will get nothing. Zero. Zilch. And to be completely frank, there is a decent chance that could happen. Imagine how your client will react when they find out they could've taken the sure cash, but you advised them not to."

Bonnie's nose scrunched. "I don't like the sound of that."

"And you shouldn't. I've got settlement authority for ten million. It's a great deal. I highly advise you act quickly and take it. Because it comes off the table in twenty-four hours."

"You really do have a lot of guts to make these demands."

"No. I have nothing to lose. You have everything. I can envision what your client will do if you don't get them any money. You'll be the one fired." Mia was putting on the hard sell. This was LCI's best and only option to get out of the lawsuit. The board was planning a dramatic reorganization, and that probably meant Lew would be taking an early retirement. It was all too much for any CEO to withstand. The headlines in the local paper had been brutal. *Disgraced LCI Executive Guilty of Homicide Commits Suicide.*

There was still the unfinished business of proving that Ed was also responsible for Howard's murder. As far as APD was concerned, it was pretty open and shut. And since Ed was dead and Morrow was locked up, the threat had been neutralized. But Mia wanted to finish the job and make sure they fully understood what Ed had been doing and why. And that there were no more turncoats in the LCI ranks.

Bonnie jotted down some notes. "I'll take this offer to my client. I obviously can't make any guarantees."

"And I wouldn't expect you to." Mia's whole world was topsy-turvy. Nothing that Bonnie could say or do would faze her right now.

Bonnie leaned back in her chair. "I have to give it to you, Mia.

Most lawyers would've lost it by now, but you've held it together. I didn't give you enough credit. I was too hard on you earlier."

Was Bonnie actually apologizing to her? Talk about things Mia had never expected. "Thank you. It's been a difficult time and something that I wouldn't wish on anyone. Law school doesn't prepare you for stuff like this, and neither did my eight years of practice."

"Mia, nothing prepares you for stuff like this."

For the very first time, Mia was seeing a softer side of Bonnie. She didn't really know how to respond. "I guess you're right," she said softly.

"Are you happy here?"

"What do you mean?"

"Doing this type of work on the corporate defense side."

"I enjoy my work well enough, but working in a big firm like this is out of necessity. I have major student loan debt. Emory Law will do that to you. I can't afford any other options."

Bonnie nodded. "We have a different compensation model at Warren McGee, but we still pay well, especially for top talent."

Mia almost choked. Was Bonnie recruiting her? "Are you saying what I think you're saying?"

"I'm saying that an opportunity exists for you at Warren McGee if you'd like to explore it once we tie up this litigation. I'd personally mentor you."

Mia about fell out of her chair. She felt her mouth gape open.

Bonnie smirked. "I see I've surprised you. I realize you think I treated you awfully during this case, but really I was testing you. Seeing what you were made of."

"And I passed the test?"

"With flying colors. Once we get this case wrapped up, we can talk details. How does that sound?"

Mia nodded before she could even process it.

Bonnie smiled and packed up her laptop. "I know my way out. I'll let you know what the client says."

Mia sat there in shock once Bonnie had gone. Everything . about her life was changing rapidly. She had to fight to keep up.

She closed her eyes for a moment. She could fall asleep right there. Her exhaustion level was off the charts.

"Mia."

She looked up and saw Nancy Wayne walking into the room. This wasn't who she wanted to face right now.

"Can we talk?" Nancy asked.

"Yes." Mia wanted to say no, but that wouldn't be right.

Nancy took a seat and crossed her hands on the table in front of her. "I've wanted to talk to you for the past few days, but it's taken me this long to get up the nerve to do it."

Mia wasn't sure what she was in for. "Go on."

"I don't even know how to say this, but I owe you a big apology." Nancy paused. "I was awful to you, and you didn't deserve it."

"Why the change of heart?" Mia couldn't help but ask.

"Knowing all you've gone through, I shouldn't have acted that way. Chase and I never dated. I made it all up to get under your skin. I was jealous because I had a crush on him, and he never gave me a second look. Then you got to take over the case even though you're not a partner, and I was being very petty. I'm sorry." Nancy's eyes filled with tears. "Before I knew it, things had gotten out of control, and I couldn't back out of all the lies I was telling."

Mia couldn't believe this. She felt vindicated but then immediately felt sorry for Nancy. "I accept your apology. I'm glad you came to me."

"You don't have to accept it. I probably wouldn't if I were in your shoes. I'm a complete mess. When I found out that your house burned down, I couldn't believe I'd been so mean to you. Is there anything I can do to make it up to you?"

Mia shook her head. "No. Your apology is enough."

"I've got a spare room in my apartment if you need a place to stay."

"Thank you for the offer. I'm still trying to figure out what I'm going to do about that."

"The offer stands if you need it."

Mia couldn't imagine taking Nancy up on it, but it was kind of her to offer. "I appreciate it."

Just when she thought the day couldn't get any stranger . . .

—◁◇▷—

Ty sat across from David in his office. It was so good to see him out of prison. Ty couldn't take much credit for David's freedom, but David was thanking him profusely nonetheless.

"You really should be thanking Noah and Mia," Ty said. "They're the ones who cracked this thing wide open."

"I have thanked them, but I also know that you worked so hard on my behalf. I actually got a phone call from the prosecutor last night."

"Really?" Now, wasn't that odd.

"She wanted to apologize and offered to help me in any way she could. She sounded sincere."

"Nice. I'm glad we saw justice done here. I'm only sorry you had to spend the time you did wrongfully imprisoned." Ty wished he could have done more. At least this time there was a happy ending for David. Ty often wasn't that fortunate, not on his side of the fence with the cases he chose to take.

David looked at him, his expression turning serious. "I never should've fought with Chase. It just shows you how one fight can lead to all kinds of bad things happening. I wish I could go back and do it all over again."

"You can't, my friend. But you do get to decide how things go from here on out."

"Yeah, that's what I'm trying to figure out, what's next for me. I need a fresh start. I need to find something else to do with my life. Being in jail gave me a lot of time to think."

"What do you want to do?"

David shrugged. "Something to help people. That's the main reason I went to ATF in the first place, to make a difference. Going back into the government isn't an option, given my history, but I think I'll be able to find another way to use my skills."

Ty felt a smile creep across his lips. "You haven't even thought about the most obvious solution, have you?"

David cocked his head to the side. "What am I missing? You're grinning like a Cheshire cat."

Ty was amused that this idea hadn't occurred to David. "You do realize that your friend runs a security company, right?"

Recognition shown on David's face as he processed what Ty had said. "Man, I didn't even think about that."

"Seems like that could be the perfect fit. You already know that Noah thinks the world of you. He stuck his neck out for you. That tells you everything you need to know."

David looked hesitant. "I just hate to ask him for anything else. He's already done so much."

"You're more than qualified. You wouldn't be asking for a handout."

"Maybe you're right. I'll talk to him about it." David paused. "There's one other thing."

"What is it?"

"Once I get a new job, I'd like to pay you for your legal services."

Ty shook his head. "No way. I took your case pro bono. I don't go back on that."

"But I'd like to be able to pay you."

There was no way Ty would accept David's money. "You can pay me by going out there, getting a new job, and making a difference. Just like you say you want to."

David smiled. "I'll never be able to thank you enough for taking my case and believing in me."

Hearing those words was more than enough payment for Ty. "That's what I do. I wouldn't have it any other way."

TWENTY-FOUR

Congratulations on the LCI settlement." Harper gave Mia a wide grin.

They sat in his office, and she had just broken the news that EPG had officially accepted the settlement offer. "Thanks. I obviously wanted this to turn out differently."

"You're being way too hard on yourself. You took on an impossible situation and made the best of it. The entire partnership is singing your praises."

She didn't respond to that.

"Is something bothering you?" he asked.

There was. "I want to know why."

"Why Ed had Chase murdered?" Harper asked.

"I think we know the answer to that, but why Ed sold out to Baxter Global to begin with."

Harper crossed his hands in front of him. "Like most everything else in life, it probably had to do with money and power."

"I just can't fathom it."

Harper shifted in his seat. "That's what separates people like us from people like them. Our conscience."

He was right about that. "Lew and Owen are happy about the settlement, and the board is debating the future of the company."

"I think Lew may just go ahead and retire, and I wouldn't blame him one bit. He doesn't need to put himself through any more headaches."

"I agree with that." There was one other thing she needed Harper to buy in to. "While Lew is still the CEO, though, there is something else I'd like to finish."

"What?"

"The work I started on the LCI internal investigation." She needed to be honest with him so he could see how much this meant to her. "I need to know that I did everything in my power to understand what happened and to ensure that we haven't missed anything. To make sure that Ed didn't have anyone else on the inside with him."

Harper gave her a warm smile. "Then you have my full support. Assuming, of course, that Lew and Owen are okay with it. The client still has to be our top priority here."

"Absolutely. Lew wants to make sure this thing is completely buttoned up. He isn't going to rest until he's sure the company is clean." She could feel herself perk up just at having Harper's blessing. "Thank you for supporting me."

"You earned it. But I will give one more word of caution. I don't want your whole life to be this investigation. Chase wouldn't have wanted you to live in the past forever. So get the answers you need and then be ready to move on."

That was good advice, but she didn't have those answers yet. One thing was certain—she planned to get them.

"Are you sure you want to do this?" Noah sat at the small dinette table with Mia. After Ed's death, she'd moved into an extended stay hotel until she could figure out what she wanted to do about housing. She was also waiting on the insurance company to do a full investigation.

"I think you understand why," she implored him.

"I'm finishing up my work and will issue a final report that Lew can take to the board." He was worried that she wouldn't let this go. "I just worry about you," he said softly.

"And I appreciate that, but I need to follow through to the end. Then I'll be able to take the next steps, knowing that I've done everything I can to understand what happened."

The two of them had grown even closer since Ed's suicide, but they were still in the getting-to-know-each-other phase. He didn't want to rush things, and they had fallen into an easy rhythm. But the black cloud of recent events still hung over them, so maybe it would actually be good for Mia to gain some closure once and for all.

"How was your day?" she asked.

"I got a very interesting phone call," he said.

"Interesting bad or good?"

"Good. David called and asked about the possibility of working at K&R."

"Really?" Her eyes lit up. "You'd hire him, right?"

"Absolutely. But I need to talk it over with Landon and Cooper and have him come in to interview. We do things as a partnership and don't make unilateral decisions."

"That's so great. Maybe something good can come out of this awful mess."

"I thought the exact same thing." He took her hand in his. "One wonderful thing already has."

―◁◇▷―

Owen sat at his desk at LCI and wondered whether he should start packing up his things. He didn't think it was good for him to stay at the company. They were most likely going to bring in a new leadership team, and he really wanted to start over.

He also knew, though, that they still needed legal counsel, especially in this tough time, and that he couldn't just walk out.

He *wouldn't* walk out. Lew needed him until everything got back to normal and a new regime could take over.

Plus, he still had unfinished business, and that was why Mia was now standing in his office doorway.

"Come on in," he said.

"Thanks." She took a seat.

"How are you doing?" He studied her and saw that she still had dark circles under her eyes.

"I'll feel better once we wrap up the internal investigation. Noah has almost completed all the computer work, and I'll be reviewing his findings."

"Level with me. Is this a wild goose chase, or do you have a specific idea of something you're searching for?"

She blew out a breath. "Honestly, I don't know. Maybe somewhere in between. I don't think it's a wild goose chase at all, but I can't point you to one specific thing. There's just this sinking feeling in my gut. Don't you feel it too?"

That was the thing. He did. "I do, but I wonder if we're both too close to this to be objective. What does Noah think?"

"He's skeptical. Everyone seems to be but you and me."

Owen nodded. "Like I said, we're also the closest, and maybe we've lost our ability to view this rationally."

"Does it matter how we view it, as long as we get to the truth?"

He sighed. "What can I do to help?"

She pushed a strand of dark hair behind her ear. "Once I take a look at Noah's findings, I'll summarize them and ask for your input. Right now, I've got some notes and files I'd like to show you. Ed planted these files on Howard's computer, and we know he also was responsible for the virus, but is there anything else we could be missing? Also, the police have questioned the VP at Baxter, but they think he's clean of any criminal wrongdoing in connection with the murders. Whether there are any other claims against him remains to be seen."

"Yeah, I got a call from the detective. It's not illegal to try to recruit an employee to join your company, and right now they can't show that any money changed hands. Baxter is also saying that any money offer that was made was for employment, not for any actual technology."

"But Ed had the know-how. Isn't that the same thing?"

"That'll be up to the police and prosecutors," he said.

"Well, we don't have any control over that at the moment, but we do have control over the LCI systems and employees."

"Let's get to work, then."

—⬦—

Mia had spent the past week reviewing every document Noah had pulled and spending countless hours with him and Owen, making sure that no one else at LCI was involved in this conspiracy. Maybe this had all begun and ended with one evil man. A man who'd had her friend killed and then was willing to take out anyone else who stood in his way.

Ed had leaned on Morrow pretty heavily, and the charges against Morrow continued to mount. The police had found an accelerant in a storage locker belonging to him, so it was pretty clear he was the one who had burned down her house. He'd also confessed to being the one who tampered with her brakes and to the fact that Ed had hired him to send the bribe letter to Ty. There was zero evidence that anyone else at LCI was a traitor, and she was almost at the point of being able to close the case and move on.

It was getting late, and she sat in her office, wanting to bang her head against the wall. Maybe she'd put in another hour and then call it a night. Going back to the hotel had become pretty depressing, but until the insurance claim got processed, she was in a financial bind and couldn't just go out and buy another house. Noah had offered to take her to a late dinner, and she was looking forward to it.

She responded to a couple of emails and was reminded that she owed Bonnie a call. True to her word, once the settlement agreement was signed, Bonnie had reached out about a possible job. Mia wasn't sure how she felt about it, especially with all the uncertainty in her life right now.

When her phone rang, she saw it was Harper. "Hi, Harper."

"Do you have a minute for me to come down?"

"Sure."

"Be right there."

Maybe this meeting would be it for the day. She shot a quick text to Noah, saying that she was meeting with Harper and that she'd let him know when she was done so they could grab dinner.

Harper walked into her office. "I didn't know if you would've already called it a night."

"What's going on?" There were always emergency projects at the firm.

"I'm glad you haven't left yet because I have some amazing news to share." His eyes gleamed with excitement.

"What?" She could sure use some good news.

"Close your eyes for a second. I want to surprise you."

She did as he said, and a few moments later, he spoke again. "Okay, you can open them."

She opened her eyes and saw two glasses of champagne on her desk beside a bottle. "What are we celebrating?" She hadn't heard of the firm winning any big cases today.

He smiled broadly. "Given the highly unique circumstances that you've been through, the partnership met earlier today and voted to make you partner-elect."

"What?" She almost squealed. Was this really happening? "Are you serious?"

"Yes. You wouldn't actually become partner for a few more months, when we make all the other partnership announcements, but the partners felt it was important to give you this news now because of everything you've been through."

Her mind couldn't process it. "I think I'm speechless. I didn't even realize this option was on the table right now."

"The client vouched for you very strongly, and everyone here knows what you went through and how you handled everything. And, of course, I put in my weighty two cents."

"Like I said, I don't think I've begun to wrap my head around this."

"Cheers." He lifted his glass.

She did the same and took a big sip. Well, this would sure change her thought process about moving to Warren McGee. There was no way Bonnie could offer her partnership. This was a game changer. It had to be.

"You deserve it," Harper said.

"What do I need to do next?"

He set down his glass and leaned back in his chair. "That's up to you. You'll have to decide what clients you want to go after."

She took another sip of champagne as she considered his statement. "Well, it might be difficult to keep LCI, but we'll have to see what Owen does." She yawned. Where was her adrenaline rush going?

"You must be exhausted," Harper said.

"Yeah. I haven't been sleeping." Her eyes started to get heavy. Too heavy. Her entire body felt weighted down. What was going on? She shouldn't be this tired.

She looked at the glass in front of her and then at Harper, then back down at the glass. "Harper?"

He didn't respond. He also hadn't touched his champagne.

Her mind raced as he avoided eye contact and sat in silence. As a heavy fog filled her brain, she was still lucid enough to put the puzzle pieces together. And the picture that came into focus was one that was so bad, she never could have imagined it.

Harper finally made eye contact again. "I see you're starting to figure it out."

"It was you." Those were the last words out of her mouth, and then there was nothing.

—◁◇▷—

Noah looked at his watch again. Mia's meeting with Harper had run much longer than he had predicted. Or at least that was what he'd thought half an hour ago.

But she still wasn't answering his texts or her cell or her office phone. And now he was getting worried.

He made a call to Owen.

"This is Owen," he answered.

"Hey, it's Noah. Have you heard from Mia?"

"Not since about six today. Why?"

"She told me at eight o'clock that she had a meeting with Harper, and now it's nine thirty. I can't get ahold of her. We had dinner plans."

"And you're worried? She probably just got caught up with a work emergency."

"Even so, she would've texted to let me know."

Owen was silent for a moment. "Let me try Harper, and maybe I can put your mind at ease. I'll put you on hold for a second."

Noah blew out a breath. "Great, thanks." He waited a couple of minutes, and then Owen clicked back over.

"I can't reach Harper on his cell or at his office," Owen said.

"She was meeting with him. Why aren't either of them answering?" Noah's frustration continued to build.

"I don't know. That is weird," Owen conceded.

Immediately, Noah knew something was off. "This isn't right."

"What're you thinking?" Owen asked.

"What do you know about Harper?"

"He's the managing partner at Finley & Hughes. Very powerful, great connections. A real mover and shaker in the community."

"How well did he know the LCI execs?"

"Pretty well." Owen took a loud breath. "Wait a minute, you aren't thinking . . . ?"

"I know I might be overreacting, but every bone in my body is screaming at me right now. I'm going to the firm to look for her."

"And if you can't find her?"

"Then my next stop is Harper's place."

"Let me know how I can help."

"Sure thing. I'll call you as soon as I know anything."

Noah hung up and didn't waste any time. He jogged out to his Jeep, calling Cooper and Landon on the way and explaining his fear.

Dear Lord, let me be wrong. Let this all be a big mix-up. Let Mia be completely safe in her office.

He completely disregarded the speed limit as he rushed from his place to Midtown. Awful thoughts ran through his head, but he also racked his brain. Harper wasn't even remotely in the equation when they were investigating. They thought everyone at Finley & Hughes was clean. . . .

—◁◇▷—

Mia woke up disoriented and confused. Then she lifted her eyes and saw Harper sitting across from her. But she was no longer sitting at her own desk. Recognition washed through her. They were in Chase's office. Nausea threatened to overwhelm her, because she had an awful feeling about how this was going to end.

The light in the office was off, but the hall light was still on, and she could see that Harper had a gun in his lap. The message was loud and clear.

"Harper, you don't have to do this," she pleaded.

"I'm not going to do anything. It's all going to be you, unfortunately. Or at least that's what everyone will think," he said calmly.

Her mind raced as she tried to figure out his endgame. "What did you put in the champagne?"

"That was just a mild sedative, but having it in your system will only add to the inevitable conclusion."

"What conclusion?" She knew it wouldn't be good.

"Mia, I actually liked you. I tried to guide you and make sure you didn't go down the wrong path. But you refused to heed my advice. Time after time, you defied me, and now you've left me no choice."

"How could you have killed Chase? He was one of us. He was family!" Raw emotion bubbled up inside her. Yes, she was afraid for her life, but she couldn't wrap her head around Harper being responsible for Chase's murder. She needed to hear it come out of his mouth.

Harper blew out a breath. "I did not actually kill him."

"But you told Ed to take care of it, didn't you?"

"You're too much like Chase. Neither of you can let things go. Chase came to me about the emails and his suspicions about Ed. At that point, he had no idea of my involvement. When I told Ed that he'd been found out, he took matters into his own hands. So no, I didn't kill Chase, and I didn't tell anyone else to. But if you looked hard and long enough, I have no doubt that you would've connected me to Ed, because you're just that good. Too good. Which is why we're here right now. I promise that I tried everything I could to avoid this, but you thwarted me at every single turn."

"What was in this for you? You already have everything."

He sighed. "I made the introduction between Baxter Global and Ed. Ed was a brilliant guy, and he didn't think that he was getting what he deserved at LCI. He should've been heir apparent, not Howard. I didn't know it would turn into anything at first, but when Ed approached me about working with Baxter Global and the money involved, I wanted a cut, since I had put my neck on the line. Given Ed's expertise and knowledge, this was a multimillion-dollar deal. They needed someone to guide them and get them in and out of the transaction unscathed and undetected. Everything would've gone off without a hitch, and no one would've gotten hurt. But Chase was too curious, too protective of LCI. And that's where things started to unravel."

"*You* should've been protective of LCI," she snapped. "They were your client. It was *your* duty. What you did was a complete breach of trust."

Harper laughed. "You're even more naïve and idealistic than I thought. The real world doesn't work like that. You make the deals that will benefit you the most. Everyone is out for themselves in the end."

"What, and now you're just going to kill me? That seems a bit crazy, doesn't it?"

Harper leaned forward in his seat. "I've come way too far to let you be the undoing of everything. Too much blood has been spilled to run the risk that you'll just let this go. I gave you a chance, and you looked me in the eyes and made it clear to me that you couldn't walk away until you were *certain* that it ended with Ed. I gave you every chance, Mia."

"You put me on the LCI case, Harper. That was on you."

"Because I thought that was the best way to contain the situation. I never thought you'd go down the path you did. I believed you'd throw yourself into the case to win it for Chase. Instead, you veered down a completely different path when you started playing investigator."

She thought for a moment about trying to convince him that she could be paid off. That she could be quiet. But who was she kidding? He would never believe her, and he definitely wouldn't take that kind of risk. She'd always have blackmail on him.

"I can tell you're gaming out scenarios here, Mia. You're a brilliant girl, which is why I have to do this. It will be painless, I promise. I'm not out to cause you any physical harm."

"Except to kill me!" she couldn't help exclaiming. *Lord, I've learned you can do anything. Now is the time when I need your intervention.*

She stood up, and Harper pointed the gun at her.

"Don't do anything stupid," he said in a stern voice.

"It's late, but there could still be people here. They'd hear the gunshot. They'd hear me scream." She knew she sounded desperate.

"No. I checked during your little catnap. This wing of the hall is empty. There was a Georgia Bar event tonight, and a lot of people went. Everyone else has long since gone home."

Could things get any worse? Then her mind went to Noah. Her sweet Noah. Would she never get the chance to be with him? To know what real and honest love was like? Then a thought hit her. They were supposed to go to dinner tonight. He would get worried when she never contacted him. Maybe there was a chance he'd find her.

She needed more time. The longer she could keep Harper engaged, the better chance she had of leaving the firm alive tonight.

"Was there really that much money in it for you, Harper? You make millions here."

"Tell that to my two ex-wives. They bleed me dry. Like I said, I never set out with the intention to cause all this, but sometimes there is collateral damage. Life isn't fair. You know that better than most."

She flinched at his usage of the term *collateral damage.* "What about Baxter Global? Are you going to kill the people there who know too?"

"No. Only one person there knows of my personal involvement, and he and I will live or die by this thing together. We both have too much to lose. Mutually assured destruction."

"And if I told you that if you let me walk out this door, I'd move on with my life?"

"I only wish it were so simple. If I truly believed you could actually do that, I would have no issue. But you've shown me time and again otherwise. I gave you the out, and you didn't take it. Remember how you sat in my office and told me that you couldn't let this go?"

She realized he was wearing gloves. That couldn't be good. He reached into his jacket pocket and pulled out a pill bottle.

"What's that?" she asked.

"It's the end, Mia." He rose from his seat and placed the bottle directly in front of her. "Everyone will think this was all just too much for you to bear. That you took your life in Chase's office."

She knew he was going to force her to take the pills, and she couldn't allow that to happen. She screamed loudly, not worrying about him shooting her, because she knew he'd want to save his hide, and shooting her would be obvious murder.

He grabbed her tightly from behind, clamping a hand over her mouth to muffle her as she struggled and tried in vain to scream.

"Let her go," a loud voice barked from the doorway.

Her eyes traveled upward and saw that Noah stood there with gun drawn and pointed at Harper—but that also meant it was pointed at her, given that Harper was behind her.

"I'll shoot her." Harper pulled her even closer and shielded his body with hers, his grip tight around her neck.

"Not before I kill you," Noah said, his voice oddly calm.

"You wouldn't dare," Harper seethed. His grip tightened on her even more.

She knew in her gut that Noah would take the shot. If there was a risk that Harper would kill her first, Noah wouldn't hesitate. His dark eyes were trained on them, and silence filled the room.

"Harper, it's over," Noah said. "Too many people know your secret now. Even if you somehow manage to kill Mia and me, which there is no chance of, there are others who know the truth. You're a deal maker, aren't you? Turn yourself in and cut a deal. Because the alternative right now is a bullet through your brain."

Mia gasped at Noah's cold, calculated tone. He wasn't a killer, but she knew he would kill to protect her life.

Harper was strangely silent. That let Mia know he hadn't fully thought this out. He hadn't considered that Noah would check on her and that his plan would start to unravel. But that also meant Harper was desperate. And desperate men did desperate things.

She heard loud noises coming down the hallway.

"I guess it's over, then," Harper said.

She looked at Noah one last time and then closed her eyes, knowing this was the end. But at least she knew she wasn't the same woman she had been even a year ago. That there was something more in store for her than just this fleeting life on earth. And even though fear gripped her entire body, that thought gave her peace. Her faith would sustain her.

She could feel Harper shift. He was going to make a move. She opened her eyes as Harper pointed his gun at Noah. She screamed as Harper started to pull the trigger, but Noah fired back quickly. The loud, rapid gunshots pierced the air. Harper's single wild shot had missed Noah, but Noah had hit his target.

Mia stood, unmoving, as Harper's dead body slumped over Chase's desk in a pool of crimson blood. She had now seen two bloody scenes in her life. She couldn't tear her gaze away as she stared at the man she once believed with all her heart was her fierce advocate. And now she knew him to be nothing better than a murderous traitor.

Unscathed, Noah ran to her and guided her out from behind the desk as police officers swarmed into the room.

"You're safe now," he whispered into her ear.

And for the first time in a long time, she truly believed it.

TWENTY-FIVE

Mia sat in one of the Warren McGee conference rooms across from Bonnie and a smiling Kate. It had been two weeks since Harper's death, and while Mia was still reeling, she knew one thing clearly. She could no longer work at Finley & Hughes. There were far too many painful memories and too much baggage for her to move forward in her career there. The other senior partners had been completely understanding of her decision—and it was probably best for them too. Everyone wanted to put this horrible chapter behind them, and having Mia around would be a constant reminder of Chase's death and Harper's bitter betrayal.

"We'll be flexible with your start date," Bonnie said, "but the biggest question is whether you're truly interested in the job."

Before Mia could answer, Kate spoke up. "And please, Mia, you need to think hard about this and not think about me. I'd hate for you to accept a position out of some sense of loyalty to me. This decision needs to be for you and your career."

Mia smiled at her friend. "Thanks, Kate. I really appreciate those words." And she had done a lot of thinking. "At the end of the day, it would be nice to be in the same firm as you, but that's not my driving factor. I've experienced so much over the past couple of months, and I think working on the plaintiff's side would give me a fresh purpose for being a lawyer."

Bonnie cleared her throat. "And we already know she'd have the best mentor at the firm."

Mia's relationship with Bonnie had been one of the many surprises to come out of this experience. She didn't agree with many of Bonnie's tactics, but she thought she could learn a lot from her.

There was something else bothering her, though. "Can I ask you something?"

"Sure," Bonnie said.

"Do you think the other lawyers at the firm will be okay with this move? For the same reason Finley & Hughes is fine with me moving on, I'm worried that people here might be wary."

Bonnie leaned forward in her chair. "The people who matter are welcoming you with open arms. And if there is any idle gossip, it will soon pass once you start working your cases and life becomes more mundane again. People have a very short attention span these days."

"And for what it's worth, I've only heard positive things about your possibly coming here," Kate added. "Absolutely no one thinks any of the craziness that happened was your fault. If anything, your true character has shown through all of it. You're a woman of principle and integrity, and that's exactly the type of attorney we need at Warren McGee."

Bonnie nodded. "I'm never quite as idealistic as Kate, but I agree with what she's saying. You'd fit right in here and be a great addition. I think you'll find that doing our type of work is good for you."

Mia was sold. Her mind was made up. "When can I start?"

—◁◇▷—

"I owe you an apology." Anna's dark eyes met Ty's. They sat in a Midtown coffee shop. She had invited him to meet, and he'd accepted. "And I should've done this much sooner. Honestly, things just got a bit crazy, and I was trying to do damage control. But that's no excuse."

Ty was moved by the sincerity in Anna's voice. "You were put in a very difficult position, and I believe that you acted on your conscience. And at the end of the day, you got it right."

"But I was wrong for too long, and in my business, being wrong can be costly. So costly it can result in the conviction or even the death of an innocent person. I realize that you probably think the worst of me, but that's the last thing in this world I would ever want."

He couldn't help himself as he reached out and squeezed her hand. "That didn't happen here, Anna. You can't beat yourself up over this. Mistakes happen, and everyone was fooled here."

"Not you. You said the entire time that McDonald was innocent."

"Right, but I didn't have any idea what a tangled mess this was. Everyone was taken off guard by how this all played out."

Anna tucked a curly lock behind her ear. "And I only get one guilty party to prosecute. Ultimately I think Morrow will try to cut a deal to get a reduced sentence, and the Feds may pressure me if Morrow can give us Van Thompson. Morrow's already given us the backstory on how Ed sought him out."

"What all did Morrow tell you?"

"That Ed talked to Chase about the fight—saw his black eye. Chase had asked Ed if he had any contacts at the apartment management company. Armed with the information about David, Ed went to work, discovered David's background story, and in that found the perfect fall guy. Morrow was more than happy to oblige—he got the money for the hit job plus he made Thompson happy."

Ty could see how much this was eating at her. "I know courtroom justice would've been preferable, but at least they can't ever hurt anyone else again. They're either dead or locked up."

He paused. "And don't forget, you still haven't come to complete closure on Baxter Global's involvement."

"Oh, you don't have to remind me. If there's anything criminal there that I can make a case on, I will do it. The process is just slowgoing, and the evidence isn't there at this point." She took a sip of her coffee. "Ty, the bottom line is that I really hate being wrong—especially about something this important. I was bullheaded and didn't fully take into account what you were trying to tell me. And for that, I'm sorry."

"Really, Anna, it's okay. An innocent man is free to live his life, and the bad guys have been stopped. I won't lose any sleep, and you shouldn't either."

"Thank you." She gave a weak smile. "What's next for you?"

"Always the next case, right?"

"Yes. I hope I won't see you in the courtroom again for a while. It's easier to do my job when I dislike the opposing counsel."

He laughed. "Thank you, I think."

"I've learned from this experience and hope that I can be a better lawyer going forward."

She took her work as a prosecutor more seriously than most. And even though they would rarely see eye to eye, he had formed a respect for her. "We can all learn from this. And while you're right, I did think you were a bit stubborn in this case, we need more straight-shooting prosecutors like you. Ones who really eat and breathe their jobs and aren't influenced by external forces."

They sat in silence for a moment. "I appreciate you saying that. Coming from you, it means a lot. Thanks for meeting me," she said. "I know you have many other things you could be doing."

"No problem." And he really meant that.

"I won't take any more of your time." She stood. "Take care, Ty."

He watched as she walked away. He felt he hadn't heard the last from Anna Esposito.

—◁◇▷—

"What do you think?" Mia asked Noah. They were walking through an apartment in Midtown.

"Do you like it?" That was the more important question for him. After everything Mia had been through, he wanted her to feel comfortable in her new home.

"I think for now it's a good short-term solution."

She'd told him that she wasn't ready to think about getting into another mortgage, and it was going to take a while to get all the insurance issues vetted. But she couldn't live out of a hotel anymore, and he totally got that.

"I think it will work well. You're close to your new job too." She smiled. "You're right."

"I know you're making the right move. I can see it in your eyes, and I feel it in my gut." He closed the gap between them and wrapped his arms around her.

Mia sighed as she rested her head on his chest. He breathed in and had never felt more content in his life. He knew they needed time together in more normal circumstances to build their relationship. That was for the best, especially so that Mia could know for certain how she felt. But he didn't need more time. He was completely in love with her and wanted to be with her every single day for the rest of their lives. But she was more than worth the wait.

"How long is the lease?" he asked.

"A year," she replied softly.

A year. He could work with that. He would be patient, because he knew Mia needed time to heal. But in the meantime, he needed her to know how he really felt. He pulled back a little so he could look into her pretty brown eyes. "Mia."

"Yeah?"

He debated a long prelude or explanation, but that wasn't him. What he felt for her didn't require rambling. It was pure and simple—but also everything. He wanted to open his heart. "I love you."

Her eyes softened. "I love you too. I didn't think it would be possible for me to feel this way about anyone, but you've changed so many of my preconceived notions about men and relationships and what love can really be."

"You've changed me too. I never thought I'd be able to open up again and trust someone after being burned so badly, but you've made it easy. I only wish I could've taken your place and borne your pain, because I hate seeing you hurt. If I could take it away, I would."

Mia nodded. "I know that, and you've done so much for me. Now I just need to get back to having some sense of normalcy. I hope you'll stick around for that."

"I wouldn't want to be anywhere else."

He pulled her close again and pressed his lips to hers, sealing his words with a kiss.

EPILOGUE

Let me help you clean up," Sophie told Mia.

"No way." Mia smiled at her very pregnant friend. "This was your baby shower. You're not doing any of the cleaning." Mia had hosted the party at her apartment, and all the guests had scattered except for the guest of honor and Kate. The past eight months had flown by, and Mia was over the moon for her best friend, who was due in just a few weeks.

"I should be congratulating you too." Sophie hugged her. "All this baby talk, and we haven't even touched on your big success."

Kate grinned at Mia. "Yeah, Ms. Win a Huge Verdict."

Mia had just won her first major case as a plaintiff's lawyer. It had taken her this long to fully adjust to life on the other side of the fence, but it suited her. "Thank you both. I finally feel like I'm doing what I need to be doing with my career. It's an amazing feeling to help people."

"Speaking of helping people, I think the guys just arrived. They told me they were coming to help us clean up," Kate said. "I think we'll accept the reinforcements."

"Good." Mia laughed. "I also think they're hoping for the leftovers." She heard deep male voices waft through her apartment.

"There you guys are." Kate laughed as the three men walked into the room.

Landon and Cooper immediately made a beeline for the food still set out on the table. But Noah made eye contact with Mia and walked her way.

"Hey, you have a minute?" he asked.

Mia looked up at him. "You want to help me clean? This place is a mess."

"Sure, but can we talk for a minute first?"

It seemed like something was bothering him, so of course she said yes. She took him by the hand and led him into the kitchen, away from the others.

"Noah, what's going on? Is something wrong?"

He shifted his weight from foot to foot. "Nothing's wrong at all. I'm just nervous."

His strange behavior was confusing her, and she hoped nothing had happened. It had been such a wonderful day so far. "Nervous about what?"

He took her hand. "About this." He dropped to one knee.

She sucked in a breath but didn't say anything.

He pulled a ring out of his shirt pocket and held it up. The diamond glistened under the kitchen lights. "Mia, I love you more than I could have ever imagined. I don't have the words to describe how much I love you. All I can say is that I would lay down my life for you. I will protect you and love you until my dying breath." He paused, and she felt tears form in her eyes. "Mia, will you marry me?"

She knew her answer without reservation. "Of course I will."

Noah stood and slid the ring on her finger as her hand shook with excitement. He wrapped his strong arms around her and spun her around the kitchen before giving her a big kiss.

He set her back down. "I love you."

"I can't believe this. Do the others know?" she asked.

He laughed. "Yeah. They were all in on it. I've been a nervous wreck all day, but I had some great accomplices. Since I'm the last one to do this, believe me, they gave me a lot of advice. But I was still so worried."

"Why? You knew I would say yes."

"Because I love you so much, and I didn't want to mess up this special moment."

"It's a moment I'll never forget."

She heard voices behind her and knew her friends were coming to congratulate them, but she couldn't let this moment pass without stealing another kiss from the man she loved.

ACKNOWLEDGMENTS

I t's been a joy to write the ATLANTA JUSTICE series, and I couldn't have done it without the help and support of many others.

To everyone at Bethany House, including Dave, Jessica, Noelle, and Amy, I appreciate all you have done for me and my books. Dave and Jessica, thanks for your editorial support to make these books the very best they can be.

Sarah, it's been a wonderful journey to work with you for the past five years! I look forward to many more. You're an amazing agent and friend.

Aaron, thank you for your encouragement and tough love about my writing career. I love you.

Rachel's Justice League, thank you for being a constant source of encouragement and fellowship, and for being such avid readers of my books.

Thanks to my entire family for supporting me and my books. It means so much to me! Mama, I love you. Thanks for always being my biggest fan.

And finally, I thank God for everything He has done for me. His love is relentless.

Rachel Dylan writes legal thrillers and legal romantic suspense. She has practiced law for over a decade, including being a litigator at one of the nation's top law firms. She enjoys weaving together legal and suspenseful stories and writes the Atlanta Justice series, which features strong female attorneys in Atlanta. *Deadly Proof*, the first book in the Atlanta Justice series, is a CBA bestseller, an FHL Reader's Choice Award winner, a Daphne du Maurier Award finalist, and a Holt Medallion finalist. A southerner at heart, Rachel now lives in Michigan with her husband and five furkids—two dogs and three cats. She loves to connect with readers. You can find her at www.racheldylan.com.

Sign Up for Rachel's Newsletter!

Keep up to date with Rachel's news on book releases and events by signing up for her email list at racheldylan.com.

More from Rachel Dylan

Attorney Kate Sullivan has been appointed lead counsel to take on Mason Pharmaceutical in a claim involving an allegedly dangerous new drug. She hires a handsome private investigator to do some digging, but when a whistleblower is killed, it's clear the stakes are higher than ever.

Deadly Proof by Rachel Dylan
ATLANTA JUSTICE #1

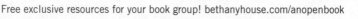

More Gripping Suspense!

When an anonymous poem predicts a string of murders, ending with her own, FBI behavior analyst Kaely Quinn is paired up with special agent Noah Hunter, who resents his assignment. But this brazen serial killer breaks all the normal patterns, and soon Noah and Kaely are tested to their limits to catch the murderer before anyone else—including Kaely—is killed.

Mind Games by Nancy Mehl
Kaely Quinn Profiler #1
nancymehl.com

A century apart, two women seek their mothers in Pleasant Valley, Wisconsin. In 1908, Thea's search leads her to an insane asylum with dark secrets. In modern-day Wisconsin, Heidi Lane answers the call of a mother battling dementia. Both confront the legendary curse of Misty Wayfair—and are entangled in a web of danger that entwines them across time.

The Curse of Misty Wayfair by Jaime Jo Wright
jaimewrightbooks.com

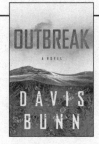

Along the coast of The Gambia, strange algae is growing and mysterious deaths are rising—until suddenly, with the sea currents' shift, the deaths stop. Professor Theo Bishop and biological researcher Avery Madison are the only ones who know the truth. Will the authorities heed their warning before it happens again?

Outbreak by Davis Bunn
davisbunn.com

BETHANYHOUSE